“I ain’t never go

Working in the fields

chore. “I just don’t see

anyway.”

Mary Ruth laughed. “Farming is in our blood, isn’t it?”

“Not mine!”

Samuel’s quick rebuttal made her laugh again. “Oh, Samuel, you say that now. But we are all farmers, aren’t we? We harvest a lot of things in our lives, even if it’s not crops from soil!”

There was something about the look on his face that caused Mary Ruth’s heart to flutter. He was staring at her, studying her, yet he still appeared so distant, as though he was deliberately putting up a barrier between them. She wondered if she had been too forward.

“*Ach, vell,*” she whispered. “I reckon I should be going.”

Indeed, she would be thinking of how Samuel had stared at her, as though seeing her with fresh eyes, eyes that were curious and interested.

Perhaps, she told herself, there was hope for him after all.

Sarah Price comes from a long line of devout Mennonites. She strives to write authentic and accurate stories that reflect over forty years of firsthand experiences with Amish communities. Ms. Price has advanced degrees in communication (MA), marketing (MBA) and education (PhD). Previously, she was a full-time college professor. Since being diagnosed with breast cancer in 2013, Ms. Price writes full-time from her farms in Florida and New Jersey.

VALLEY OF HOPE

Sarah Price

ISBN-13: 978-1-335-00600-4

Valley of Hope

This edition published by arrangement with Harlequin Books S.A.

For questions and comments about the quality of this book, please contact us at CustomerService@Harlequin.com.

Printed in U.S.A.

Chapter One

Rather than walk down the gravel lane to his parents' house, Samuel decided to cut through the valley between the front and back pastures. It was faster and easier, despite the fact that his boots would be muddy from the recent spring rain. It had rained a lot this spring and the fields were muddy because of it. However, the air was crisp, cooler than usual, and the grass was green. It was a perfect day for a good long walk, and he knew that would do him some good.

After a long day of work at his brother's carpentry shop, Samuel liked to be by himself. It gave him time to think and to just be alone. Jonas Junior wasn't one for wasting time when there was work to be done. There wasn't much time for idleness during work hours. Projects seemed to keep stacking up. And Samuel was tired of listening to his older brother telling him what to do.

Being the youngest of ten children, Samuel had enough of being bossed around by everyone else. For as long as he could remember, everyone seemed to tell him what to do, when to do it, and how to do it. If it wasn't his father or mother, it was one of his older brothers. It didn't help matters that he worked for Jonas Junior at the carpentry shop: just more order taking. And Samuel Lapp was tired of taking orders from everyone else in the family. He was tired of following the authority of brothers, father, and ministers.

For as long as he could remember, he had been the one that was always left behind on Communion Day or sent away whenever there was an adult conversation. For years, he had stood in their shadows, watching them take the kneeling vow, settle down, and start families. He seemed to be the tail end of a long line of people who had been there, done that. No one seemed to recognize his own individuality and need for standing on his own two feet, especially now that he was almost twenty.

Yes, Samuel thought, it sure is nice to walk home alone and not have to listen to his brother: no one to tell him what to do, what to think, or even where to walk. Besides, it gave him time to reflect and think, a time to be by himself, a time when he didn't have to listen to others telling him what to do or how to behave.

In the middle of the field, he paused for a moment. He could hear the engine of a fast car on the lane that ran parallel to his father's farm. Samuel shielded his eyes with his hands and stared in the direction of the sound. As the noise grew louder, Samuel squinted in anticipation. A red Ford Mustang raced along the road. It slowed down at the stop sign before turning left onto Hess Road and disappearing over the hill.

Samuel frowned and shook his head as he continued on his way through the small valley. A car, he thought. If only he could drive a car…just once. He wanted to feel the wind on his face as he drove sixty miles per hour down a highway. He'd drive with his arm hanging out the window and the radio turned as loud as it could play. The speed of a car, especially a Mustang, couldn't even be compared to the old-fashioned horse and buggy that he was forced to drive through the streets of Leola, Pennsylvania, that was for sure and certain.

A small flock of Canadian geese flew overhead, squawking in harmony as they passed. Samuel paused for just a moment to watch them, admiring the perfect V formation of their flock. When the one leading them began to tire, it would fall back and let another take the lead. They flew by unspoken rules and supported each other...no questions asked.

Just like the Amish, Samuel thought with another frown on his face.

He was approaching his parents' house. Just two years back, his parents had moved from the main house into the *grossdaadihaus* that was connected to it. It was a smaller house with three small bedrooms upstairs and one larger bedroom downstairs. Samuel and his older brother, David, had moved with his *mamm* and *daed* into the *grossdaadihaus* so that Junior and his family could move into the main house. They had six children now and needed the extra space.

Samuel didn't mind the move. In fact, it was quieter in the *grossdaadihaus* since the little children didn't come visit as much. With more space to live and easier access to the front yard, the children seemed more content on their own side of the house. Their *mamm*, Lillian, had her hands full taking care of the house and the children, too. And with David helping brother Daniel in the fields during the day and courting Susie Miller on the weekends, it was plenty quiet on the farm, and that suited Samuel just fine.

When he rounded the bend of the valley and began to climb up the back hill, Samuel noticed his *mamm* standing in the driveway talking to brother Daniel's wife, Rachel. She had just had their second baby, another little girl, and was enjoying the fresh air. Samuel took a deep breath and exhaled. He hoped he didn't have to coo over that new baby for too long.

"Samuel!"

He looked up at his mother and frowned. Her tone was less than friendly. "What is it, *Mamm*?"

"You know the pastures are muddy! You couldn't walk down the lane like the others? You'll track mud all through my kitchen! And I just cleaned the floors today!"

Samuel rolled his eyes. "I'll take my boots off, *Mamm*." He glanced at Rachel and the baby in her arms. But rather than say anything, he merely nodded and hurried up the steps into the *grossdaadihaus*.

Before he disappeared into the kitchen, he noticed that Rachel frowned, lifting one eyebrow in displeasure at his lack of a hospitable greeting. Inwardly, Samuel groaned, knowing that he'd hear about that later from his brother, Daniel. But he couldn't help it. In the four years since Rachel first arrived on their farm, they just hadn't seen eye-to-eye on much of anything. When it came to Rachel, Samuel knew that avoiding any and all interaction was the best policy, even if it meant getting the what-for from his brother later on.

Inside the kitchen, his eyes quickly adjusted to the dim light. With the sun starting to set, the natural light in the room was fading rapidly. He paused in the doorway, leaning against the wall to kick off his boots before padding across the clean linoleum floor to light the kerosene lantern hanging over the kitchen table. Within seconds, a bright light lit up the room and Samuel sank into a chair by the table to glance through *The Budget*, the weekly newspaper for current news and happenings in the Amish community.

"You could try to be a little more pleasant, Samuel," Katie said as she walked into the room. Her voice was strained and even. He could tell she was fighting to maintain her patience. "You didn't even say hello to Rachel or look at the baby."

He rolled his eyes and waved his hand dismissively, ignoring his mother and keeping his attention on the newspaper. Without even looking, he could sense the frown on his mother's face. Again. It seemed to be permanently engraved there, at least whenever Samuel was around. He had grown used to ignoring it, letting her displeasure bounce off of him as though he was surrounded by a shield. It was just easier that way.

"You'll understand one day, Samuel. Mark my words," Katie sighed.

"*Ja*, one day when I'm an old man and finally ready to settle down, mayhaps!" he retorted.

Katie laughed, shaking her head as she turned toward the kitchen counter. "Oh, it'll happen, son. Sooner than you think. Just you wait and see."

This time Samuel ignored her, and to his relief, his mother didn't pursue the conversation further. The silence that fell upon the kitchen was just fine with him as it allowed him time to read the paper in peace, without more interruptions that required him to answer questions or engage in conversation. After working all day with Jonas Junior, his eldest brother, Samuel was ready to unwind before supper and evening chores. And silence was top on his to-do list.

"*Onkel*!"

Samuel rolled his eyes. Forget about the news, he told himself as he set down the paper and shoved it across the table. Clearly, the silence was broken for good, and without doubt, he'd have no peace for the rest of the evening. Forcing a smile onto his face to mask his irritation, Samuel turned in the direction of the noise. "Linda! Jacob! I suppose I should be surprised to see you here, but then again, seems you're always here!"

His nephew Jacob ran across the kitchen floor and flung himself at Samuel's legs. Despite being eight, he was very small for his age. It was a concern of the family, and Samuel knew that his brother Junior was thinking about taking him to a fancy medical facility in Philadelphia. But Jacob didn't seem to notice that he was small in stature. He made up for it through a large personality. "We just finished supper and wanted to see if you needed help milking the cows!"

Samuel tousled the little boy's brown curly hair, so typical of the Lapp boys. "Tell you what, Jacob. You can milk all the cows for me!"

"Really?" the little boy said, his eyes wide and hopeful.

His older sister leaned against the table, frowning at her brother. "No, silly. He's just teasing you!" At twelve, Linda was growing into a pretty young girl. Unlike Jacob, she was tall for her age and willowy with pretty brown eyes and dark, shiny hair. She wasn't wearing her prayer *kapp*, but her hair was pulled back neat and tight in a traditional Amish bun at the back of her neck. "Ain't so, *Onkel*?"

Samuel sighed. There was no fooling around with Linda in the room. She was much more serious and direct than the other *kinner*.

"*Ja*, it's true." He reached down and tweaked Jacob's nose. "But you can help me, that's for sure and certain. You know how much I love milking those cows!"

Both Jacob and Linda giggled. It was a known fact that Samuel Lapp detested farm work. He didn't like getting up at four in the morning to milk the cows or mucking out the stalls or chasing cows through muddy paddocks. He much preferred working with his hands, building the storage sheds and garden houses that Junior's company sold throughout America.

Katie dried her hands on a towel as she walked over to her two grandchildren. There was a concerned look on her face as she stood before them. "Your *mamm* had an early supper tonight, *ja*?"

Linda nodded. "She's feeling poorly."

Katie glanced down at Jacob. Clearly, she wanted to ask more questions but didn't want to upset the young boy. With Lillian expecting her seventh baby toward the end of summer, she had been especially sluggish and weary for the past month. Yet, Katie was still concerned. "Where's your sister?"

"Lena's helping *mamm* with the dishes," Linda replied.

It wasn't unusual for Lena to be lingering in the kitchen. Of all the *kinner*, Lena was the one who enjoyed spending time with her *mamm* and avoided the outdoor farm work. She was only a year younger than Jacob but quite different, quiet and serious with searching eyes that seemed to observe everything with curiosity but nary a word to say about it.

That left Linda to watch the little ones, since Lena was glued to Lillian's side. "You tell your *mamm* that I'll be over after we've had our own supper to help her with the little ones, Linda," Katie said.

"Yes ma'am," Linda replied solemnly. Everyone knew that if something needed to get done, asking Linda was a sure way to insure that it was done properly.

"Now, I think if you look in my cookie jar, you'll find some fresh sugar cookies," Katie said lightly. "One each. And take one for Lena, Abram, and little Anna, too."

Both children ran over to the counter, Jacob watching expectantly as his older sister carefully removed the lid from the jar and pulled out their booty. She made certain to give him the larger of the cookies, a simple act that made Katie smile.

"*Danke*, *Mammi* Katie!" Linda smiled at her grandmother. "*Es gut!*"

Jacob scowled at his sister. "Of course it's *gut*! *Mammi* Katie makes the best cookies in all of Leola!"

Samuel laughed and shook his head.

Katie frowned at Jacob. "No better than any other *mamm* with hungry children, Jacob," she said modestly. Compliments were for the vain, after all. But it was clear that, secretly, she was pleased with her grandson. "Now, Linda, mayhaps you should run along to help your *mamm*. If she's feeling poorly, you should take care of the little ones until I come over. Get Lena to help, too," Katie said. She glanced around the kitchen.

"Need to prepare the supper meal here then I'll come over to see what needs fixing at your house, *ja*?"

Linda nodded, taking her charge seriously, and quickly disappeared through the door that connected the two houses. Jacob, however, stayed behind. For a moment, he stood in the middle of the room, looking at Katie then at the door where his sister had left. With a shrug of his shoulders, he returned to the table and leaned against Samuel's leg while eating his cookie.

"How many sheds did you build today, Samuel?" he asked.

"More than you can count!" Samuel grumbled, still trying to read the newspaper.

Jacob's eyes grew large, a cookie crumb falling from the corner of his mouth. "Really? That's a lot!"

"And tomorrow the big truck will come to haul them away to New York State!" Samuel added, leaning down so that he was closer to Jacob. "That truck must be awful powerful to be able to take those sheds so far, don't you think, Jacob?"

"Why, I bet our horse couldn't pull even one!" Jacob exclaimed, his eyes shining.

"That's right," Samuel said, brushing some cookie crumbs off of his leg. "Imagine how many horses it would take to move four sheds!"

"Oh!" the little boy replied in pure wonder at his uncle's words.

The kitchen door opened and Samuel's older brother, David, walked inside, pausing only to take off his dirty boots. He set his straw hat on a peg in the wall and greeted his mother with a smile. When he saw Jacob at the table, pushing against Samuel's leg, David laughed.

"*Ach*, Jacob! You are a permanent fixture in this house, *ja*?"

Samuel frowned. "Wouldn't I know it!"

Jacob was immune to their banter. "How many horses would it take to pull the sheds, *Onkel*?"

David glanced at his brother. "Come again?"

Samuel shrugged.

Jacob rolled onto his back, leaning over Samuel's knees. He stared up at the ceiling. "Samuel said it would take a lot of horses to move one shed! How many would it take to move four?"

David laughed and tweaked Jacob's nose before pulling out a chair and sitting at the table next to his brother. "Oh, my!" he said. "I'd think at least a hundred."

"A hundred!" Jacob said, his eyes wide and bright.

Samuel nodded. "*Ja*, a hundred!"

David laughed with his brother. "That's right! A whole field or two of horses!"

"Or three!" Samuel added.

"Wow!" Jacob drew in a deep breath. "That sure is a lot of horses!"

David winked at his nephew and lowered his voice. "The same number of horses that it would take to drag your *onkel* Samuel to the youth gathering tonight!"

Samuel groaned. "*Ach*, no! I've been trapped!" He leaned down and began to tickle Jacob's belly. The little boy giggled and twisted his body, trying to get away from Samuel. "See what you've done!"

"Jacob! Come get cleaned up and help me with the meal," Katie said, laughing with her sons. Jacob groaned and sank to the floor in a heap. "Come on, young man! You can help your *Mammi* Katie!"

Reluctantly, the young boy scraped himself up from

the ground. David and Samuel laughed at his theatrics but let him mope over to Katie, half-heartedly helping her with her chores. They were thankful for the break in entertaining him, despite Samuel's dread of the conversation that he knew would follow.

"Brother, come with me tonight," David said as he sat down on the chair beside Samuel.

"*Nee*," Samuel said, shaking his head. "You know I'm not into those gatherings."

Katie kept Jacob busy, even though she was leaning toward the table so that she could hear the conversation. She was too aware that her youngest son seemed to avoid any type of Amish youth gathering. It was a concern to her. David was clearly walking the path of the Amish while Samuel was creating great concern for the family. After having almost lost Emanuel and Sylvia to the world of the Englischers, she was not about to lose Samuel.

"You know how I feel," Samuel whispered. "My interest lies elsewhere."

David rolled his eyes. "Those two Mennonite fellows are no *gut*, Samuel."

Samuel frowned, his eyes narrowing as a dark look crossed his face. "I don't know what you are talking about, brother."

"*Ja vell*, you think you're fooling everyone, but you ain't," David sighed. "Besides, it's time for you to start socializing more with our own, Samuel. You're spending too much time outside the fold." David glanced at his *mamm* and winked. "Besides, I hear that Mary Ruth is going to be there."

Samuel straightened his back and raised an eyebrow. That certainly caught his attention. “Mary Ruth Smucker?”

“*Ja*!”

“As in our neighbor, Mary Ruth? At one of your friend’s gatherings?” he said, emphasizing the word *your*.

“It’s harmless and you know it.” David leaned forward and lowered his voice so Katie couldn’t hear. They both knew that she had the best hearing ability in the county when it came to conversations that weren’t meant to be overheard. “Music and all is okay if you haven’t taken the kneeling vow.”

Samuel smiled mischievously. “And I sure bet that she’s going to take it soon…like you?”

“Mayhaps,” David replied. “We haven’t taken it yet so we can still listen to the music.”

Samuel snorted. “I’m not intending to take it for a long time…if ever.” He ignored the hurt look that crossed his mother’s face as she glanced over at him. But she had given up on talking to him about the baptism. After all, he argued, his *rumschpringe* was his right, and until he took that vow, there was naught that the community or church could do about it. But standing around and listening to music near an empty schoolyard was not his idea of a wild *rumschpringe*. Nor did it sound remotely exciting. “No interest in going, David.”

David laid his hand on his brother’s shoulder. “Wouldn’t hurt you to come by, see the fellows, and put a sparkle in that Mary Ruth’s eye. It’ll be the highlight of her week, for sure and certain.”

With a big sigh, Samuel nodded. “All right, all right,” he relented, forcing himself to look inconvenienced. Truth was that he hadn’t seen much of Mary Ruth outside of the church services recently and he was interested in having a private word with her. "I'll go tonight. But not because Mary Ruth is going to be there," he stated, trying his best to sound convincing.

"Of course not," David said with a solemn expression. "Not because of Mary Ruth." But the twinkle in his brother's eye told Samuel that he didn't believe him.

Samuel stared at his brother, casting a stern look at him as though warning him against matchmaking. He wished he could tell his brother that he was happy enjoying his *rumschpringe* and certainly didn't need a proper Amish girl to tell him how to behave or hold him back. Mary Ruth would be sure and certain to do such a thing. True, she had grown so much in the past few years, changing from the neighbor girl into a pretty little Amish doll. Her blond hair was different than most of the dark-haired girls, and he sure did notice her sparkling blue eyes. But Samuel was not the settling down type.

"Not because of Mary Ruth at all," he mumbled and, ignoring the chuckles from his nephew, brother, and mother, reached for the paper.

Chapter Two

The lights from the buggies lit up the empty field. Samuel leaned back against his brother's buggy, his hat tipped down over his head despite the fact that the sun was down. He didn't want to be there. If anything, he'd rather be at the Maple Grove Racetrack in Reading, Pennsylvania. He loved watching the car races, loved the energy from the crowd and the loud noises. It was so foreign to his insulated world of farming and horses and church. Unfortunately, Samuel knew that the cars weren't racing tonight and his brother, David, had tricked him into attending the gathering at the end of Hess Road near the schoolhouse.

One of the boys had produced a music box attached to an iPod and was playing loud hip-hop music. Samuel thought he recognized the lyrics of Viper, a popular singer for the Englischers and one that he knew from the racetracks. The words were hard to understand, especially since the singer had a thick Latino accent and sang in both English and Spanish. But the beat made him want to tap his toes, despite not knowing how to dance.

"Samuel Lapp! I don't believe it!"

Samuel sighed and glanced over at the young man who approached him. "John Bucher," he said with a smile. A good friend when Samuel was growing up, John was certainly not one to be associated with such gatherings that were more worldly in nature. "What brings you here?"

John laughed and clapped Samuel on the back. "That young gal, Millie Ann. She said she'd be here." He glanced around at the small clusters of Amish youth as though looking for her. It was clear that he didn't spot her in the crowd. "But I don't see that she got away from her *mamm*'s eagle eyes."

"Bound to happen with the good ones," Samuel said, his eyes skimming the crowd. While it was true that these youth were in their *rumschpringe* and gathering to talk while listening to music was harmless, many of the parents would certainly hold their daughters close to the farm. They viewed the gatherings as dangerous since there was no one to chaperone. And everyone knew that a woman's reputation once tarnished was hard to ever get clean. It was no wonder that Millie Ann hadn't shown up, especially if her *mamm* had caught wind of the event.

"*Ja*, *vell*..." John remarked, letting the conversation fade between them.

"You'll see her on Sunday, anyway," Samuel added. He laid a hand on his friend's shoulder in a friendly, good-natured manner. "And her *mamm* will let her go to the singing, for sure and certain."

Before John could answer, a voice called out "Samuel!" Both Samuel and John turned their heads at the same time when they heard the voice that called out

Samuel's name. A young woman dressed in a pink dress with white prayer *kapp* emerged out of the shadows, bouncing over toward them. The battery-operated lights from the buggies cast a soft glow on her path, illuminating her way. She was a pretty girl with high cheekbones and soft pouted lips. Her bright eyes, a light shade of blue, seemed to take in everything around her. Now, as she approached Samuel and John, a smile lit up her face.

But Samuel maintained his stoic stance. He straightened his back and stood taller. "Mary Ruth," he said coolly.

"I see your girl had no problem escaping from her *mamm*'s clutches," John chuckled under his breath.

"Ain't my girl," Samuel retorted, his voice lowered so that Mary Ruth wouldn't hear as she approached. "No time for courting, John Bucher. Not this fellow." But John didn't look convinced. He just smiled and quietly moved away, letting the two of them have some rare privacy.

"I can't believe you are here!" Mary Ruth said, trying to contain her enthusiasm. She stood before Samuel, a smile on her face and her hands behind her back. She seemed to rock back and forth on her feet, her exuberance too hard to hide. "You never come out to the youth gatherings!"

"*Ja*, David dragged me," Samuel said, glancing over her head to see if he was being watched by the others. It wouldn't do any good to have tongues wagging, despite the fact that his heart pounded just a little harder when she was standing next to him. She was such a lively young girl, so unlike many of the Amish women who tended to be quiet and shy, withdrawn into their common world of quilting frolics and canning bees.

Mary Ruth's family had grown up in the same *gmay* as the Lapp family, attending school and church together. In truth, she had been more like a little sister when they were younger. Now, however, was a different story. Even during their younger years, Samuel had felt protective of Mary Ruth. Her quick smile and pure heart had always been one of the reasons he made certain no one had bothered her at school or after church service. And, in return, she had always seemed to stick up for him.

Now, he did his best to maintain his composure and seem aloof. She was at the age of settling down, and Samuel knew that he was a long way from such decisions. He wanted to explore the world before he considered the lifelong ramifications of joining the church and taking on the responsibility of a wife and family. So, despite the way his heart raced, he didn't want to lead Mary Ruth into thinking that he was interested in her.

"Heard you were coming but I didn't believe David when he said it," she gushed, her blue eyes sparkling. Those eyes, so light in color, reflected even in the shadowy darkness. "You've been so reclusive! You never seem to have much time for social time. In fact, I haven't seen you in ages, outside of church Sundays."

He leaned back against the buggy, crossing his arms over his chest. His eyes skimmed the crowd, trying to avoid eye contact with Mary Ruth. "Been busy."

"So I heard."

Her comment surprised him and he turned to look at her. He was taken with how pretty she looked in the glow from the buggies' lights. He also hadn't realized that he was so much taller than her. She was willowy thin so she didn't appear short. Except now, as she stood before him, he realized that he towered over her. Despite having known her for years and having grown up on the farms next to each other, he knew that he didn't really know her at all.

Oh, he knew that she had always been one to say a kind word to him, even when others frowned at his behavior. He was always aware that she was the first to stick up for him in the schoolyard and among their peers. And over the years, there had been quite a few times when Samuel had found himself on the far end of the favorite stick for many people, both at school and church. But tried and true, there was Mary Ruth, the first to smile at him when others would have just as soon turned their backs but couldn't.

Yes, Samuel thought, Mary Ruth had grown from a sweet child into a sweet young woman, indeed. Sweet and pretty young woman, he corrected himself quickly as he stared at her. But he also knew that she was Amish, through and through, despite being at such a "wild" *rumschpringe* gathering with Englischer music and no chaperones.

Snapping out of his quick whirlwind of thoughts, he looked away again. The crowds were still mostly separated by the sexes, the men in one area and the young women in another. Some of the women were swaying in time to the music, the closest they dared to get to dancing. Samuel thought he saw a group of young men smoking cigarettes in the distance but couldn't be certain. Wild *rumschpringe*, he thought. Indeed.

"What brings you here anyway?" Samuel asked, nonchalantly. "Your *mamm* must surely object."

Mary Ruth laughed, glancing over her shoulder at her group of friends. They were watching Mary Ruth's exchange with Samuel with great interest. "Simon brought me so she didn't say much. Besides, it's something to do, I reckon," she explained, looking back at Samuel. He could see her eyes sparkling in the dim light from the buggies. "I like the music, and after all, it's our time to explore a bit, *ja*?"

Samuel spared her a rare smile. He couldn't imagine Mary Ruth exploring the world of the Englische. Not with the fast pace of life, the noises, the people. The little that Samuel had explored had shown him the truth about the non-Amish world that surrounded their communities. There were unstructured pleasures out there, pleasures in food and activities and culture. But there was also unstructured evil and temptation that lingered around every corner.

He knew that he had only touched on the tip of it and there was so much more to explore. But he had mixed feelings about it. There was an element of danger to the exploration. He never knew what would happen next. On the other hand, he often worried about how far he was crossing the line. Would it ever get to the point of no return, and if so, would he be able to live with that? Yet, he also knew that the alternative was to stay exactly where he was, listening to music on a cheap, battery-operated radio in the dark of an empty schoolyard. And that was a little less exploration than he wanted, for sure and certain.

But for Mary Ruth? No, he thought. Exploring for Mary Ruth needed to be confined to exactly what she was doing…meeting in that dark schoolyard to talk with her friends and listen to music from that cheap radio until she was ready to join the church and settle down. Exploring much more beyond those perimeters would ruin the very essence of what it meant to be Mary Ruth Smucker: innocence. After all, when he really thought about it, the more time Samuel spent with his other friends, the more bored he became with Amish ways.

"Don't explore too much, Mary Ruth," he said wistfully.

"Funny you say that, being that you are here, too," she said. As she did so, she raised an eyebrow and tilted her head, looking at him from beneath long lashes. He felt as though she was staring right through him and reading his thoughts. It made him feel uncomfortable, especially when she continued, "Besides, it sure seems you are quite the explorer these days, too!"

His smile faded. She was right. After all, he was usually away from his Amish friends, watching the fast cars at the racetrack with his Mennonite and Englischer friends. But how had she known? Could Mary Ruth have heard about his time among the Englische? It wasn't that he was ashamed of it, but he wasn't aware that the community knew. "I have no idea what you mean," he said casually, not certain why he was denying it.

Mary Ruth leaned forward and lowered her voice to a soft, musical whisper. "You know your secret's safe with me." He could feel her warm, sweet breath on his cheek and it sent a shiver up his spine. He looked at her, scarcely able to hear her as she added, "I would never tell." Then, with a quick smile and a wave of her hand, she disappeared into the darkness to return to her small group of friends.

For the next hour, Samuel stayed on the periphery, watching the groups interact. Just as before, for the most part, the Amish women stayed to one side and the Amish men stayed to another. Yet there was an element of something heavy hanging in the air. Samuel didn't have to ask what it was. He knew. It was the unspoken element of courtship. The youth gathering wasn't about rebelling against the church or doing forbidden things like listening to music. It was about being out there and meeting someone, getting to know them outside of the careful eyes of a chaperone.

To be truthful, Samuel never had understood the courtship routine of the Amish, despite having been surrounded by it for his entire life. For years, he had watched his older brothers as they secretly courted their future wives. It was never a big surprise when the announcement came, so Samuel wondered why they bothered to sneak around so much.

In fact, he often had wondered why everything was kept such a big secret. He knew that Amish people didn't ask questions about courtship. It was always such a private matter. And why, he often asked, did courtship presume marriage? He much preferred the Englischer way of friendship and dating before settling into a future-promised courtship. Besides, the Amish way hindered the couple from really getting to know each other, and that was something that had always bewildered Samuel. A few buggy rides home from church singings, a walk or two on a Sunday afternoon, and maybe a few secret moments stolen under the hint of a setting sun where people couldn't see. That was courtship—the foundation for forever.

Yet, despite their feigned acts of secrecy, it was easy to see who was courting. In the beginning, there would be a stolen glance, a shy smile, perhaps a blush across the girl's cheeks. Then, she might serve him lemonade at fellowship before any of the other men. Finally, as the relationship progressed, from time to time, they'd sneak away from their respective groups to steal a few minutes of quiet conversation. Even when they stole away into the darkness, Samuel knew that none of these youths had anything to worry about their reputations. Most of them wouldn't even chance a wayward kiss in the darkness.

Samuel sighed, wondering why he had bothered to come with David. During the nice spring nights, some of the younger folks liked to get together and spend time outside of the regular social gatherings such as the traditional Sunday singings that followed the church services every other week. It was harmless, that was true enough. While their parents might frown on the loud rock music or the youth being without any adult chaperones, everyone was respectful of each other and their *rumschpringe*; and that was boring to Samuel.

Some of the groups from other church districts were more exciting. The men would openly smoke cigarettes or even sneak in some beer. While Samuel wasn't interested in the smoking or drinking, he was interested in the other thing that they snuck into their *rumschpringe*: cars. He had even heard of some Amish youth that bought their own cars and hid them at the houses of non-baptized family members. Samuel was almost disappointed that all of his family members had been baptized. There would be no car sneaking in his family.

"What are you doing over here by yourself, Samuel? Come join the group," David said, emerging from the shadows.

"Nah," Samuel said, shaking his head. "Seems to be dying down, anyway. Think I might head home."

David laughed. "Or over to see what those Miller

Lane Mennonites are doing?" Quickly, he became somber and leaned closer to Samuel. "Seriously, brother, I hear those two boys are causing their own district quite the stress. Wonder that you are mixed up with them."

Samuel cast a stern look at David but didn't reply. For years, David and Samuel had run around together. They were often in trouble, whether from chasing girls with frogs or racing horses down the lane. His mother had often given her head one of her subtle, disapproving shakes as she frowned at their antics. But times were changing. Samuel knew that David was focusing more of his time and energy on conforming to the church ways. After all, he was planning on taking the kneeling vow in the fall. And Samuel wouldn't be surprised if he made another announcement soon thereafter. Pretty Susie Miller was certainly anxious to see that happen, that was for sure and certain.

It bothered Samuel that, now that David wanted to settle down, he was becoming judgmental of the choices that Samuel was making. After all, it wasn't anyone's business, especially David's, if Samuel wanted to spend time with the Mennonite fellows that lived on Miller Lane. Samuel hadn't committed to taking the kneeling vow yet and didn't intend on doing so for quite a few years to come. Until that time, Samuel knew that he could do what he wanted with his own free time. Just as he knew that he couldn't stop his older brother from moving forward with his own life.

"You take the buggy then," his brother conceded when Samuel didn't respond. "I'll have Mary Ruth's brother drop me at home."

Grateful that the lecture had ended, Samuel nodded his thanks and hurried over to the buggy. He didn't like being told what to do and he certainly didn't care for his brother David to interfere with his friendship. Robert and Paul were good fellows, fun to be around and always eager to take Samuel with them in their car. Samuel smiled as he quickly pulled the light blanket off of the horse. Driving in cars was a whole lot faster and more fun than driving a horse and buggy, he thought as he folded the horse blanket before putting it onto the back seat of the buggy.

The evening had cooled down a bit since he had arrived at the gathering with David earlier in the evening. He was glad that he had brought his light jacket with him. He'd need it, for he intended to take a trot down to Miller Lane. He wanted to see if his friends were out on this fine spring evening. After all, it was too early to go home.

The horse's hooves made their soothing music on the macadam, hitting it with the solid two-beat rhythm of a brisk trot. He always liked taking the buggy out for night rides. The darkness made everything seem faster. Plus, there was a dangerous element to driving the buggy in the night. It always made his pulse quicken and his senses feel more alive. Now, if he could only get behind the wheel of a car…just once, he thought.

As he drove the buggy down Miller Lane, he saw two figures leaning against the side of a car. He pulled the buggy to a stop and slid the door open to lean out.

"*Wie gehts*?"

One of the young men looked up and smiled. "Hey, Samuel! Thought we might be seeing you around tonight!"

Samuel held the reins in one hand and nodded to the other man. "What are you two fellows up to, Jacob?"

"Waiting for Peter Bartlett. You meet him yet?"

Samuel shook his head. He had heard of the name but wasn't familiar with it. He was fairly certain it wasn't Amish or Mennonite. "*Nee*," he replied.

Paul glanced over his shoulder, looking down the lane. "Friend of mine that I met last summer. A college boy." The way Paul said that seemed impressive to Samuel. He had never hung out with someone who had gone to college. "We're heading into Lancaster proper for a while. You want to come along?"

Samuel scratched at his cheek, thinking quickly. Lancaster meant a car ride and highways. He'd taken short rides with Robert and his friends, usually to the racetrack on a Friday or Saturday night, but never into the city. He wanted nothing more than to join them but it was late already.

"Need to work early tomorrow," he said, more to himself than to his friends.

"That's the problem with farmers," Robert laughed. "Getting up when we're going to bed!"

"No fun in that," Paul said.

"Besides, tomorrow's Saturday. You can sleep in the afternoon," Robert said.

Samuel held up the worn leather reins. "Got the horse here."

Robert waved his hand, dismissing Samuel's excuse. "Park the buggy at Miller's Store. That's my cousin's place. He won't mind and no one will bother it, Sam. You know he leaves stalls open during the night because no one is there."

Samuel took a deep breath and hesitated. As long as he made it back in time to help milk the cows in the morning, no one would know what time he came home.

And the horse would be fine at Miller's. After all, he reasoned, this was his *rumschpringe* and exploring the world was its purpose. What harm could come from a night out with his friends?

"All right," he said reluctantly, as though he was still undecided. He had never gone out with Robert and Paul at night, and he just hoped they wouldn't be back too late. "Let me tie her up and I'll be right back."

As he drove his mare down the dark lane, his buggy lights cast a slight glow in front of him. His heart pounded as he realized that he could still keep driving down the lane instead of leaving the horse at the small barn behind Miller's Store. But that would mean facing the ridicule of his friends, who would think he had been too scared to go into Lancaster for the night.

After unhitching the mare from the buggy, he led her into the stall and made certain that there was a bucket of water and plenty of hay. No one would be the wiser if he cleaned up after the horse before escaping back to his parents' farm. Samuel had often heard of other young men in their *rumschpringe* who left their horse and buggy at Miller's Store.

Then, after patting the horse gently on her neck, Samuel turned toward the darkness outside the empty barn. The lane was dark and he could barely make out the lights of the car waiting where he had left Robert and Paul. Peter must have arrived. He took a deep breath and stepped through the doorway, his feet heavy as he hurried down the dark lane and toward his friends.

Chapter Three

Sunday was a church day. The early morning air was cool but the sky was a rich blue, completely clear of any clouds. It was a beautiful spring day. A gentle breeze flowed over the fields toward the farm where the grey-topped buggies were pulling down the lane. There was a large paddock along the road with green grass and trees that were just beginning to sprout green leaves from their red buds.

In the paddock, two horses grazed. One lifted its head and watched as the line of buggies began to roll past the paddock. The horse started to run, its legs tall and gangly. Leaping and kicking out its back legs, the horse twisted in the air, its black mane flowing behind it. The other horse stopped grazing for a moment and watched as its youthful companion began racing along the paddock fence, leaping and twisting in pure delight of a beautiful spring day.

The horses pulling the buggies wore blinders and couldn't see the antics of the young horse in the paddock. But they tensed up, sensing the excitement in the air from a fellow equine. The drivers of the buggies tightened their reins, speaking softly through the open window on the driver side of the buggy in order to calm down the horses.

Behind the paddock was a two-story house with a barn even farther back. In front of the barn was a gravel parking area. It was in front of this building that the Amish men stopped their horses, and once they were in position, the doors would slide open to let the occupants emerge.

Slowly, the driveway began to get crowded. Men in black suits with white shirts and black vests quickly unharnessed their horses and led them inside to the stalls. There was fresh hay on the floor and everything had been swept to perfection. Some of the horses snapped at each other, trying to quickly establish dominancy with their new, temporary stall mates. Several of the Amish men took off their fresh, crisp straw hats with black bands and wiped the sweat from their brow as they finished the task of taking off their horse's harness. The sun was over the horizon now and the air was warming quickly.

While the men took care of the horses, the women carried their wicker baskets or boxes of food and disappeared through a doorway at the front of the barn. Inside the main door, there was a narrow flight of stairs to the second floor where the church service would take place on this day of worship.

Several women had small children in tow, each of the little girls dressed in the same color dress with white aprons covering the front. Smaller children wore a simple one-piece apron that covered the front of their dresses and was pinned at the back of the neck while the older girls wore a white replica of their mother's black apron with an upside-down triangular bib that covered the top of their dresses and was pinned at the waist and shoulders.

At the top of the stairs, Mary Ruth glanced around and smiled at the older women who were already forming a haphazard line in the kitchen room. She took a deep breath before she followed her sister and walked toward the line, pausing to shake the hand of each woman in the line and lean down to give her a soft kiss. It was the ritual for each church Sunday, to humble oneself and ponder upon the importance of extended community. Some of the older women held her hand longer than others while some of the younger women barely touched her hand at all. She always knew which women would brush past her. It was something Mary Ruth was too familiar with, but it always made her smile.

After she had greeted all of the women, she stood at the end of the line beside her sister. Now, they would be the ones greeting any newcomers to the service. The process always seemed to take a long time, especially as younger women with children began to arrive. The little ones would slow their *mamm* down, and there was more of a lapse between greetings.

While she waited, Mary Ruth glanced over her shoulder at the large room behind her. There were three windows on each of the walls in addition to the large open doorway where she stood. The room was divided into two sections. She knew that one was for the men who would sit facing the other section, the one reserved for the women. The backless church benches were lined up in perfectly neat rows. Separating those two sections were two rows of cushioned folding chairs that faced each other. The bishop, ministers, and deacons would sit in those folding chairs, facing each other, with the rest of the congregation sitting behind them.

On each bench was a worn, thick copy of the *Ausbund.* Those copies had been in their *gmay* since the 1950s, cherished by generations of Amish. Mary Ruth loved the feel of the books when she held them in her hands. It was almost as if she could feel the love from the years long past. And she could certainly hear the voices of those people, ancestors of her family and her neighbors, as they lifted together to sing the many beautiful songs within those books.

Mary Ruth leaned against the doorframe, smiling at the women who entered the kitchen. It was taking longer for the newcomers to make their rounds to greet everyone, especially since most of them had four or five little children crowded around their legs. She loved to see the little ones, especially the little girls.

On church Sunday, their little black shoes shone from having been polished to perfection. Most mothers dressed their daughters in the same color dresses, something which helped to identify which children belonged to which mother. Some of the youngest ones had tiny little braids on their foreheads to help keep their growing hair out of their eyes and under their prayer *kapps.*

Mary Ruth watched the children as she stood next to her older sister, Leah. They were just two years apart in age and as close as sisters could get. Since they shared a room together and split all of the kitchen chores, they were rarely apart, despite Leah being twenty and eager to take her kneeling vow in the fall.

"Look at him!" Leah whispered, interrupting Mary Ruth's thoughts. Her older sister had narrowed her eyes and pursed her lips as she glared over Mary Ruth's shoulder.

"Who?" Mary Ruth glanced in the direction where her sister was staring. She saw nothing or no one that was out of the ordinary. "Look at who?"

"That Samuel Lapp," Leah hissed under her breath. Her displeasure was more than apparent.

Mary Ruth looked again, scanning the men that were still downstairs. Her eyes fell upon Samuel. He was at the bottom of the stairs, standing apart from his regular group of friends. He leaned against the wall, waiting for the men to climb the stairs to join the women in the worship room. Mary Ruth still saw nothing unusual. Samuel wasn't doing much of anything and certainly nothing to call attention to himself. Confused about what her sister meant, Mary Ruth turned back toward Leah and asked, "What about Samuel?"

There was no mistaking the disapproving look on Leah's face. It was as though a dark cloud had passed overhead, casting shadows upon her. Leah tilted her head forward and lowered her voice so that no one could overhear her next words. "He's falling away from the Lord and taking his *rumschpringe* much too seriously." She paused, more for dramatic effect than any other reason. "I heard that he was running with those three car-driving Miller Lane Mennonites over the weekend."

This statement caused Mary Ruth to laugh softly. "You heard that? Shows you what good your ears are!" She smiled and whispered, "He wasn't with those Miller Lane boys. He was at the social gathering on Friday night. Not only did I see him with my own two eyes, I spoke to him!"

Leah arched an eyebrow. "Really? Then I suspect

that you, too, arrived home at morning milking time on Saturday? I'm sure *Mamm* and *Daed* were none too happy with you, too!" Her voice dripped with sarcasm.

Morning milking? Mary Ruth had spoken to him at nine o'clock. By ten, he was gone and she had left for home shortly thereafter. Was it possible that Samuel had left the group and not returned to his farm? Could he have continued his journey and run off with the Miller Lane Mennonites? "He was out until morning milking? How would you know such a thing? You shouldn't spread such gossip," Mary Ruth said disapprovingly.

"You know that our brother Simon works at the carpentry shop with him, Mary Ruth. Where else would I hear such a thing? His older brother, Jonas Junior, was terribly upset with Samuel because he was tired and lazy all day. And Simon overheard that his *daed* was furious with him. He came home while the rest were doing morning chores."

"I don't believe you," Mary Ruth whispered.

Leah nodded. "*Ja*! And he left his horse at Miller's Store all night. Eli Miller was right upset because Samuel didn't clean up after the horse, nor did he replace the hay that Eli had left there for his own horse."

"Leah!" Mary Ruth gasped. "That's simply cannot be true!"

"Simon said there was quite a row at the Lapp farm about Samuel's misbehavior," Leah said with conviction. "Seems he's conforming more to the world these days than he is toward Christ."

Mary Ruth looked back at Samuel. He was leaning against the wall, his hands thrust into his pants' pockets and his hat was tipped forward, casting a shadow on his face. She couldn't be certain but she thought he might be sleeping, even though he was standing up. No wonder, she thought. He was probably exhausted from being out late on Friday and working all day on Saturday. "I don't believe you," she repeated softly, even though she wasn't certain that was true.

Leah pursed her lips and frowned, staring at her younger sister with a concerned look on her face. "I'd hang my bonnet on someone else's peg before I fell sweet on that one, Mary Ruth." She lowered her voice. "He's hopeless, if you ask me!"

Before Mary Ruth could respond, a silence fell over the gathering and the energy in the room started to dissipate. Socializing time was clearly over as the ministers began to emerge from the stairwell and make their rounds in the greeting line. When they finished shaking the hands of the women, they single-filed to the chairs in the middle of the room, silently announcing that service was to begin.

The elderly women sat down behind one row of the men. Then the married men began to enter the room and take their places on the other side. Only when they were seated did the young women with children enter the room and take the back rows, leaving an empty two rows in between them and the elderly women. Mary Ruth knew that it was where she was to sit with her sister. They waited until the women were seated before they followed and found their place. And, finally, the single men entered the room and sat on the benches between the married men and elderly men.

As soon as they sat, without any word or indication, the men reached for their straw hats and took them off their heads. The men along the back row reached up and hung the hats on the row of nails over the windows while the other men slid their hats under their benches. Other than the noise of shuffling feet and benches scraping against the floor, the room was quiet.

Then the singing began.

One man at the back of the men's section of the room started singing the first syllable of the selection from the *Ausbund.* Mary Ruth shut her eyes, listening to the long, drawn-out word and the rhythm of the song. Then, when it was time for everyone else to continue singing the rest of the song, Mary Ruth joined in, knowing both the words and the tune by heart. After each line of the song, the same man would start the next by singing the first syllable, creating the rhythm for the song with his loud voice so full of adoration for the Lord. It was Mary Ruth's favorite part of the church service.

She watched as the ministers stood up and left the room once more. She knew that they were returning to the back room to discuss the sermon for the day. Between the bishop, ministers, and deacons, two would be selected to preach. She hoped it would be the bishop, for he always gave *wunderbaar gut* sermons and sometimes quoted poetry in German. Mary Ruth liked the songlike quality of his poems.

Someone opened the windows along the front of the building, letting in the rising sunshine and a fresh breeze. It was the perfect day to worship the Lord.

While Leah sat up straight and stared ahead as the church elders emerged from the back room, Mary Ruth took a quick moment to look once more over her shoulder at Samuel. Her mind was in a whirl. She had noticed that he had left shortly after their brief conversation but hadn't thought to inquire about his disappearance. Truth be told, she had been surprised that Samuel had shown up at all. She had naturally presumed that he had returned home, especially since she knew that he had to work early in the morning.

But to think that he had left the gathering, driven his horse and buggy over to Miller Lane to be with the Mennonites? She wondered about such a decision. After all, her *mamm* always said that birds of a feather flock together. And that group of Miller Lane Mennonite youth had a fast reputation, one that troubled the Amish *g'may*. It was also a fact that this small group was causing issues among their own church district and leadership.

Yet, Mary Ruth knew, while Samuel was known for marching to his own drum, he wasn't worthy of such a rebellious reputation, of that she was certain. He always seemed to be at the center of scuttlebutt, people loving to talk about him and his outrageous behaviors. He liked to provoke his brother's wife, Rachel, that was a known fact. And when they were younger, he often skipped school to go fishing in a nearby pond. Once, she remembered, he had even snuck out of a church service to take up the fishing rod.

Of late, Samuel seemed to be less of a problem, but she wondered if it was because he wasn't around much. She had heard that he spent his free time away from the farm. He rarely attended social gatherings, and no one seemed to talk about where he was. She had wanted to presume that he was home with his family, but she knew that would have been foolish. Someone like Samuel wasn't bound to sit home at all.

She tried to put Samuel Lapp and the wild story of his Friday evening out of her mind as she sat on the hard bench and focused on the church service.

The first minister was preaching about faith and how Abraham's people had such faith in God. His voice took on a song-like quality as he talked, his voice stretching over the heads of almost two hundred and fifty people who were seated on those backless benches, listening to his words.

"Abraham and Sarah. The parents of many nations, not one single nation, but *many* nations. God's hand was at work in both of their lives. Out of barrenness and emptiness, God promised them life and hope. But this divine covenant, established by God, was meant to reach far beyond Abraham and Sarah. This covenant extends to all the generations that came from their offspring. This covenant of life and hope extends to you."

Mary Ruth shut her eyes, listening to his words. A covenant of life and hope. She liked the sound of that. Did she have a strong enough faith? She often wondered about that. She tried to live a pure and faithful life. But she often felt as though she was lacking. Something was missing and she wasn't certain what it was. The discussion about Samuel had really struck a chord with her. If people thought that Samuel was so wild, what would they think of her for going to those unchaperoned gatherings? She certainly didn't want people talking about her and questioning her faith, not the way that people were questioning Samuel's.

I'll not go to any more of those gatherings and I will follow God more closely, she told herself. And immediately, a great weight was lifted from her shoulders. She felt lighter and free, knowing that God was pleased with her decision. Mayhaps, she wondered, Samuel might feel the same way if only he, too, would open his heart to commit his life to God.

The sun was high overhead when the service finally ended. The men hurried to help set up the tables. They took wooden boards and quickly lifted the benches so that the legs slid into the boards, raising the benches off the ground and quickly converting them into tables. The remaining benches were slid underneath, in expectation of the first seating of people for the noon fellowship meal.

While the men prepared the tables, the women retreated to the kitchen to make certain that the food was ready for serving. Mary Ruth and Leah filled up the pitchers that lined the counter with cool water and squeezed fresh lemons into it. Millie and Marie Alderfer walked before them, setting plastic glasses down by each plate while Mary Ruth and Leah followed, filling up the glasses with the fresh water.

The older and married men ate at one table while the older and younger married women ate at another. The bishop, ministers, and deacons sat at the table in-between the two other tables, accompanied by several elderly men with long white beards. Without a word, the room fell silent and heads bowed for a short silent prayer. Then, the eating commenced.

The tables were piled high with fresh bread, homemade jam, cup cheese, bowls of chow-chow and pickles, and plates of sliced meats. There were even bowls of brown-sugared pretzels that the children were eyeballing with temptation. And, of course, there were fresh, homemade pies that the hostess for the service had prepared for everyone to enjoy. It was a communal meal, one that was prepared by every household, with the exception of the elderly who didn't have to bring any of the food items.

Since the older men and married men ate first, Mary Ruth kept her eyes open, looking for Samuel to join his regular group of church friends who were lingering near the open window in the back corner. However, he was nowhere to be seen. She was still looking for him when the room grew silent. She quickly bowed her head for the silent prayer that signaled the end of the first seating.

As soon as everyone got up and started to move away from the table, the younger women hurried to clear the dishes and bring the used cups over to the wash station. Once the dishes were washed and dried, Millie Ann and Marie hurried to set them out by the new place settings. The movement of over two hundred people through the room for fellowship, some having been fed and others eager to claim a seat, was certainly organized chaos and one of the greatest parts of worship Sunday, at least in Mary Ruth's mind.

But now, as she watched, she saw David Lapp and John Bucher sit down. Mary Ruth knew that Samuel must be nearby, so despite not seeing him, she hurried over to that table to make certain that his brother and friends had fresh lemon water to go along with their midday meal.

"Five in the morning?" she heard John Bucher say, laughing as he shook his head. "Sure bet your *daed* wasn't too happy with that!"

David scoffed. "Me, neither! Had to milk all those cows without his help!"

Another young man seated next to David leaned forward. "He said where he went all night?"

David shrugged. "Wherever Samuel went, only he knows the answer. He ain't saying nothing of where he went all night."

"Mayhaps he was with one of those Englische girls that hang out with those fellows?"

The young men laughed at the joke, but it was an uncomfortable laugh. There were groups of Englische girls that liked to hang around the more conservative Mennonite and less conservative Amish men. Those girls were notorious for being too willing to corrupt. It seemed like a challenge to them, and most Amish men stayed far away. But there were always stories about Amish youths who gave into the temptation and satisfied the curiosity of those less reputable girls. No one ever spoke of what happened, whether it was a simple kiss or more involved intimacy, but the rumors always ran rampant whenever the story reared its ugly head.

When David's eyes looked up and spotted Mary Ruth, he quickly sobered up. The other men quickly did the same and bent their heads over their plates of food. "*Gut martiye*, Mary Ruth," David said.

She looked around the table. "Seems your group is missing one, *ja*?" She smiled as she reached for David's glass and poured more water into it.

"Samuel, you mean," he said, quickly lowering his eyes. He hoped that she had not overheard their conversation. "I'm not certain where he made off to."

Setting the glass down in front of him, she smiled at John Bucher and reached for his glass. "Well, it sure would be a shame if he missed such *wunderbaar gut* food on a beautiful day." Her eyes scanned the groups of men that were lingering near the open windows, catching up on the weekly news.

"I'll make certain a plate is set aside for him," she said softly to David. "You let him know, *ja*? No *gut* if he's hungry, especially if he was feeling poorly yesterday."

David nodded in response but said nothing as he watched her finish serving the rest of the group. Clearly she had overheard their conversation but gave no indication of disappointment or disapproval in Samuel for taking his *rumschpringe* further than most Amish men. That wasn't too surprising, however. Mary Ruth had always been known to have a kind heart to everyone, not just Samuel. Yet, while any one of the men at the table would have been eager for her attention, they all knew that her eyes seemed to sparkle the most when Samuel Lapp was nearby.

It wasn't until the second seating of worshipers was finished with the meal that Mary Ruth finally found Samuel. She had been helping the women clean up, wiping down the tops of the make-shift tables so that the men could take them apart and carry them downstairs for stacking in the wagons used to carry the church benches. The room was almost empty now, and she noticed that many of the young men were helping to carry the benches downstairs. As she was standing in the kitchen, drying the cups that had been used by the congregation, she happened to look out the window and saw him.

He was standing in the back paddock, staring at the recently plowed fields. He was facing away from her so she couldn't see his expression, although she suspected that he was deep in thought. He always seemed to be deep in thought when his hands were tucked into his pockets and his shoulders slumped over. She wondered what he was thinking and decided to excuse herself from the rest of the cleanup in order to go find out.

After all, it was Samuel, and the talk of the congregation wasn't smiling too favorably on him on this fine day. Mayhaps, she thought, he was in need of a friend.

She walked down the stairs and smiled at a few of the older men who were lingering in the lower level of the barn. While the women cleaned the fellowship area, the men stood near the horses and exchanged whatever news they had from their farms and family. No one seemed to pay her much mind so she slipped away and headed out the back door toward the paddock where she had seen Samuel.

He was still standing there, his hands in his pockets and his head hanging over his shoulders. It was clear that he was tired and also deep in thought. She stood for a moment, her hand tucked under her chin as she watched him. Clearly, whatever he was thinking wasn't making him happy, and that worried her.

"Samuel?" she called out.

He turned around, startled by her unexpected presence. "Mary Ruth!" He lifted his head and straightened his back. "What are you doing here?"

"Saw you from the window," she said, gesturing toward the barn behind her. With the windows over the kitchen area on the second floor, it was clear that anyone else could be watching them. "Wanted to make certain you had something to eat."

He frowned. "Dinner's over, then, *ja*?"

She nodded. "But I set aside a plate for you, Samuel."

"Aw, Mary Ruth," he said, shaking his head. "No need for that."

A smile crossed her lips. She knew that she didn't have to do that, but she also knew that she wanted to make certain he didn't miss a meal. "I know," she whispered. "But I did it just the same."

His mouth twitched from side to side, as though he had something that he wanted to say but chose not to say it. Instead, he inhaled the fresh air and looked around the meadow. "Sure is a pretty farm, ain't so?"

She followed his gaze. The grass of the green pasture waved in the slight breeze, moving like water on land. A bird swooped down from the sky, dancing in the air as it flew toward the trees in the distance. "Oh, *ja*! I love the buttercups in the field!" She pointed toward the back pasture where black and white cows grazed amidst small yellow flowers. "Looks like God was painting the tips of the grass in yellow. It's so beautiful."

Samuel nodded. "*Ja*," he said. "Beautiful, especially for those who want to farm." He glanced at her. "I ain't never going to farm," he quickly declared.

"Nothing wrong with that, Samuel," Mary Ruth said. "Many of the young folks don't have farming opportunities now, do they?"

With a simple lift of his shoulders, he signaled his thoughts about farming. "Not important if you don't want to farm, I reckon." He paused and stared back over the field. He was glad that he had the work at the carpentry shop. Working in the fields seemed to be a never-ending chore. But many of the youth seemed to always lament not having enough land to follow in the footsteps of their fathers. "I just don't see why so many want to farm, anyway."

She laughed. "Farming is in our blood, isn't it?"

"Not mine!"

His quick rebuttal made her laugh again. "Oh, Samuel, you say that now. But we are all farmers, aren't we? Whether it's a small garden or a large backfield, we all plow something for a harvest. And if you think not, think about the words we speak and the lives we touch. We harvest a lot of things in our lives, even if it's not crops from soil!"

There was something about the look on his face that caused her heart to flutter. He was staring at her, studying her, yet he still appeared so distant, as though he was deliberately putting up a barrier between them. She could sense his discontent, and it made her take a step backward. She wondered if she had been too forward and the thought shamed her.

"*Ach*, *vell*," she whispered. "I reckon I should be going."

"*Ja*. Reckon your *daed*'s looking for you," he said slowly, his words even and deliberate.

She took another step backward and lifted her hand to wave goodbye before she turned around, hurrying back toward the barn where her father was most likely harnessing the horse to the buggy while her *mamm* said her goodbyes. They'd be waiting for her and it wouldn't do anyone any good if she kept them waiting. But she was glad that she had walked down to speak to Samuel. Indeed, she thought, for she knew that, during the short ride back to their farm, she would be thinking of how Samuel had stared at her, as though seeing her with fresh eyes, eyes that were curious and interested. Perhaps, she told herself, there was hope for him after all.

Chapter Four

The Sunday singing was well attended. When the weather grew warmer in spring, the youth seemed more inclined to venture out at night. After receiving the what-for from his *daed* and *mamm* for being out so late on Friday, Samuel had decided to join David at the singing, even if only for the chance to escape the tension in the house. He had enough of his *mamm*'s sighing behind his back and his *daed*'s disapproving scowls. Yes, he had told himself, time to escape the house, even if it meant going to a Sunday singing.

David had insisted that they take separate buggies. He intended to ask someone if he could bring her home. While he didn't divulge to Samuel which girl had caught his eye, David did tell him that he didn't want to be burdened with having to figure out how to get Samuel home. Samuel hadn't commented, knowing that Susie Miller was the girl riding home with him these days. But he respected his brother for wishing to keep the matter private.

The singing was being held at a farm too far away for him to walk. Samuel didn't mind taking his own buggy, for it gave him that little bit of liberty that he liked to have handy. Plus, he was still tired from the weekend and wanted to escape early so that he could get to bed before ten o'clock. Six hours of sleep would perk him up right quick!

He stood in the back of the large room, his hat tipped over his eyes so that he could shut them. They burned from exhaustion. Yet he wouldn't have traded his Friday evening for anything in the world. Driving into Lancaster with his friends had been exhilarating. They sped along the highway, the windows open and the music blasting inside the car. Robert drove fast and took curves as if he were behind the wheel of a racecar. Samuel had laughed with the other men as they passed slower cars and weaved through the traffic.

Lancaster at night was bright and alive. There were cars and people enjoying themselves until the wee hours. It was around one a.m. when they had stopped at a diner to get some food. They had even met a group of Englischer girls who looked as if they had spent their evening at a bar. With disheveled hair and bleary eyes, the girls had found the ragtag group of men curious and, as such, spent some time chatting with them. It was well after 3 a.m. when they had finally left Lancaster to return to Leola in the car. And Samuel still had to fetch the horse and buggy to get home.

The only problem with his plan was that he hadn't counted on his *daed* being up already. The sun was barely casting an orange glow along the horizon of the fading night sky. He wasn't certain what time it was. After all, he didn't wear a watch or carry a cell phone. Yet, as Samuel was unharnessing the horse when his *daed* walked into the horse stable, he realized that it was well into the hours of morning chores and he knew he was in trouble.

"Samuel Lapp!" Jonas had said, his voice sharp and loud. Startled, Samuel spun around and saw his *daed* standing in the barn door, his hands on his hips and a scowl on his face. "Where have you been?"

It wasn't often that Jonas spoke sharply to his children. In fact, Samuel couldn't remember ever hearing his *daed* raise his voice. The fact that he was on the receiving end annoyed Samuel. After all, he rationalized, a *rumschpringe* was that time in a young man's life to explore. So why would his *daed* be so angry?

So, in response to his *daed*'s question, Samuel had merely glanced over his shoulder and scowled back. "Out with friends. I'm back in time for chores."

His father had given his head a firm shake, clearly dissatisfied with Samuel's nonchalance toward the matter. "I won't be having none of this, Samuel. Running around is one thing but coming home in the early morning? You'll be worthless at work and the people will talk! Already your brother has been helping by himself for almost an hour!"

An hour? Samuel glanced at the sky. Could it be that close to five o'clock? If he felt sheepish or ashamed, he hid it behind a stoic face of indifference. "I'm here now," he said stubbornly, refusing to apologize or look ashamed. Instead, he rubbed his hand on the horse's neck before turning to walk past his father and heading to the dairy barn.

For the rest of the day, he had received the silent treatment from his family. Even David had given him a dirty look and ignored him, annoyed that the bulk of the dairy chores had fallen on his own shoulders because of Samuel's lack of responsibility. After Samuel had finished at the carpentry shop, his father had given him an endless list of chores to do around the farm as if trying to break his spirit of defiance. Truth was that Samuel was too stubborn to be broken by chore after chore. He knew that he could retire early that evening and by the next night, he'd feel fit and rested.

But, to his surprise, the tension remained through the next day, including the church service. Samuel had sensed his parents' displeasure with his behavior from the previous Friday evening. In fact, they hadn't spoken to him unless it was absolutely necessary. Their silence was irritating and getting on his nerves. So, when David mentioned the singing, Samuel had jumped at the opportunity to escape the house and mend broken fences with his brother. Attending a youth singing was bound to help, he thought.

Now, as he stood at the back of the room, the same room where church had been held earlier but where the youth were now gathered to sing and socialize, he wanted nothing more than to be back at the farm and in his bed.

He shut his eyes and remembered the young women from Friday night. They had smelled sweet, like crisp flowers. He had never been close enough to a fancy woman who wore perfume. He had liked the smell. And the lanky blond woman had seemed to pay special attention to him. She had sat next to him, her leg brushing against his as they talked. Once, her hand had even touched his leg and he had felt a shiver up his spine. No one had ever been so bold or brazen toward him in a physical manner, and to both his delight and shame, he enjoyed the physical attraction between himself and a woman. It was a new feeling for him and brought him great pleasure.

How different the social activities are for the Amish, he thought, opening his eyes to observe the singing. The women were on one side of the barn and the men on the other. Their voices carried through the barn as they sang fast-paced religious songs in both German and Englische. The sound was beautiful. Samuel had to admit that. The voices lifted together in an unspoken harmony, faster than they sang during the church service but just as beautiful. However, the songs and voices sounded nothing like the fast beat of Englischer music.

"This is three times in one week," a soft voice said by his side.

Samuel opened his eyes to find Mary Ruth staring up at him. She was so petite and small, a wisp of a woman with such soulful eyes. Despite his own vow to not get attached to anyone in his community, he found himself smiling at her. "Who's counting, Mary Ruth Smucker?"

She raised an eyebrow. "Three's an easy number to count to, ain't so?"

He laughed but didn't reply.

Quickly, she changed the subject. "Thought you might be thirsty," she whispered and handed him a glass of iced tea. "Might wake you up a bit to join the singing."

With a quick glance around the barn, Samuel was glad to notice that no one was watching them. It wouldn't do to have people observing their quiet interactions, especially since Mary Ruth had brought him a refreshment. Doing such an act in front of everyone was a very intimate gesture and worthy of gossip. "*Danke*, Mary

Ruth, but you didn't have to do that," he said gently, a reminder that he was not her beau.

As usual, his rebuke didn't appear to bother her. She merely laughed and shrugged her shoulders. "I know I didn't, but you looked thirsty and I wanted to say hello, anyway." Without another word, she smiled and hurried back to join her friends, leaving him to stare after her as she disappeared amidst a sea of women wearing colorful dresses and white heart-shaped prayer *kapps*.

During the break between songs, David and Simon joined Samuel at the back of the barn by the open door. It was warm inside the barn, a sharp contrast to the cooler spring air outside the open barn door. The stars were sparkling bright against the dark night sky.

"Samuel, *gut* to see you outside of work," Simon said, clapping him good-naturedly on his back. They had always gotten along well, even during his troublesome school years. Now that they were working together, their friendship had seemed to grow even more. "All work and no play...," he teased.

"Who says I'm not playing?" Samuel shot back, smiling devilishly. For some reason, he felt proud of the fact that he was walking outside of the line that was expected of the Amish youth.

"*Ja*, so I heard," Simon retorted, the tone of his voice not going unnoticed by Samuel. "And you seemed to be dragging at work yesterday. Mayhaps the result of too much playing the night before, ain't so?"

Samuel frowned. Dragging? He didn't like that comment coming from Simon one bit. It sounded very judgmental and that irritated him. He made a clucking noise with his tongue, shaking his head slowly. "Seem to be powerful interested in what I do with my free time during my *rumschpringe*, Simon Smucker. Is there a reason for that, I wonder?"

"Actually, there is," he said, tipping his head closer to Samuel so that no one could overhear their conversation. "David said you brought your own buggy tonight. Mayhaps you could give my sister a ride home, if no one else asks her? I have my own plans but want her home safe." Simon pulled back and stared him in the eyes. "Trusting you won't be whisking her off until milking time, *ja*?"

"Leah or Mary Ruth?" Samuel asked, trying to act noncommittal and disinterested. He hadn't intended on taking anyone home from the singing. Fact was that he had been contemplating seeing if Robert was around later. Taking one of the Smucker girls home would hinder that idea. And he didn't want tongues wagging, especially given the interest that Mary Ruth displayed toward him. "Reckon I could. As a favor to you, 'tis all."

"I'll let Mary Ruth know then," Simon said. "And *danke*, Samuel. Although I'm sure it's not too much of a hardship for you." He laughed. "Taking Mary Ruth home, that is." With that, he turned on a heel and walked back toward the other men.

David waited until Simon was gone before he cast a stern look at his younger brother. "You be careful with that Mary Ruth," he said sharply. "You know she's ripe for heart ache when it comes to you. Too quick to defend you when others are willing to turn their backs. I won't have you hurting that girl, Samuel."

"I'm not looking to court anyone, David. You know that and she does, too," Samuel snapped. "I can't help it if she's looking for signs that ain't there!"

"Just be careful, brother," David warned solemnly before he, too, disappeared to rejoin his other friends.

It was close to ten when the group began to break up and pairs of Amish folks began to disappear into the darkness. Samuel sighed as he scanned the crowd, looking for Mary Ruth. She was standing near the refreshment table with two of her friends and a lone Amish man. Samuel frowned, recognizing Elias Lantz. He was standing next to Mary Ruth and clearly paying more attention to her than was normally warranted unless there were ulterior motives. He clenched his teeth and took a deep breath, too aware of how annoyed he was that Elias was making a move on his Mary Ruth.

His Mary Ruth.

The words lingered in his mind and he quickly shook his head. She wasn't his Mary Ruth, he corrected himself. After all, he didn't have any intentions of settling down. Not yet, anyhow. He knew that his brother had set his sights on Susie Miller and his friend, John Bucher was secretly courting that Millie Ann. That was all well and good for those fellows. But Samuel Lapp had no intentions of courting anyone for several years to come, he told himself.

Yet, despite this argument, he had made a promise to Simon Smucker. His sister needed a ride home and Samuel had promised to give it to her. A promise was a promise, he argued. And there was no issue with courting when a promise was made, even if the promise involved Mary Ruth.

Approaching the group, Samuel strode up to Mary Ruth. He noticed that she stopped talking when he came near and he liked how she lifted her blue eyes to look at him. She smiled, just slightly, but enough so that he noticed it. With a feeling of protectiveness, Samuel positioned himself between Elias and Mary Ruth, tipping his head in greeting to the other women but ignoring the man at his back. "Mary Ruth, your brother Simon mentioned you'd be needing a ride home, *ja*?"

She beamed at him, her eyes sparkling and her cheeks flushing pink. "That would be *wunderbaar gut*, Samuel. I think he's left already and walking don't suit me tonight, if I can avoid it."

"You don't have to walk," Elias offered, an eager smile on his face. "I'll take you in my buggy, Mary Ruth."

Samuel reached for her arm, slowly guiding her away from the group. He ignored the tightening in his chest when Elias had tried to change the plan. "*Danke*, Elias, but I have this covered tonight." And, within seconds, they were far away from a disappointed Elias and a stunned group of young women who watched as Samuel led Mary Ruth toward the outside in order to find his horse and buggy.

Once inside the buggy, Samuel glanced at Mary Ruth as she sat next to him. He wasn't certain how this had all happened and he didn't want her to make any presumptions about why she was sitting there. Oh, she sure was pretty all right and would make a perfect Amish wife, he told himself. But Samuel knew that she'd be settling down with someone sooner rather than later and that someone was not him, that was for sure and certain. He wasn't near ready to settling down.

With a deep breath, Samuel cleared his throat. "I'm taking you home because your brother asked, Mary Ruth."

She smiled, staring straight ahead. "I know."

Her nonchalant response irritated him. She was too calm and easygoing, too willing to agree with him. He wondered if she was teasing him. "Don't go thinking that I'm interested in courting you," he blurted out. "I ain't."

She laughed and looked at him. "Samuel Lapp!"

"What?"

"I know that, too!" She shook her head, still laughing. "But it sure is neighborly of you to take me home. My brother surely appreciates it." Gently, she laid her hand on his arm and waited for him to look at her once again. "As do I," she said softly.

He glanced down at her hand. It was warm and soft on his bare arm. Her skin was clear and white, unblemished from working indoors all winter. When Mary Ruth removed it, he felt tingles where it had rested. His heart pounded inside his chest. "Well, just so we have that straight. Don't need no tongues wagging or false hopes setting store in something that ain't so, *ja*?"

She returned her gaze to look out the window, another smile playing on her lips. "*Ja*!" she retorted playfully.

Samuel cleared his throat and looked back to the road. "Still," he began carefully. "Can't have just anyone taking you home, I reckon. No *gut* having that Elias Lantz chasing after you."

"What's wrong with Elias Lantz?" she asked, laughing at Samuel's comment.

"Aw, you can't tell me you don't see how poorly he treats his horse! That mare is bones and needs a lot of grooming. He sure don't see fit to rub her down before he takes her out, that's for certain!" Samuel said, shaking his head. "A man treats his horse poorly, he sure ain't gonna take care of his girl."

"I'm not his girl," she said quickly. Then, after the briefest of hesitations, she added, "And why would you care anyway?" Mary Ruth tossed back at him lightly. "You just set the story straight between us, ain't so?"

Samuel glanced at her out of the corner of his eye and shook his head. "Mayhaps but can't have you running with that Elias. He's no *gut* for someone like you."

She laughed again. The sound was light and cheerful, two words that just about summed up everything when it came to Mary Ruth. Nothing seemed to bother her or make her feel poorly. A smile always graced her face and a sparkle twinkled in her eyes. People were naturally drawn to her, wanting to have just an ounce of her happiness rub off on them. He fought that same urge, knowing that settling into a steady courtship with anyone, especially with Mary Ruth, would hinder his adventures with his Mennonite friends.

When he pulled the buggy up to her house, he made a fuss about getting out and walking around the buggy to open her door. He reached out to take her hand in his as she climbed down with a spring to her step. For a moment, he held onto her hand and she paused, looking up at him.

"I never said *danke* for saving me a plate earlier today," he said softly.

"Why, Samuel," she replied, her voice barely a whisper. "You knew that I would. I always do."

He still held her hand, and for just a moment, he took a step forward, the toes of his boots brushing against hers. "What I said back there..." He nodded toward the buggy. "Well, it ain't that I wouldn't court you," he added, stressing the word *wouldn't*. For a moment, just one, he rubbed his thumb over the back of her hand. "It's just that…*vell*…just that I'm not about to court anyone right now." He stumbled over the words, his voice low and soft with a rare gentleness that was saved only for moments like this.

She bit her lower lip and stared down at the ground. Even in the darkness, she could sense the color rise to her cheeks. She was glad that he couldn't see. "I understand, Samuel."

He raised her hand to his lips and brushed his lips against the back of it. "You always do, don't you, Mary Ruth?" He chuckled softly, liking the way that she looked away from him at his gesture. He had startled her by kissing the back of her hand, an innocent gesture but one that presumed much for a man who claimed not to wish to court her. "I don't know why you always stick up for me but you do."

She smiled in the darkness. "Reckon old habits die hard."

"Hmmm," he whispered under his breath, his voice low and soft. "Mayhaps that old habit can stick around a bit, Mary Ruth. If only you'd wait it out…" He let his voice trail off, leaving the rest unspoken. But his intent was clear.

"Good night, Samuel," she said softly, pulling her hand from his grasp and slipping away from his presence. "You be careful driving home and think twice about running over to your Miller Lane fellows. It might do you some good to walk the path a little straighter… stop those tongues from wagging anymore." And with that, she turned and hurried to the door.

Her words lingered in his mind as she disappeared

into her parents' house, one light still burning in the window to help her find her way. She had always been so good to him, sticking up for him when others wouldn't. Now, she was sending him a kind warning that people were talking. And Samuel knew that, once a reputation was established, it was hard to erase it.

He waited until he saw her *outten* the light before he turned back to the buggy and climbed inside. His mind whirled at the turmoil of emotions that he always felt when he was near her. If only he didn't have such an interest in exploring the world and living life. Yet, no matter what he did or how much trouble he found himself in, there was Mary Ruth, championing him despite unpopular opinions and seemingly waiting patiently for his wild ways to die down.

The only problem, Samuel thought to himself, he didn't know if they'd ever die down enough to be the kind of Amish man someone like Mary Ruth deserved. He slapped the reins on the horse's back and clucked his tongue. As the buggy lurched forward, he leaned back in the seat. No, he told himself, Mary Ruth deserved better than the likes of him, no matter how much she hoped that he would change.

Chapter Five

A few afternoons later, Samuel used the gasoline powered weed whacker, cutting down the overgrown grass along the fence line of his father's far pasture. The sides of the pasture ran up along the hill, parallel to the road. Then, at the top of the hill, it cut along Musser School Lane. His father often asked him to cut the weeds along the fences on Saturday afternoons when he finished working at the carpentry shop. Samuel didn't mind since he liked to be by himself and ponder different things.

He often thought about what he wanted to do with his life. His daydreams included everything from seeing the ocean to visiting the big city, Philadelphia. These daydreams focused on travel and exploration, learning more about the ways of the Englische and enjoying the world of technology. They included things like cell phones and computers, cars and planes. But those daydreams never once included a future of weed whacking twenty acres of fence line.

Despite having grown up within the community, Samuel had always wondered why the Amish church permitted gasoline-powered machinery for certain types of yard work but not others. Their rules seemed conflicting, maybe even a little hypocritical. But when the chores fell onto his shoulders, he certainly wasn't about to question it. Of course, the decisions on what could or could not be used varied from district to district. Just two miles down the road, the families couldn't use gasoline-powered lawn mowers. Instead, they had to use the old-fashioned push mowers with the metal blades that spun around, moving faster if it was pushed faster. Living in a progressive *gmay* had its benefits, that was for certain, he thought, as he shut off the machine to take a break and drink some of the water he'd carried along.

"Hey, Samuel," someone called out as he took a long pull from his bottle of water.

He lowered the bottle. "Who's that?" he called out.

Samuel set the water bottle on the ground and started walking toward the hill. He took his straw hat off of his head and wiped at his forehead with the back of his arm. Small pieces of grass clippings clung to his sweaty skin, which was tanned a golden brown. He tried to brush the clippings away, but they seemed glued to his arms.

"Peter!" the voice called back.

As Samuel crested the hill, he noticed the car just below and his friend leaning out the open window. "*Wie gehts*?" Samuel asked as he crawled through the fencing and jumped down the incline.

He didn't know Peter Bartlett very well. After all, it was only a week ago that Robert Miller had introduced them, and that adventure hadn't gone very well. Unlike his other friends, Peter was not Mennonite. He came from a family of Presbyterians who didn't regularly attend church. Samuel hadn't been able to understand how anyone could affiliate himself with any church if he never attended. But he had figured that it was an Englische tradition.

The one thing that Samuel knew about Peter was that he was quite smart. At twenty-one, Peter would be starting his senior year of college in the autumn at Penn State. He was studying agriculture and wanted to eventually farm. When Peter went back to school, he spent his time studying and socializing with his Englische friends. But he was home for the summer now and, according to Paul, he worked at a local outlet mall. Apparently he hated it, preferring the farming environment to the retail industry. That was one of the reasons that Peter liked to hang out with Robert and Paul. Samuel suspected that was also why Peter now considered him a friend.

"Headed into town to get some food. Want to come along? I'm picking up Paul and Robert on Miller Lane," Peter said. He leaned out the window, his arm tapping on the side of the car door.

With tanned skin and a dazzling smile, Peter was definitely a good-looking Englischer. With that, Samuel knew, came the Englischer girls. He had noticed how the young women were attracted to him the other night when they went into Lancaster. Just one more of the many strange things about the Englische culture that he didn't understand: their emphasis on outer beauty instead of inner strength and goodness was foreign to Samuel. In fact, he had thought about that fact just the other night as he watched the young Englische women laugh at Peter's jokes and lobby to sit next to him at the diner.

But now, that thought was long gone from Samuel's

mind. Forgotten were his questions about the non-Amish culture. All that mattered was that Peter had stopped by to see if Samuel wanted to grab a quick bite to eat. If only I didn't have so many chores, he complained to himself.

Samuel glanced back at the top of the hill. The weeds were growing high by the fencing. It always amazed him how high the weeds could grow in just one week. Unfortunately, his *daed* liked a neat and tidy farm. No weeds. No overgrown grass. Clean fence lines. Samuel knew that his parents felt that the care of the property and house reflected on their own faith. The better it was maintained, the more loyal to God. He never had understood that philosophy, but having accepted it, Samuel just did as he was told to help keep that image of loyalty through a well-maintained farm.

"I don't know," Samuel started to reply. "My *daed* will be awful sore if I don't finish this fence line tonight."

That was the truth. Neither one of his parents had said so much as a word to him over the past few days. Samuel wasn't quite certain what to make of that. It wasn't as though he had been out drinking alcohol or even smoking cigarettes. He knew that plenty of Amish young men did experiment with those things, some even trying drugs. But Samuel had no interest in that. He just liked the freedom that came with *rumschpringe.*

"Aw, come on," Peter said, hanging out the window. "You'll be back in two hours. Plenty of time to finish."

Samuel scratched at the side of his head. With the other fellows being picked up next, Samuel would get to ride in the front passenger seat. He'd be able to roll down the window and hang his arm outside, feeling the cool air on his skin as Peter drove along the winding back roads. It was quite tempting. "*Ja*, *vell*, he's still mad about the other night."

Peter laughed, his eyes mocking Samuel. "I thought *rumschpringe* was a time of no questions asked." The way he said the word *rumschpringe* dripped with sarcasm.

"There's questions, all right," Samuel quipped. It annoyed Samuel that Peter was mocking him. "Especially when others are stuck doing my morning chores!"

With a casual shrug of his shoulders, Peter started the car engine again. He seemed disappointed that Samuel wasn't going to skip out on his chores and take the trip into town. But it was clear that the trip was going to happen, with or without Samuel. "Maybe next time, then," Peter said, shifting the car into gear as he prepared to drive down the road.

"Wait!" Samuel called out. Two hours, he told himself. The sun would still be high enough in the sky, and in all likelihood, his *daed* wouldn't even notice that he was gone. He could always say that he ran out of weed whacker cord and took a quick break to run over to Jake's to get some more. He was about halfway between the two farms, anyway. It was a logical excuse.

He hurried back up the hill and glanced down at the farm. No one was in the barnyard or in the lower field. Certainly no one had seen him disappear down the hill, nor was anyone keeping track of his progress. Satisfied, Samuel hurried back down the hill and ran around the side of the car. "I'll go. I'm hungry from all this work. Nothing wrong with a little break, *ja*?"

"That's more like it," Peter said, a smile lighting up his tanned face as he waited for Samuel to buckle his seat belt before he started to drive down the road toward their friends' house. "This is our time to have some fun. All work and no play sure does make for some boring weekends!"

The sun was setting when Samuel jumped out of the car and ran back up the hill to crawl under the fence. He waved once at the car and watched as they drove down the road, Peter flooring the gas pedal and the engine roaring away. He even sped around the corner, the noise of the car lingering far longer after the car had actually disappeared from view. Peter drove too fast, that was for certain. While Samuel didn't mind going fast on the highway, especially with the windows rolled down and the music blaring, he always felt that Peter was taking chances on the back roads.

The first thing Samuel realized was that the weed whacker was missing. He walked up and down the fence line, looking for it. He was certain he had left it by the tenth section of fencing, but just to make certain, he walked up and down the row, looking for the machine. But it was gone.

He sighed, annoyed at himself for having gone and even more annoyed at Peter for insisting that they go into Lancaster for a bite to eat. When Peter had said he wanted to get some food, Samuel had assumed he meant into New Holland or Bird-in-Hand. But Peter had his own ideas and had taken the three young men thirty minutes away to a small, dark pub in Lancaster. Samuel also had not liked that Peter had two beers. So when Peter wanted to walk around, Samuel was supportive, knowing that the fresh air and time would insure that Peter wasn't intoxicated when he drove them back to Leola.

Samuel also noticed that Peter had his own idea about time. In Peter's world, time was meant to be wasted and used, but only at his own convenience. Samuel had tried to act unconcerned about the time, but as two hours slipped into three and then into four, he began to worry. He'd never get the weed whacking finished, and with the sun starting to set in the sky, he knew he'd never make it home in time for evening chores. Once again, Daniel and David would be stuck with extra work. Not only would Samuel hear complaints from his *daed*, his brothers were certain to give him an earful, too.

So, as he walked down the hill toward the farm, he tried to think of a dozen different ways to explain his absence from the farm. But, short of outright lying, he quickly realized that there was no escape from the angry words of his parents and brothers. He quickly understood that he had no choice but to accept their reprimand, promise to not do it again, and hurry away to his room for the rest of the evening. He was tired anyway so that plan seemed the most sensible.

"Samuel Lapp!" his mother said sharply as he walked into the kitchen. "You had us worried half to death!" She was sitting in her chair, working on cross-stitching some squares for a quilt. She set the fabric on her lap as she looked up. "You best go to see your *daed* in the barn! He's quite unhappy, Samuel."

Samuel stared at his mother, unable to speak, as he realized that nothing ever changed. The routine was the same, day in and day out: Rise, chores, eat, work, eat, chores, sleep. Every night, after the supper was served and enjoyed, his *mamm* would clean the dishes, dry them, and put them away before sitting in the same chair to mend clothing or work on her cross-stitch. His father would sit in the chair next to her, the kerosene lamp hissing overhead as he read *The Budget* and shared stories about other Amish communities throughout the country.

That could be me, he told himself as he stared at his *mamm*. Same routine, same life. One day, he'd wake up and be older, tired and weary. Gray hair, gray beard, lots of wrinkles, and when he looked back on his life, he would only see what he saw every day: the routine. Samuel just didn't see what was so appealing about it.

"Did you hear me, Samuel?" his mother snapped.

"Huh?" he uttered out of his daydream.

She gave two quick *tsk*, *tsk* under her breath as she shook her head. "You need to go apologize to your *daed* and make this right, son. It's time you start taking responsibility for your actions and become the man you will need to become to support a family."

Samuel frowned. "A family?"

Katie pressed her lips together tightly as she stared at him. "While you think you will never settle down, you still have a family, even if it's only your *daed* and me! You are almost twenty years old. You need to stop acting like a wild child and start behaving like a proper man!" He was used to her sighs and disapproving looks but not to these words. Never had she spoken so harshly to him. "You think that *rumschpringe* means you can run wild, Samuel, but there is a limit to the tolerance that people will have for such poor choices and behavior," she said, snapping the thread that she was using on the quilt square.

There was a sharp edge to her look, one that caused

Samuel to feel forced into a corner. Fight or flight, he thought. Since fight was clearly not an option, he turned on his heel and hurried back out the door. Better to face his *daed* without his *mamm* within hearing distance. Her willingness to forgive was clearly not in order this evening.

But the wrath of his father was even worse. Silence. His father was finishing with the chores, Daniel and David letting the cows out for the evening, when Samuel walked through the barn doorway.

David saw him first and frowned. "Nice job, Samuel!" he snapped sarcastically.

Samuel lowered his eyes. "I'm sorry, David."

"You should be! Getting sick of pulling your weight around this farm. Mayhaps you should do some of my chores for a few mornings to see what it feels like!"

Daniel walked over to his younger brothers and set his hand on Samuel's shoulder. "Best be rethinking some of your choices, brother." His words were not unkind, but the message was clear. "Some of them are not making you too popular around here."

But Jonas didn't say a word. He continued with his chores, ignoring Samuel who stood behind him, waiting for his reprimand. Jonas moved in slow motion, his eyes clearly avoiding any connection with his youngest son. The unspoken message was even louder and clearer than his *mamm*'s harsh words: If Samuel continued on the path he was traveling, he risked becoming an outcast from the family and that meant a separation, both physical and spiritual. It was clear that his father was reminding Samuel that a separation from the family would be filled with such silence, and if his behavior continued, a separation was exactly what would happen.

Chapter Six

Mary Ruth sat quietly at the kitchen table, playing with her fork while she listened to the conversation between her two older brothers. She pushed the scrambled eggs back and forth on her plate, not eating because of the growing pit in her stomach. She felt her heart flutter and her pulse quicken as they shook their heads. There was a dark cloud looming overhead, a tenseness in the air that was palpable, contrasting with the bright mid-May sunshine outside. The conversation was not the normal jovial one, filled with stories that brought rounds of laughter to the family. Instead, Samuel Lapp was the topic at hand, and while his antics were of great interest among her brothers, his parents clearly did not find them as humorous.

Breakfast was always the liveliest family time in their house. It was also the only meal where everyone was present on a regular basis. Most days, for the noon meal, her older brother, Simon, was at his job at the Lapp carpentry store while her other brother, Stephen, might join them for the meal or might take some time to run his own errands. The rest of Mary Ruth's siblings had married and were living at their own houses. The Smucker farm was not as big as some of the others in the immediate area, and especially since the crops had already been planted, her father and brother Stephen often had some free time in the afternoons to visit with friends and neighbors if they wanted. Yet, always, they gathered in the morning to start their day off with a silent prayer, good food, and family fellowship.

But this morning, despite the wonderful smells of sizzling bacon, scrambled eggs, and morning potatoes, there was something unpleasant in the air and Mary Ruth sensed it. Indeed, there was an unspoken tension that lingered above their heads. Quietly, she sat next to her older sister, Leah, and listened intently as her two brothers bantered back and forth about Samuel.

"*Ja*, Junior was quite upset with him yesterday," Simon said. "Seems Samuel arrived late for work in the morning. Overheard them arguing about it."

"Again?" Stephen shook his head in disbelief. "That's the third time you mentioned it in two weeks! What's he thinking?"

"He's taking his *rumschpringe* further than most, *ja*?"

Stephen frowned. "Running free is one thing, but I ran into his brother David at the supply store, and he said that Samuel's hardly ever at home at night." It was a known fact that Stephen was preparing to take his baptism classes during the upcoming summer months in preparation for his kneeling vow in the fall. The eldest of the four remaining children living at the Smucker's home, Stephen was always quick to set an example for his other siblings. After all, it was certain that he had his eye on a particular young woman and would be announcing his own marriage soon enough.

Simon spread some butter on his toast. "I must say that he works hard enough during the day at the shop, but he sure does seem to like those fellows from Miller Lane. Spends a lot of time with them, I hear."

"Bad news, that crowd," Stephen added.

Her *mamm* sighed, listening to the story with a somber expression on her face. "I heard from Susan Weaver that the Mennonites are beside themselves with those boys. Buying fast cars, staying out late at night."

Shaking his head, Mary Ruth's *daed* chimed in. "Seems their church leaders don't know what to do with them, either. I heard Bishop Peachey talking about it with Whitey and Eli Stoltzfus."

Miriam's eyes looked sorrowful, and Mary Ruth knew that she felt the pain for Katie and Jonas. If one child went wild, it certainly reflected poorly on the entire family, and that was bad news for the Lapps. "Seems that boy has just fallen into a crowd that's simply no *gut*," her *mamm* said. "His poor *mamm*, Katie, must be at her wit's end."

"Everyone sure is putting an awful lot of importance in stories," Mary Ruth said quietly.

The room fell silent and all eyes fell upon her. It was unlike Mary Ruth to speak up during the meal and especially about so controversial a topic. She felt a flush of warmth spread across her face because of their attention. Her *daed* narrowed his eyes and stared at his youngest child. "How so, Daughter?"

"The Bible teaches us to help one another and to turn a deaf ear to gossip," she said meekly. "Unless Simon was there that night, we can't be sure that Samuel was with those Mennonites, can we? And it sure seems that Samuel isn't saying it's true. Seems to be gossip, that's all." She hesitated, trying to think of the right words to say but quickly realizing that she probably shouldn't have said anything at all.

"You know I wasn't there, Mary Ruth! You shouldn't suggest such things," Simon said quickly.

Mary Ruth raised an eyebrow and looked at him. "And I'm surprised at you, Simon. Didn't Samuel give me a ride home as a favor to you the other night after the singing? At your request?"

Simon narrowed his eyes at his sister. "*Ja*, I asked him to take you home. But don't think I didn't talk to him first. Didn't want him dragging you over to Miller Lane!"

"He would never do such a thing!" she gasped. "He's nothing but respectful with me and you know that, Simon!"

"One can't be too sure," her brother mumbled.

"Where there is smoke…," her *mamm* started.

"There's fire," her *daed* finished. He pointed his finger at Mary Ruth. "Don't be getting any thoughts of sweetness for that one, Mary Ruth. That family has been riddled with problems for the past few years. You know that as well as I do."

"*Daed*," she pleaded.

But her father held up his hand, stopping her before she could say too much. "That Samuel will be having the bishop knocking at their door soon enough, and I don't need our family name associated with such discussion."

"They've been naught but *wunderbaar gut* to our family," Mary Ruth said meekly. "Doesn't the Bible teach us to love our neighbor as ourselves in both joy and affliction?"

"And I'll not be having you talk back," her *daed* said sharply. "Katie Lapp is a right *gut* woman, but her children seem to stray toward walking crooked on the path. They seem drawn to worldliness. I won't have my daughter involved or associated with such a boy."

Her mother nodded her head in agreement. "A reputation soiled will never be clean."

Mary Ruth hung her head, her appetite vanished and her heart pounding inside of her chest. If only there was some indication that she had reason to hope that, mayhaps, Samuel Lapp might have a serious interest in her, she would defend him. But he was too independent and rebellious to be taken seriously, even in those moments of intimacy, when he shared a kind word or caressed her hand.

For the rest of the meal, Mary Ruth remained quiet, too aware that her sister Leah and brother Simon were watching her. She didn't need their concern, she thought to herself. She knew what she was doing. And she knew that Samuel Lapp was not walking a crooked path…at least not one that was so far removed from the way of the People. He would be redeemed and take that kneeling vow. And, Mary Ruth hoped, she would be beside him shortly afterward.

"Don't you fret none about *Mamm* and *Daed*," Leah whispered to her while they were washing dishes after the meal. "But you might want to use caution."

Mary Ruth raised an eyebrow. Her older sister had always been more serious and cautious than Mary Ruth. She had learned to question Leah when she made such statements. "What do you mean, Leah?"

"Caution with that Lapp boy," Leah said. However, when she saw that Mary Ruth's face fell, becoming serious and drawn, her sister tossed some sudsy water at her. "I know the talk is poor about Samuel, and we all know you mean well."

Mary Ruth glanced over her shoulder. Her father was talking with her mother near the kitchen door. He held his tattered straw hat in his hand. Clearly, he was getting ready to leave for the day, ready to cut some hay in the backfields. Mary Ruth knew that the others couldn't overhear the conversation she was having with Leah. "I mean well?" Mary Ruth repeated. She wasn't about to ignore the opportunity to find out what her sister meant by that statement.

"Your heart, Mary Ruth," Leah replied, her voice low so that their conversation would remain private. "You like to take care of those in need. Samuel Lapp has been your special project for years, *ja*? Always defending him, always supporting him. Mayhaps, however, it would be good to start looking at some of the other young men, don't you think? Sure would cause less talk among the folk."

There was a long moment of silence. Mary Ruth wasn't certain how to respond. Courting among the Amish was typically kept private, and truth be told, Mary Ruth didn't want to engage in any conversation dealing with Samuel Lapp. But, as she had for years, she always felt the need to defend him. "Don't see why people should be talking," she said softly. "I'm not courting him, not that it's anyone's concern."

"*Gut*," her sister added. "Glad to hear that, sister. Remember what *mamm* said about a woman's reputation."

Mary Ruth didn't reply. For a young Amish woman,

the one thing that needed protecting over all else was her reputation. No Amish man would marry someone with a questionable past, not that this was something Mary Ruth feared. After all, she was naught but God fearing and community loving. She had never given anyone reason to question her virtue or honor.

Without another word to her sister, Mary Ruth bent her head to the task of finishing her part of cleaning the kitchen. Her sister's words echoed in her mind. It hurt her feelings that her sister would hint about Mary Ruth's reputation, Mary Ruth who was always the first to take care of others, putting everyone else's needs before her own. A bad reputation was more than just idle talk, Mary Ruth told herself. It usually meant something bad had actually happened. Certainly her sister wasn't accusing her of poor behavior, Mary Ruth thought.

Yes, she was annoyed at Leah for even suggesting something so mean to her. Even worse, she was increasingly mad at herself for caring what Leah or anyone else actually thought about her.

Chapter Seven

Samuel narrowed his eyes against the sharp glare of the sun. He saw the willowy figure of an Amish woman walking down the road, a basket in her hand. She wore a light green dress with a black half-apron covering the front of her skirt. There was something very determined about the woman and Samuel found himself watching, amused. She was clearly on an important mission, the basket swinging by her side as she walked.

He leaned on the pitchfork in his hand and tilted his head backward, his hat shielding his eyes from the sun. As she came closer, he began to make out her features. A bouncy step, a smile on her face… Mary Ruth Smucker. He glanced around the barnyard to see if his brothers were nearby. To his surprise, Junior and David were not within his line of vision, so Samuel set the pitchfork to the side and wiped his dirty hands on his black pants. He walked toward the edge of the mule paddock.

At the edge of the property, he leaned against the fence and waited, watching her walk down the road. Clearly, she hadn't noticed him yet. So he enjoyed the anonymity of no one being aware that he was staring at this young girl walking down the road, admiring her beauty and zest for life.

He had known Mary Ruth for his entire life. Thinking back upon his childhood, he was unable to remember one moment that didn't include her. Church services, playing in the school yard, skating on the small pond, sleigh-riding down the back hill, and tending the crops alongside their fathers. All of those memories evoked images of Mary Ruth and her family. Indeed, Samuel thought, she is more like family than some of my own cousins and siblings.

But more important was the fact that Mary Ruth had always been the one who stuck up for him. He smiled as he leaned against the fence post, watching her, as he remembered the time that he had accidentally tripped one of the girls at school. It had been Mary Ruth who had defended him. Even at such a young age, Mary Ruth had been his staunch defender.

That day had been the beginning of a lot of problems for Samuel. He was just eleven, maybe twelve. The children were playing outside at mid-morning break. Some of the older boys were keeping the ball away from Samuel, teasing him so that they could see him get angry. And indeed he did. He had turned away from the boys, ready to stomp off to play his own game. Who needed them anyway, he had thought to himself.

When he had turned to run off, the laughter of the older boys still ringing in his ears, he hadn't seen Katie Stoltzfus behind him and had bumped into her, knocking her down to the ground. She had hit her nose and it bled. Boy, did it bleed! Samuel had stood there, shocked at the amount of blood that could come from someone's nose. He was so shocked, he didn't even reach down to help her back to her feet.

Everyone had been so angry with him, claiming that he did this on purpose. In hindsight, Samuel often felt that it was as if the other boys had been looking for a reason to make him an outcast. But then and there Mary Ruth came to his defense. She had been the only one who stood by his side, declaring that it was surely an accident. The others had scowled at him, shunning him in the way that only children can do. But Mary Ruth maintained his innocence. She had even sat next to him at noon, sharing her dinner while the others stayed far away, pointing at him or talking about him behind his back. Samuel wasn't proud of the fact that others thought he had tried to hurt another person intentionally. That certainly spoke a lot about what they thought of his character. But he sure had been pleased that Mary Ruth had believed in him.

Now, as he watched her walking down the road, he could only blink away the memory and smile to himself. Mary Ruth Smucker, he thought. The only girl who would have interested him…if only he was interested in settling down.

He waited until she was almost beside him until he poked his head out from the shadows. "Mary Ruth!" he called out, deliberately startling her.

Indeed, she jumped at the sound of his voice, clearly frightened by his sudden appearance. Her hand fluttered to her chest, and when she recognized him, a wide smile broke onto her face. "Samuel Lapp! You scared me!"

He shrugged his shoulders casually. "Didn't mean to," he said softly, his head tipped forward and his eyes shielded by the shadow of his hat's rim. He knew it was a white lie but he couldn't help himself. She was so pretty when she was flustered, her pale white hand against the front of her green dress and the color flooding to her face.

The brisk pace of her walk was broken and she wandered over to the fence. Setting the basket on the ground, she looked up at Samuel, her blue eyes bright and lively. "Well, you sure could have called out before now, *ja*? No need to frighten me half to death," she teased. The laugh that escaped her lips was soft and gentle, not holding anything against him. Typical Mary Ruth, he thought.

"Now, what fun would that be?" he said, a smile crossing his face. "Do you know that you blush when you're scared? Your cheeks turn pink and your eyes glow."

"Aw, Samuel!" she teased. "You like scaring people walking down the road? Just to see my cheeks turn red?" She lowered her voice and leaned forward. "That's scandalous, for sure and certain."

"Scandalous," he said, repeating the word. He liked the way that it sounded when she said it. Indeed, everything about Samuel seemed to be scandalous these days. But, as usual, it didn't seem to bother Mary Ruth. Just as it didn't bother her when he reached out to brush a piece of hay from her shoulder. Sure, he noticed that her eyes glanced at his hand when he made the motion. But she didn't seem to mind the intimate touch. "And where, exactly, are you walking to, Mary Ruth, that you didn't notice me standing here?"

Too aware of his overpowering presence, she took a step backward and glanced down the road. "Whitey's wife has taken ill, you know," she began to explain.

"*Mamm* asked me to bring her some soup and fresh bread."

"Amish recipe for good health, *ja*?"

Mary Ruth shrugged her shoulders but didn't respond. She felt strange under the strength of his gaze. He was staring at her and it wasn't in his usual way. There was something alarmingly close about the way he looked at her. Deciding to change the subject, she looked around the farm behind his back. "You helping with the chores instead of working at the carpentry shop today?"

He took a deep breath and looked up toward the sky. "Not working in the shop today, no."

"Why?"

He rolled his eyes back down to meet hers. For a long moment, he held her gaze and said nothing. There was a connection, that was for sure and certain. Since the ride home a few weeks ago, he had done nothing but think of Mary Ruth and his declaration that he didn't want to court anyone. That was, indeed, true. He kept telling himself that. But the fact was that Mary Ruth was not just anyone. She was much more than that. She was *the* one. Only Samuel was too aware that the timing was off. "I was out late last night and Junior told me to not work today."

A gasp escaped from her throat. "Oh, Samuel!" The sparkle faded from her eyes. Unlike other people, she didn't look disappointed in him but concerned. Unlike other people, Mary Ruth was always concerned when it came to Samuel. "Again?"

He shrugged, trying to act nonchalant about it. "It doesn't matter. I'll just help my *daed* today, listen to some grumbling tonight, and be back at the shop tomorrow."

Mary Ruth shook her head, her smile gone and the sparkle vanishing from her eyes. "Seem to be a lot of grumbling where you're concerned these days," she said softly, averting her eyes. "Might not be as exciting as your new Mennonite friends, but mayhaps you should stick closer to your own people, Samuel."

"Not you, too," he said sharply. He noticed that she flinched and he was immediately sorry that he had raised his voice to her. "I'm sorry, Mary Ruth. I didn't mean to speak harshly. I'm just tired of everyone sharing their opinion with me. It's not as though I've taken the kneeling vow, and I am not going to apologize for enjoying my running-around time!"

"If you enjoy it too much, it might be hard to return to the fold," she said, forcing herself to lift her eyes and meet his gaze. "Women aren't the only ones who can have their reputations soiled beyond repair, Samuel."

"Aren't you ever curious, Mary Ruth?" He leaned forward again. His eyes seemed to sparkle as he looked at her. "Don't you ever want to see what it's like out there? To drive in cars, the window rolled down as you fly down the highway? Or go do some of the things that Englischers get to enjoy like movies or concerts?"

"No," she said, her voice firm and flat.

He stood up straight, surprised by her quick response, spoken with such conviction. "Just like that? No?"

She lifted her chin defiantly. "There's nothing out there that interests me, Samuel. For there is nothing worth losing my faith, my family, and my future among my community."

He laughed at her. "Spoken from the girl who was tapping her toe to that loud hip-hop music the other night!"

Mary Ruth tilted her chin. "You won't be seeing me at those gatherings anymore, Samuel. I recognized the worldliness in that music and made a promise to God that I would focus more on His Word and not Englischer music." He stared at her, his eyebrows raised as he listened to her. "I made that promise to Him after listening to the sermon on Sunday."

Before he could respond, their conversation was interrupted as Rachel walked around the side of the mule shed. She was carrying her baby and headed down the lane. "Is that Mary Ruth?" She waved and smiled a happy greeting. "Was just talking about you inside," Rachel said as she approached, ignoring Samuel, who didn't even smile a greeting hello.

"Ooo, let me see little Katie," Mary Ruth said, hurrying over to see the baby. "She's getting so big!"

Rachel smiled with pride as Mary Ruth cooed over her two-month-old daughter. "And Lovina is such a helper with her new sister, although she's with *Mammi* Katie right now."

"I just love the wee ones!" Mary Ruth said, happily taking the baby from Rachel's arm. Samuel watched with amusement as Mary Ruth rocked the baby in her arms. Being the youngest daughter, Mary Ruth was in a similar position as him, being exposed to babies only through nieces and nephews rather than having their own younger siblings to tend. He wondered why she didn't seem to resent that birth order as much as he did.

Rachel tucked the blanket around her daughter's bare feet, shielding her skin from the sun. "Glad to know that, Mary Ruth. That was what we were talking about just moments ago at *Mammi* Katie's." She smiled when Mary Ruth looked up with an unspoken question on her face. "*Ja*, talking about how *wunderbaar gut* you are with the wee ones!"

"Oh?"

"Lillian has been feeling poorly and could really use some help. Can't help her myself, I have my hands full with my own *kinner*. Katie suggested that we inquire if you'd be willing to help in the mornings, perhaps spend just enough time to give Lillian a small break until she's feeling better and Linda is out of school," Rachel explained.

Mary Ruth glanced over at Samuel. He raised an eyebrow but looked away, too aware of the expression on Mary Ruth's face. If she were to help Lillian during the day, she'd be at the farm on a regular basis. Not only was it likely that he'd see her more often, she'd also be privy to his personal life. He wasn't certain how he felt about that.

"I reckon I should ask my *mamm*, *ja*?" Mary Ruth smiled, turning her attention back to Rachel. "But I sure hope she says that it's right fine with her!"

"What's wrong with Lillian?" Samuel asked.

Rachel looked over at her brother-in-law, her eyes cold and distant. They had never gotten along and avoided each other like the plague. Clearly she was surprised that he had been paying attention, never mind the fact that he actually inquired about his sister-in-law's health. "Tired, drained, not eating." She frowned. "If you paid any attention to your own family, you'd have recognized the fact that your mother has been tending to Lillian and the children at night."

Samuel rolled his eyes at the reprimand from Rachel. He'd never understand what his brother Daniel had seen in her. She was different than the other Amish women he knew, testy and strict with a quick tongue and flashing eyes. "If you paid any attention, Rachel, you'd have recognized the fact that I work in the dairy or shop both morning and night and I'm not around to see what *mamm* is doing most times, never mind Lillian or anyone else!"

"Samuel," Mary Ruth said softly.

Rachel shrugged her shoulder at Samuel, dismissing him casually as she turned her attention back to Mary Ruth. "You ask your *mamm*, and if she says that is fine, you come over in the morning, *ja*? Lillian will sure be grateful if you could, that's for sure and certain, Mary Ruth." She reached out for the baby and smiled. "Now, I'll get the mail and leave you two to whatever you were discussing." As she turned to leave, she scowled at Samuel. "Can't imagine that will be a long conversation," she scoffed under her breath and hurried along to the mailbox.

A long moment of silence fell upon them as Rachel left. It felt as though the energy vanished with her. Her parting comment, though discreet, had been heard by both Mary Ruth and Samuel. Neither one knew how to respond, so rather than try, they simply stared after Rachel. She was a tall young woman and she carried herself with a measure of reserve that was unusual for Amish women. Yet Mary Ruth admitted that she liked Rachel Lapp for many reasons. There was something stoic about Daniel Lapp's wife from Ohio.

"Well," Mary Ruth said finally, breaking the silence. "You two sure have a unique relationship."

Samuel snorted. "Unique!"

Mary Ruth laid her hand on Samuel's arm. "You should try to be more patient with her."

Despite the fact that her gesture startled him, he found himself annoyed. "Why does everyone keep saying that?" he asked incredulously.

"You know what she's been through," Mary Ruth reminded him, her expression softening under his intense gaze. "Everyone needs some degree of understanding, Samuel. You should certainly know that these days." She took a deep breath then reached down for her basket. "Best get moving along to Whitey's so that I can get home in time for evening chores. You have a wonderful rest of the day, Samuel Lapp!"

He didn't reply but watched her thoughtfully as she hurried down the road, her basket swinging gently at her side and her gait full of life and happiness. For a few minutes, he leaned against the fence post, his eyes following her until he couldn't see her anymore. It wasn't until he returned to his work that he realized the image of her smile and the light touch of her hand on his arm remained on the forefront of his memory, even though she had long disappeared over the rise of the road.

Chapter Eight

Outside playing with the children, Mary Ruth felt as though she was being watched. Laughing at Jacob and Lena as they chased after a ball that she had rolled on the grass, Mary Ruth stood up and covered her eyes with her hand. The sun was directly overhead, burning bright against the beautiful blue sky. There was a figure standing in the doorway of the barn, watching her. For a long moment, she stood there, her eyes trying to make out who was standing just inside that doorway. But it was too dark and the sun was too bright. Without being able to fully make out who it was, she simply presumed that it was Samuel.

For the past few days, she'd been helping Lillian and she found herself enjoying the change in her daily routine. The Lapp children didn't tax her overmuch, and Lillian was always so grateful for her help that she was glad to come. And of course, there was Samuel…

Glancing at the children to make certain that they were all right, she started to walk in the direction of the dairy barn. But the figure disappeared, slipping further into the shadows. She hesitated and paused, just for a moment. It was Samuel, she thought. Wasn't it? But she couldn't understand why he would watch her only to retreat into the dairy barn when she noticed him.

Curiosity got the best of her. "Jacob," she called out. When he looked up, she motioned toward the barn. "I'll be right back. You watch the little ones, *ja*?"

He stood up straight, puffed out his chest, and nodded. It was clear that he was taking his charge quite seriously, and as Mary Ruth started to turn back to the barn, she saw him round up Lena, Abram, and Anna, leading them toward the grassy knoll behind the *grossdaadihaus*. She smiled at his authoritative demeanor, watching for just one more minute before hurrying across the driveway into the dairy barn.

It took her eyes a minute to adjust when she walked through the doorway. The cows were outside and the aisles were cleaned, ready for the evening milking. In the distance, she heard the hooves of a horse pulling a buggy as it ambled down the road, just behind the barn. The sound grew louder until it passed. Whoever was in the buggy had somewhere to go that didn't involve stopping at the Lapp farm.

Mary Ruth looked around. She had never been inside the dairy barn. It was much larger than her *daed*'s, understandable since the Lapps had a lot more acreage than her own family. It was well tended and fairly clean for a dairy barn.

As she walked down the aisle, she let her hand run along the wall. It was built of stone and felt cool to her fingers. The sweet scent of hay rose to her nose as she passed a wagon full of hay, ready for the next feeding. But she didn't see anyone or hear anything. For a moment, she wondered if she had been mistaken. Perhaps he hadn't been there, watching her from the shadows.

Just as she was about to turn around and return to the *kinner*, she felt his hands on her waist, quickly spinning her around and pulling her close to him. His action scared her and a startled scream escaped her lips as she found herself in his arms, staring up into his face. He was laughing at her but didn't loosen his hold.

"Samuel!" She tried to push him away but his hold was tight. "You nearly stopped my heart!"

He shifted his hands slightly which caused her to press closer against him. Her heart pounded inside of her chest and she feared that he would feel it against his own. Her hands were pressed flat against his broad shoulders and she leaned backward, pulling away as much as she could.

"You sure are easy to scare," he teased.

She pressed her lips together, frowning at him. "Easy to scare if you keep sneaking up on me." His hand pressed against her back and she wiggled in his embrace. "You can let me go, please."

"*Nee*," he whispered.

"Samuel!"

But he didn't listen to her. Instead, he stared down into her face, his deep blue eyes glowing. He seemed to be studying her face and she felt uncomfortable. Why would he pay her such attention, she wondered. It was not like Samuel to do so. Besides, she reminded herself, he had been quite adamant that he was not interested in courting her. Yet, she marveled, he certainly wasn't acting that way. Had he changed his mind?

"Mary Ruth," he said, his voice low and soft. "You sure do feel nice in my arms."

For the briefest of moments, she relaxed. The throaty sound of his voice, so deep and strong, sent tingles down her spine, and she could only just keep herself from melting against him. But certainly he would think her too bold and forward if she did. And Mary Ruth was well aware that such intimacy was saved only for married people and only in the privacy of their own home.

"You set the story straight, Samuel," she reminded him, gently rubbing one of her fingers along his shoulder. "Remember?"

He nodded slowly but didn't say anything.

"And I'm not much for waiting around," she added.

Within a blink of the eye, his left hand released his grip on her waist and covered her hand. His skin felt warm and strong against hers as he held onto her. Slowly, he dragged her hand down until it was pressed against his chest. She lifted her eyes to stare at him. "Feel that?" he whispered.

She did feel it. The beating of his heart. It was beating just as fast and furious as hers was beating inside of her own chest. Yet, here he was, holding her in his arms, pressing her hand against his flesh so that she could feel it. A beating heart, she thought. His beating heart and it's beating for me, she corrected. Immediately, the color flooded to her cheeks and she pulled away, using more force than she had before.

"I think that's quite enough teasing, Samuel Lapp," she said, her voice soft and cracking just slightly. She pushed away from him again.

He responded with a smile. A gentle smile that sent tingles down her spine. Indeed, when he smiled at her, she felt a flutter inside of her body, as though her blood carried tiny butterflies coursing through her veins. It was a different smile, one that she had never seen before and one that made her knees feel weak.

"*Ja*," he whispered, releasing her this time but gently so that she wouldn't stumble backward. "Enough teasing."

She took a moment to compose herself, smoothing down her apron and running a hand over her hair. "I came in here because I thought I saw you watching me," she said. "It's impolite to do that, Samuel, and not say hello."

"Hello," he said softly.

Another frown crossed her face. "That's not funny."

He shrugged.

"I best get back to the children. No *gut* to leave them alone for too long," she said and turned to leave the barn. She glanced over his shoulder at the open doorway. She could barely make out Jacob and the little ones, seated on the grass in a semicircle. "And I reckon Junior will be looking for you back at the shop, *ja*?" But from the look on his face, she immediately knew that he had once again missed work, and that explained why he wasn't at the shop. "Oh, Samuel," she said, shaking her head sadly. How long would Junior tolerate Samuel missing work? And if he lost his job, what would happen then? "Not again. This is the fourth time in just a few weeks! You're going to lose your job!"

"Who's keeping count, Mary Ruth?" he asked, a mischievous smile playing on his lips.

Her mouth fell open at his question. Had she really just heard him correctly? Was he really smiling at her as though it was a big joke? A few minutes ago, when he had smiled at her, she had felt a thrill down her spine that sent shockwaves throughout her body. But the smile that crossed his lips now made her angry.

"When did you become so bold?" she retorted and immediately wished she could take the words back. But, once spoken, there was no taking back the spoken word. "I think everyone's right. You *are* taking this *rumschpringe* too far," she said, her voice angry. "Just because you haven't taken the kneeling vow, Samuel Lapp, doesn't mean you don't have responsibility to the people around you."

The smile faded from his face. Her words didn't sit well with him. Not from anyone but especially not from Mary Ruth. "I'm getting tired of everyone telling me what to do!" he snapped. "All my life I've been hearing it. I sure don't need to hear it from you!"

"Telling you what to do?" she asked angrily. "No one is telling you what to do."

"Everyone is telling me what to do!" he retorted. "If it's not my *mamm* and *daed*, it's one of my older brothers or the church! Everyone wants to control me!"

She shook her head. How could he not see the obvious? That people cared about him. That the church was there to help the people, not hurt them. It was all because they cared. Instead, Samuel saw it as a matter of being controlled? That seemed backwards to Mary Ruth. The church wasn't controlling them but providing them a structure with which to live. Instead of recognizing that, Samuel was rebelling and continuing to make bad choices, increasingly alienating everyone who loved him.

"You have it wrong, Samuel," she said. "No one is telling you what to do, but they are warning you that you are going to have to deal with some consequences that you just might not like."

He waved his hand at her. "I'm exploring the world. That's what it's all about, *ja*? No one is getting hurt. Staying out late or having dinner in town doesn't hurt anyone."

"Oh, Samuel," she whispered. "I pray that you see what you are doing to your family, to your friends." She hesitated before adding, "To yourself."

"I'm not hurting anyone," he declared before lifting his chin defiantly and narrowing his eyes at her. "Mayhaps it wouldn't hurt you to explore a bit before you make some lifelong decisions. You don't know what you are missing."

Once again, she shook her head. "*Nee*, Samuel. I don't need to explore the outside world to know that I'm happy with myself and with my life." She lowered her eyes, hoping to hide the tears that touched the inner corner of her eyelids. "I just wish you were, too."

With that, she turned and hurried back toward the children, leaving Samuel in the dairy barn to stare after her. She didn't want him to see how upset she had become by his words. It wasn't that he didn't want to spend his life with her. No, that wasn't it. It was that she was becoming afraid of the possibility that he didn't want to spend his life with the Amish. And, if that happened, she was afraid that he would be lost forever.

Chapter Nine

"Twins?" Mary Ruth exclaimed as she dried one of the dishes in Lillian's kitchen. She set the dishtowel on the counter and stared at Lillian, who had just returned from the doctor. Junior had insisted on taking her into the city for a proper medical examination, and Mary Ruth had volunteered to stay later than usual to watch the children. Now she was glad that she had stayed. After all, she got to hear the glorious news right away. "Oh, Lillian! How exciting!"

Lillian set her shawl over the back of a chair and collapsed into the green sofa by the window. Her eyes were glowing and her face flushed. She looked more energetic and alive than she had in weeks. With a smile on her lips, she shook her head, laughing. "I can't imagine such a blessing," she gushed and stared at Mary Ruth and Rachel.

For the past two weeks, Mary Ruth had been helping Lillian during the mornings. Convincing her *mamm* and *daed* hadn't been easy, especially given what they referred to as the Samuel Situation. But after Mary Ruth pointed out that Katie was too old to help take care of so many small children and Rachel had her own growing brood to care for, Miriam had relented and pushed her husband to agree that their youngest daughter could do the Christian thing and help their neighbor. Besides, Samuel worked at the carpentry shop during the day, and the chances of Mary Ruth interacting with him were slim.

During that time, Lillian's condition hadn't improved. She was deathly ill all day, couldn't keep any food down, and slept incessantly. The more her condition seemed to deteriorate, the more concerned everyone had become. She had never been so incapacitated with her previous pregnancies. So Junior had insisted that his wife visit an Englischer doctor, demanding only the best care for her and clearly not caring what the bishop might have to say about it. With Jacob Zook's wife having passed several years back from the cancer and Whitey's wife not faring well, Junior wasn't about to take any chances with his beloved Lillian.

Now, as they returned from the doctor, Lillian greeted the anxious Mary Ruth and Rachel with the joyous news that she was, indeed, not facing some dreadful illness but the beauty of two additions to their family.

"Do twins run in the family?" Rachel asked, a look of trepidation in her eyes.

Lillian laughed. "I don't think you have to worry, Rachel. I've yet to hear of twins from Junior's cousins."

Rachel looked relieved and turned back to drying the dishes.

"What else did the doctor say?" Mary Ruth asked, eager for any news.

"*Ach, vell,*" Lillian began. "Said that twins tend to be more taxing on the mother, which is why everything has been so extreme—the fatigue, the illness, the swelling. It might not get better and, come midsummer, I may be bed-bound." She frowned, obviously not liking that piece of the news. "But the doctor felt that they will probably come early. Mayhaps September… mayhaps August."

"He?" Mary Ruth asked, her eyes wide. Amish women used Amish midwives. The thought of a male doctor for something so intimate was startling to Mary Ruth.

Lillian flushed. "Junior took me to the clinic in Lancaster. He wanted a specialist, not just any doctor. But it's all fine, Mary Ruth. Junior was with me the whole time."

The side door opened and Katie emerged from the room adjoining the two houses. She smiled at Lillian. "What *wunderbaar gut* news, Lillian!" She gave her daughter-in-law a rare hug. "I was so worried about you, but once again, the good Lord has proven that He cares for His flock in many ways!"

Junior emerged from behind his mother, a sheepish smile on his face. Young Jacob trailed behind, sensing that something important was afoot but not understanding. Mary Ruth retreated back to the sink, helping Rachel to finish washing the dishes while Katie gushed over Lillian.

"*Wie gehts*?" Samuel asked as he walked into the house from the joining room. "Such a fuss. Must be important," he said. He glanced over and saw Mary Ruth next to Rachel. He nodded once but turned back to his brother. He was still sore from their words from the other day in the barn.

"Doctor said Lillian's fine. Be even better in September when our twins arrive," Junior said, trying to mask his pride as his eyes glowed at his wife. As usual, Lillian could do no wrong in Junior's eyes. His adoration of his wife was more than apparent to everyone in the family.

"Twins, *ja*?" Samuel rubbed at his chin and shook his head. "What's that make? Eight?" He tousled Jacob's curly head. "You best be moving in with us, Jacob. Gonna get awful crowded and noisy over here."

"Samuel!" Katie scolded him. "Don't be putting ideas in the boy's head." She leveled her gaze at her youngest son. "Words spoken can't be retrieved," she reminded him.

Junior sighed and shook his head, clearly uncertain how to deal with Samuel. "You didn't head back to work yet, eh?"

"Just finished dinner," Samuel explained.

Lillian reached up and took Samuel's hand. "Mayhaps you could drive Mary Ruth home? She was kind enough to stay late to help Rachel watch the *kinner*." She smiled at Mary Ruth, silently thanking her with her gaze. "I'm sure her *mamm* would be right thankful if you could. Would spare her that extra time walking."

The room fell silent and Mary Ruth watched expectantly. She knew that her *mamm* would be anything but thankful if Samuel drove her home in his buggy. But she also knew that she would like nothing more than to spend a few minutes alone with him. During the past few weeks, she had caught only some passing glances of Samuel when he came home for the noon meal. He usually disappeared into his parents' house and rarely stopped at Lillian's. She wondered about his behavior toward her, almost as if he was avoiding her since their encounter in the barn.

Now, as the room stared at Samuel, waiting for his answer, she meekly heard herself say, "I don't mind walking."

Lillian waved her hand at Mary Ruth. "Don't be silly. It won't take but a moment to harness the horse. Right, Samuel?"

Samuel grimaced as his sister-in-law turned expectant eyes to stare at him. Like the rest of the family, it was near impossible for him to say no to Lillian. She was similar in temperament to Mary Ruth, positive and cheerful, full of belief and support. Disappointment was not an option when it came to dealing with Lillian. Besides, Samuel knew that he owed her one. After all, she had been responsible for calming Junior down recently when he had overslept and missed work this past week. Like Mary Ruth, she seemed to be a staunch supporter of Samuel, and for that, he couldn't say no.

"I'll go harness the horse," he mumbled and spun on his heel, disappearing through the doorway to return to his mother's kitchen. Within seconds, they heard the screen door open and shut from next door. Samuel walked past the kitchen window, his straw hat on his head and his eyes cast downward.

Mary Ruth set the dishtowel on the counter, smoothing it before she turned to Rachel, smiling a silent goodbye. "Guess I can go help," she said and hurried to the door. "I'll see you tomorrow, Lillian," she called over her shoulder before she disappeared through the mudroom and outside to help Samuel.

It took a moment for her eyes to adjust to the darkness in the horse barn. Samuel was in the stall with his horse, a black mare with a high-stepping gait. When he had purchased the horse, more than one person had raised an eyebrow at the expensive horse that was fancier than most standardbred horses that the Amish used for their buggies. This one was a different breed, a warm blood, with large hooves and a proud head.

"Samuel," she said quietly as she peered over the stall door. "Truly, I can walk."

He glanced up, his hat tilted back on his head as he brushed down his mare. He lifted up his hand and rested it on the horse's withers. The intensity of his gaze on her face caused her to look away. "You step back now, Mary Ruth. I can harness the buggy faster without your help and don't want you getting hurt," he said, his voice low and soft.

She did as he instructed. Leaning against the wall, she watched as he led the horse outside the stall and over toward the buggy. She liked to see him working with the horse. Besides the fact that, indeed, he worked swiftly, there was a gentleness to how he handled the horse.

First, he slipped the harness saddle over the back of the horse, resting it just behind the withers and making certain that the girth was secure so that it wouldn't slip while supporting the shafts of the carriage. He ran his hand along the side of the horse as he moved toward the tail, a kind and calming gesture showing how much he cared for his horse. He gently slapped her hindquarters before attaching the crupper, a V-shaped piece of leather latched around the tail, buckling it at the dock, preventing the harness from sliding forward. Then, in one quick motion, he reached over the mare's head and slipped on the breast collar, a wide piece of padded leather sawn to two long tugs that would attach to the buggy to allow for pulling and steering it.

Crossing the leather tugs over the back of the horse,

Samuel then moved to the buggy, pulling it toward the horse while positioning the shafts into their holders, one side at a time, and after clipping the holdback straps to the breeching, Samuel uncrossed the tugs and secured them to the swiveling base.

Mary Ruth couldn't help but admire how patient, yet efficient he was with the horse, speaking softly in Deitsch to the animal and pausing to reassure it with a loving touch on the neck before he slid the bridle with blinders onto the horse's head, checking to make certain that the bit was comfortably positioned in the horse's mouth over its tongue. In less than three minutes, Samuel was done, with the mare harnessed to the buggy and ready to be driven.

"Ready?" he asked, leading the horse and buggy outside, pausing just long enough to slide open the door and reach for her hand. She hesitated before touching his hand and letting him help her step up and into the buggy. After she settled down, he climbed up and sat next to her.

Mary Ruth felt awkward next to him. The only other time she had been with Samuel in a buggy had been masked by the cover of night when he had brought her home from the singing as a favor for Simon. Now, in broad daylight, she couldn't help but steal a look at him, admiring the way he held the reins with one hand, staring straight ahead as he steered the horse down the lane and toward the road.

"That sure is *wunderbaar gut* news for Lillian and Junior," she said, breaking the silence.

"If you like babies," he replied dryly.

She laughed. "Everyone likes babies!"

"Not me," he said, his voice void of emotion. "They're noisy and underfoot all the time."

"Oh, Samuel," she said. But she stared at him, trying to assess whether or not he was serious. When his expression didn't change, she waved her hand at him. "You don't mean that!"

He raised an eyebrow and glanced at her. "Babies are for women, not men."

She pursed her lips and rolled her eyes. "Now you're just trying to be difficult."

"Difficult?" That had taken him by surprise.

Mary Ruth turned on the seat to stare at him. "I'm getting to understand you, Samuel Lapp. You think it makes you interesting to be so aloof and act so distant, but I know you!" She raised her voice as she pointed at him. "Yes, I do know you…better than you think."

Now it was his turn to laugh. "So you think you do," he said. She didn't like the tone of his voice. It was dark and sinister, a new side to Samuel that she hadn't seen before this day. Yet she knew that it was just more of the bravado façade that he liked to show the world. So she wasn't surprised when he added, "You don't know me at all!"

"I know what you are thinking."

He chewed on his lower lip for a long second as if deep in thought. Then, slowing the horse down, he pulled the brake and turned to face her. His blue eyes glowed and stared into her own. For over a month now, ever since he took her home after the singing, he had been thinking about her. He doubted that she knew that. He had avoided the house while she had been helping Lillian, not wanting to run into her, which would surely give him more reason to spend his free time daydreaming about her. He doubted that she knew that, too.

"Really?" he asked. "What am I thinking now?"

"That I don't know you and never will!" she shot back at him.

"Wrong!" he said, a smile playing on his lips. With one hand, he reached for her shoulder and pulled her close to him. He leaned forward and pressed his lips against hers, forcing her to kiss him as he held her close to him. She could feel the strength of his arms around her and the muscles of his chest pressed against her own.

For a moment, she didn't resist his kiss and found herself lost in it. After all, hadn't she wanted this? Been dreaming of this moment for years? Yet the shock broke through and she placed both hands on his chest, pushing him away. "Samuel! How dare you!" She moved away from him, pressing her back against the side of the buggy. "You will not soil my reputation!"

"It's what you wanted, isn't it?" he said, moving closer to her. He reached out to brush his hand across her cheek. "And I think you liked it."

None too gently, she slapped at his hand. "I'm not one of those fast Englischer girls that you run with!"

He grabbed her wrist and held her hand away from her body and also away from his. "You don't know me at all, Mary Ruth. Mayhaps it's better that way," he murmured as he leaned down to kiss her one more time.

This time, she didn't kiss him back. When he pulled back, she glared at him. She had never before felt anger toward Samuel. The way her heart was pounding inside of her chest conflicted with the way her stomach felt twisted and weak. How could her Samuel Lapp have stolen her honor in such a brutish manner? They weren't even courting and he had thought to kiss her? Kissing was for marriage and they weren't even a true couple.

Mary Ruth felt tears coming to her eyes but refused to give him that satisfaction. "Mayhaps you're right," she whispered, reaching for the door and sliding it open. "Thank you for the offer of a ride, Samuel, but I think I will walk from here." Before he could object, she slipped out of the buggy and began walking along the road toward her home.

Her lips stung from the weight of his kiss. Yes, his lips had been soft and gentle, and true, she had enjoyed the kiss…at least until she realized what he was doing. He was trying to make her not like him, to show her what a scoundrel he truly was. And, for the first time, she was inclined to believe him. She knew that he cared for her, that deep down he was as interested in her as she was in him. But the fact remained that he had done something so scandalous just to prove her wrong.

Perhaps, she thought as she fought the tears, everyone was right about Samuel. Perhaps he was heartless and beyond hope for change. Truly he couldn't care for her if he wanted her to feel hurt and pain. Even worse, she realized, he wanted her to feel shame. The disappointment that she felt was a new feeling for Mary Ruth. She let the tears fall freely as she walked, realizing that she didn't like this new feeling, especially since she was beginning to think that the only truth about Samuel Lapp was, indeed, a feeling of disappointment.

Chapter Ten

At least forty people sat at the five long wooden tables under the tall oak tree at Sylvia and Jake's farm. The tree provided enough shade for the afternoon fellowship meal that Sylvia had arranged for their non-church Sunday. Besides her own family, she had invited her neighbors, the Smuckers, as well as Whitey Hostetler's family. With his wife being so ill, it was a welcome invitation for him, and everyone was glad to see his wife join him, even if she spent most of the day sitting on a chair in the shade of the porch.

A small brood of children ran through one of the paddocks, chasing each other despite the late-June heat. Most of them were the grandchildren of Katie and Jonas, although Whitey's oldest son and family had joined the festivities. The men sat at the tables, discussing their plans for upcoming crops and planning for hay cutting while the women moved about the kitchen and talked about their gardens. It was an easy day, with limited work and an emphasis on socializing with friends and family.

Jake held a sleeping baby in his arms, glancing over

at the women. His eyes found his wife, and when Sylvia looked up as she carried some dishes to the tables in preparation of the meal, he smiled. "Don't know much, Jonas," Jake said, turning his attention back to the group of men seated at his table. "Your daughter seems intent on forcing my hand at adding onto this farmhouse," he teased good-naturedly.

Jonas tugged at his graying beard and laughed. "You aren't the only one. Appears Junior has a similar situation facing him."

Raising an eyebrow, Jake turned to look at Junior. "*Ja*?"

Samuel grunted. "You didn't hear about the twins? It's all anyone is talking about at our farm."

Jake gave his youngest brother-in-law a friendly kick with his boot. "Now, now, Samuel," he chided gently. "You'll understand soon enough once you settle down and burn a fire on your own hearth. There's something magical about being a family man."

With a wave of his hand, Samuel dismissed his words. "Don't hold your breath, Jake. There's not enough magic to entice me, that's for sure and certain!"

Daniel laughed. "Typical Lapp! Determined to be an old *bewe* until a woman comes out of nowhere and spins his head."

"Speak for yourself," Samuel snapped. He didn't like his brothers laughing at him. "Don't care if I'm an old *bewe*. Courting just ain't in my plans! And I sure don't know why everyone's so intent on my settling down."

"Mayhaps it's because the word in the wind is that you'd fare better settling down than running around," Jake teased.

"Bah!"

Samuel didn't wait to hear anymore from the laughing group of men. He stood up and stormed away, angry and frustrated at always being the brunt of their jokes. No one ever teased David about settling down, despite the fact that he had approached Bishop Peachey about his baptism in the fall. And Jake always had a way of turning things around, Samuel thought with a scowl on his face. It was annoying at best.

"Where you going, *Onkel*?"

Samuel groaned, shutting his eyes momentarily as he quickly counted to ten. He didn't have to guess who it was. He knew. His shadow. So Samuel wasn't surprised when he opened his eyes and saw little Jacob standing by his leg. "Why aren't you playing with your cousins and friends?"

The little boy shrugged. "Rather be with you!"

Samuel frowned. His ruse had not worked. "I'm not doing anything."

"Then take me to see Jake's baby horses!"

Trapped. Samuel cringed, further annoyed that he had been bested by an eight-year-old child. Without seeing it, Samuel had walked right into spending one-on-one time with Jacob rather than being able to retreat to a hidden corner of the barn for a nice long afternoon nap. "All right," he relented with an exasperated sigh and started walking toward the barn, not bothering to wait for little Jacob to catch up with him.

Over the years, Jake had developed his horse-breeding business, and despite his trial-and-error approach to farming crops, he had become well known for producing high-quality standardbred horses. This spring, he had four new foals which, within the next year or so, would be sold to eager Amish youth approaching their courting years and wanting to train their own horses. Even Samuel had to admit that the young colts were amazing with their large round eyes, short fluffy tails, and gangly long legs. To think that those horses would grow into a mainstay of an Amish home, Samuel thought as he looked over the stall door at a mare with her foal. Without these horses, the Amish couldn't maintain their lifestyle and would have to rely on cars, which, undoubtedly, would increase their exposure to the outside world.

He frowned as that thought passed through his mind. Indeed, it was the horses that kept the community glued together. Then why, he wondered, do I have such a fascination with cars? And it dawned on Samuel that perhaps he would never take that kneeling vow and would be forced to leave the community. Could he survive outside of the tight-knit world of the Amish? Is that what he truly wanted?

"I like that brown one with the white blaze," Jacob said eagerly, squirming against the stall door while Samuel held him up to see the foal.

"Sure is a nice-looking foal," Samuel conceded.

"Samuel!" a young girl's voice called out. He turned his head in time to see Linda run toward him. Mary Ruth was following, holding little Abram's hand, but when her eyes met Samuel's, she hesitated. "Jacob, did you see all of the babies? Aren't they just beautiful?"

Jacob grabbed his older sister's hand and dragged her toward another stall farther down. "Come and see this one!"

Linda took Abram from Mary Ruth and followed Jacob. While the children clambered over the stall doors, gushing about the different babies, Mary Ruth crossed her arms over her chest and kept her distance from Samuel. He noticed that she didn't greet him nor did she even make eye contact. It was better that way, he told himself. Yet there was something unsettling about her demeanor.

"Haven't seen much of you this past week, Mary Ruth," he said solemnly, leaning against the stall door as he watched her.

She took a deep breath and shrugged her shoulders. "Been busy, 'tis all."

He didn't like this new Mary Ruth. Where was the bubbly and sparkling girl, the one who looked at him with bright eyes and endless patience? Nonchalantly, he nodded, trying to look disinterested. "Still helping Lillian, *ja*?"

Mary Ruth snapped her head to look at him. Her eyes were narrow and angry. "You know that I am, Samuel Lapp. And you know exactly why I'm not speaking to you."

The sharpness of her tone startled him. An angry Mary Ruth? Who was this feisty young woman standing before him? "I didn't realize that you weren't speaking to me at all, given that I haven't seen you."

She took a step forward and lowered her voice, glancing quickly over her shoulder to make certain that the two young children couldn't hear. "You stole something from me that wasn't yours to take!"

"I stole..." He frowned as he repeated her words slowly. Was she referring to the kiss in the buggy? He smiled as he raised an eyebrow. "I stole nothing that you didn't want to give, Mary Ruth."

Defiantly, she tilted her chin. "My kisses shall be saved for my husband, not some confused, hopeless rebel who thinks nothing of showing such dishonor to the one person who has stood behind him for all these years."

He laughed at her. "A rebel? Is that what you think of me?" She didn't answer. "If so, then why stand behind me, Mary Ruth? Why not move on?" Despite the harshness of his words, he felt torn when she lifted her eyes to stare at him. Sorrow, he thought. She felt sorrow, despite trying to put on a brave front. Why couldn't he settle down, he asked himself. Why was he so opposed to courting her?

"Mayhaps I will, Samuel."

At those words, he reached out for her arm. She glanced down at her hand and tried to yank herself free. "You wouldn't do that," he whispered, keeping his voice low since he heard the children approaching. "I know you, Mary Ruth. Better than you think."

She succeeded in pulling her arm from his grasp just in time. Linda and Jacob skipped around the corner, dragging Abram with them, gushing about the baby horses and small fuzzy chicks in the chicken coop. They were all smiles on their faces and dirt on their bare feet.

"We'll see about that," she whispered back. Then, with a forced smile on her face, she turned to greet the children. She knelt down, holding her arms out to give them a warm hug. "Tell me about these wonderful baby animals!" she insisted, taking ahold of their hands and letting them lead her down the aisle to go look at the foals.

Samuel watched as Mary Ruth led the younger children away, noticing that she seemed to bounce down the aisle between the stalls. He was only partially surprised to realize that she wasn't going to look back at him. Her anger toward him caught him off guard. That was not the Mary Ruth that he knew. She had threatened to "move on," and that worried him. What if she did start courting that Elias? Samuel knew that it would not sit well with him at all.

It was during the fellowship meal that Samuel sat quietly at the table, his head bent over his food while he listened to his *daed* speak with Amos, Mary Ruth's father, about the upcoming auction in New Holland. Their words seemed to blur together. They were speaking about nothing that truly interested him. Auctions, equipment, harvesting. It seemed as though it was the same conversation year after year. Instead of listening, he glanced down the table at Mary Ruth from time to time. She was ignoring him as she sat next to Rachel and Sylvia, listening to their plans for the summer. Not once did she look at him, and that bothered Samuel.

But he sure did notice Amos and Simon watching him. Samuel could feel their eyes on his face, watching him as he glanced at Mary Ruth. He looked over at them, surprised by their blatant staring. He could sense the displeasure on Amos's face but couldn't quite read what Simon was thinking.

"Next Church Sunday is at the Yoders," Daniel said, passing a bowl of yellow potato salad to Junior. "They just built that big room over their new horse barn. Should be nice for them to get to use it," Daniel added.

"*Ja*," Junior said. "Hearing more and more about that. With these young folk buying more modern houses, they seem to be building the church rooms over the barns."

"Not a bad idea, if you asked me," Jonas added. "Nothing wrong with having to convert those houses to our needs, especially with so many finding non-farming ways to make a living."

Whitey shook his head. "Not enough farm land to sustain them anymore." He looked down the table at the women then lowered his voice so they couldn't hear. "Heard that some of my nephews are planning a move to another county in Pennsylvania."

That got everyone's attention. "A new county? Where?" Simon demanded.

"Don't go getting no ideas!" Amos pointed his finger at his son. "Need you here, Simon."

"That mean I can go?" Stephen added quickly, which caused the rest of the men to laugh.

Jake was the first to interrupt the laughter. "Would sure be a shame to see any of the young men leave the area. The more Amish that move out, the more the Englischers that move in."

"Spoken from an Englischer who moved in and never moved out!" Whitey added, which brought another round of laughter.

After the laughter quieted down, Jonas continued the conversation. "Jake's right," he said. "We'll have no land left here soon. We need to start planning for the next generation."

Amos tugged at his beard. "*Ja*, good point. Need to make certain no more land gets sold to those developers." His own farm was smaller than Jake and Jonas's. Everyone knew that Simon was working with Jonas at the carpentry shop because the Smucker's farm was too small to sustain his and Stephen's future families. As the youngest son, Stephen would inherit the land. The older Smucker sons had married and moved away, not finding any affordable farms in the area. In reality, if

Simon were to move away, he'd be able to open up his own carpentry business.

"Nothing wrong with not farming," Samuel added.

The older men shook their heads. Even Daniel joined them. It was Amos who replied to Samuel. "The less we farm, the further we grow away from God," he said, his eyes narrowed and accusatory as he stared at Samuel. "Seems some young folk are wandering when some good old farm work might bring them back into the fold."

"Now, now," Jake said. "Doesn't have to be that way." He sensed the tension between Amos and Samuel and tried to defuse it. "It's good to have options. Not everyone wants to farm anyway." With a quick nod to Junior, he continued. "Jonas Junior sure has made a successful go of the shed-building business. Nothing wrong with carpentry skills. Seems your own son is benefiting as well."

"I'm talking about those young men who are working with the Englische!" Amos argued. "Exposes them to worldly ways. Cars, cell phones, and Internet."

Whitey shook his head. "Not *gut*, that technology."

Jake sighed. "It has its place in the world. But we can sure avoid it by encouraging our young men to be entrepreneurs and work for our own communities, not the Englische." He looked over at Samuel and winked. "And buy up all the farm land that we can get our hands on."

The men laughed in agreement. But Samuel didn't join them. All this talk about the future and raising families was boring him to tears. He didn't understand why the older men were always so against progress. As for farming, he was glad that he worked with his brother. Junior handled all of the bill paying and business planning. All Samuel had to do was show up to work and do his job. He didn't want any of the hassles of being in business for himself, nor did he want to think about having to support a family. Instead, all he cared about was getting back to the farm so that he could harness up his horse and buggy to head over to Miller Lane to see what his friends were planning for the upcoming week.

Chapter Eleven

"You seem awfully quiet today," Lillian said. The day was beautiful with the sun shining brightly overhead and not one cloud in the crystal blue sky. The pastures were green with growing grass and the cows dotted the landscape. They were outside, weeding the garden that Lillian had planted a month ago. "Seems a shame to be so deep in thought on such a *wunderbaar gut* day."

But Mary Ruth was deep in thought. She hadn't felt good about herself since her confrontation with Samuel at the weekend gathering. It was out of character for her to be short with anyone, especially Samuel. She had lost control of her feelings, and that just didn't sit well.

"Just thanking the good Lord for such a day," she mumbled but knew that the words sounded too flat to be believable.

"*Ach*, Mary Ruth," Lillian said softly. She knelt back on her heels, wiping the dry dirt from her hands on the black apron that covered her knees. Her skin felt dry from having worked in the sun, and she was beginning to feel too hot and tired to work in this heat. But her main concern was the troubled young woman kneeling before her. "If it's Samuel who has stolen your thoughts..." She didn't complete the sentence but let the words drift between them. It wasn't proper to discuss courtship or crushes, and Lillian knew that she had crossed a line.

But Mary Ruth didn't seem to mind. She took a deep breath and turned to look at Lillian, who had become much more than a friend during the past few weeks. At one point, she had hoped that Lillian would become her sister through marriage, but now that looked ever so distant and impossible. "Oh, Lillian, it just seems so complicated." She tried to smile, hoping that she didn't look as forlorn as she felt. "If only he'd settle down from his wild ways."

There wasn't much that Lillian could say to that. She certainly couldn't downplay Mary Ruth's concern. After all, everyone was hopeful that Samuel would think twice about how he was handling *rumschpringe.* Yet, despite their concern, Samuel seemed to dive deeper into it. First, he was spending time with the Miller Lane Mennonite boys. Then he was staying out all night. Now, he had recently informed his parents that he was going to take a trip with his Mennonite friends and one of their Englischer friends to Philadelphia for a long weekend.

There wasn't much that Jonas and Katie could say or do to stop Samuel from making such decisions, no matter how upset those decisions made the family. Jonas had frowned at his son and told him point blank that such decisions could ruin a young man's life. But Samuel had laughed and downplayed his father's concern.

"It's Philadelphia, *Daed.* It's not like I'm going to California or Florida for weeks!"

"Son, you best be right careful and think twice before going to the big cities," his father had said solemnly before retiring to his bedroom for the evening. It had been clear that no one was in favor of this trip, no one except Samuel.

The story was shared at supper one night, Simon retelling it while the Smucker family ate their evening meal in awed silence. Apparently Samuel had been laughing about his *daed*'s concern during a break from work at the carpentry shop.

From his expression, it was clear that Simon disapproved of Samuel's decision to spend a weekend in Philadelphia, sharing a motel room with his non-Amish friends and roaming completely unsupervised in the big city. He had even commented that the Englischer, Peter Bartlett, was known to be a drinking man. But it was even clearer that the rest of the Smucker family were just as shocked to hear of Samuel's latest declaration.

Even Mary Ruth was shocked. Philadelphia? For a weekend and with the Bartlett boy? When Mary Ruth had heard this latest news, she felt as if her heart dropped within her chest. Was it possible that Samuel would venture into the Englische world and abandon his roots? Would Samuel actually turn wild during his running-around years? Would he refuse to return to the Amish faith? The speculation from the community sure seemed to be coming to fruition, and that worried Mary Ruth.

Such refusals were not uncommon. In fact, many Amish youths did decide to join the Mennonite churches, finding them less restrictive than the Amish church and more permissive of worldly luxuries. But Samuel wasn't even walking that path. He just seemed to be running wild, letting other misguided youths turn his face from God and toward the world.

Lillian stared at the young woman before her. Everyone in the Lapp family adored Mary Ruth Smucker. She was good-hearted and loyal to her friends, family, and God. For years, everyone had suspected that her eyes sparkled only for Samuel, but no one really understood why. He had also seemed to carry a sweet spot in his heart for her, and they had all held out hope that she could tame him. But clearly that wasn't happening.

"He'll be fine, Mary Ruth," Lillian finally said. "And, if it's God's will, Samuel will return to the fold." She smiled as she gently added, "And mayhaps to you."

"Mayhaps to the fold," Mary Ruth said softly, feeling uncomfortable sharing her private thoughts with anyone but knowing that Lillian would never share them with another person. "But certainly not to me. Waiting for a young man doesn't seem very proper, does it? And especially for one who has strayed so far from the Lord." She knew that was what her mother would want her to say. But Mary Ruth's eyes gave her away. There was a sorrow deep within her gaze as she looked past Lillian's shoulder at the carpentry shop down the lane in the distance.

Since their confrontation at the Edwards' farm last Sunday, Mary Ruth had been relieved not to bump into Samuel while helping Lillian. But, with the weekend rapidly approaching, she had hoped that she could find Samuel and warn him about this crazy Philadelphia weekend idea. If only she could find out why he wanted to rebel, she thought. If only she could make him see how these decisions were going to impact his future.

It was clear from the discussions at her own family

table that the community was losing their patience with Samuel Lapp. His own brother was forbidding him to arrive late to work at the carpentry shop, so Samuel was risking the loss of his job each time he stayed out all night. And while the bishop couldn't go so far as to shun Samuel, he sure could make it difficult for Samuel to return to the church. Despite the fact that the Amish were quick to forgive, Mary Ruth knew that they were not quick to forget.

She waited until it was after dinner before she began looking outside the window, hoping to catch a glance of Samuel leaving his mother's kitchen and trekking back up the lane to return to the carpentry shop for the afternoon. She had a plan worked out in her mind. First, she'd approach him and ask to speak to him in private. Then, she'd try to reason with him and help him see the error of his ways. She'd apologize for their harsh words in the Edwards' barn the other day and try to smooth over that bump in their relationship.

But Mary Ruth knew Samuel and knew that convincing him to stay would take more than words. She just wasn't certain what more she had to give him.

The opportunity to speak with Samuel arose about fifteen minutes after she had finished washing the dishes. She heard, rather than saw, Samuel as he stomped down the wooden stairs leading from his *mamm*'s kitchen to the driveway. She glanced out the side window in Lillian's kitchen and saw him walk by, his tattered straw hat on his head. Since no one was around, Mary Ruth hurried to the side door and opened it, trying to act nonchalant when she all but bumped into him.

"Mary Ruth!" he said, reaching out to steady her.

His hand lingered on her arm and she didn't pull away like she had the last time that they had talked. "I didn't see you bouncing out that door!" He seemed to be in a jovial mood, despite their strained relationship.

She forced a smile and took a step back. "I'm sorry, Samuel. I didn't mean to bump into you."

He glanced around as if to see if anyone was nearby to observe their encounter. "Haven't seen much of you this week. Keeping busy with helping Lillian?"

She nodded. "*Ja*, I sure am. Those *kinner* sure can keep a body busy, that's for certain!"

A moment of silence befell them. It was tense and awkward, especially since the last time they had talked had not resulted in a pleasant parting. But she was glad that he was talking to her. She had been worried that he would ignore her, settling for casual pleasantries.

"You off to work for the afternoon?" she asked, despite already knowing the answer.

He nodded. "*Ja*." He hesitated, looking at her then glancing down the road. She got the sense that he wanted to say more but didn't, perhaps because he felt uncomfortable from their last conversation. He took a step backward, his hands thrust in his pockets. "Speaking of which, I best get back to the shop," he finally mumbled, dipping his head as he started down the lane.

"Wait!" The word shot out of her mouth before she could stop it. It surprised her as much as it surprised him. She felt strange, not used to being so assertive. "Samuel, I have something I want to say to you," she began. Her voice sounded stronger than she felt. Inside, she was trembling. How bold she sounded! She didn't like that feeling at all.

Samuel seemed equally as surprised. He turned back

around and stood facing her. Because of her petite stature, he seemed to loom over her. His shirt was opened casually at his neck and he wore a belt around his waist, rather than the traditional suspenders. Even his boots were worldly, she noticed.

"What is it?" he asked softly.

"I..." She started to speak but the words became jumbled in her mind. She tried to think back to her plan, to how she had intended to talk to him. The words that she had wanted to say disappeared from her memory. Her eyes met his, and for a brief moment, she thought she saw him smile, encouraging her to speak. But when she opened her mouth to speak, nothing seemed to come out and her mind went blank.

"Yes?"

"I...well..." She paused. A new thought crept into her head and she pushed her shoulders back, tilting her chin in the air and lifting her eyes to stare into his face. "You see," she began, "I wanted you to know that I've decided that, if you aren't at the singing on Sunday, I will accept that ride home from Elias Lantz."

The expression on his face changed. The color drained from his cheeks and he squinted at her, as if not fully understanding what she had said. "What?"

Upon hearing the words and seeing his reaction, that was exactly the question that popped into her mind: *What was she thinking*? Why had she blurted that out? She had completely lost her train of thought and couldn't seem to say what she wanted. Instead, she had uttered the only thing that came to her mind as a way to try to convince him to not go to Philadelphia, to not stray from the People. But that wasn't what she had intended to say, and she felt tears of frustration burn at the corner of her blue eyes. The words were out there and she knew she couldn't take them back. So she straightened her back and stared at Samuel. "I think you heard me correctly."

He took a step toward her, reaching out for her arm. He held it gently in his hand as he moved closer to her. His eyes glanced around, making certain that no one was watching. Reassured that they were alone, he bent his head so that his lips were near her ear and he whispered, "What's this about, Mary Ruth?"

She moved away from him and forced him to meet her gaze. It was the only way that she knew he would understand how serious she was. "If you go to Philadelphia with those boys," she blurted out. "That will be the end, Samuel. I won't be waiting around anymore for someone who cares so little for his community, his family, and himself. There's nothing out there but trouble, Samuel. You are only hurting yourself…and the people who care for you."

"I never asked you to wait around," Samuel said, a frown wrinkling his brow as he stared at her.

"No," she replied, shaking her head slightly. "No, you surely didn't. But I was waiting, Samuel, and now I will no longer do so."

So there it is, she thought: The moment that she put everything out there and left the decision to Samuel. After all, it was always up to the men. But she could force his hand…as well as hers. And she knew that, if Samuel went to Philadelphia, she would have no choice but to follow through and move on. She'd accept that ride from Elias and turn her thoughts away from Samuel for once and for all.

Releasing his hold on her arm, he took a step away

from her. For a long moment, he stared at her as though sizing up this new, feisty Mary Ruth that stood before him. She held his gaze, refusing to look away, despite feeling uncomfortable under the steadiness of his eyes. He finally nodded as though coming to an understanding of what she had meant. "*Ja, vell*," he began. "You have sure given me a lot to think on, then. And I still need to get back to work. Won't do to lose my job now, would it?" He tipped his head at her. "You have a good day, Mary Ruth." And then he was gone.

His reaction had *ferhoodled* her. She didn't quite know how to read it. But she did know one thing. Sunday evening was bound to be the deciding factor. She also knew that she had done the right thing. If Samuel cared so little about himself, why should she continue pining for him? Yet part of her hoped that he would show up on Sunday and make a public claim for her attention. Despite it being several days away, she knew that the hours would pass like days and the days even longer. It would be a long, restless time between now and then.

She watched as he walked down the lane, headed toward the carpentry shop. She watched him until he disappeared from view. Her heart felt heavy and she scolded herself for having been so bold. Certainly she had expected a reaction from him, but not *that* reaction. In fact, he had no reaction, and she realized that was worse than if he had gotten upset or angry. Sighing in disappointment, she turned back to the house, knowing that the children would be in need of attention before their afternoon naps. She would have to put Samuel out of her mind for the rest of the day and week. And she knew that was not going to be an easy task to do.

Chapter Twelve

When the hired car pulled up to the barn where the singing was *supposed* to have been held, everything was dark. The car's tires made crunching noises on the driveway as it rolled over cracked macadam and loose gravel. Samuel opened the passenger door and stepped out, looking around. He wasn't certain what time it was, but he did know that he was running late.

"You want me to leave you here?" the driver called out, leaning over the seat toward the open door.

Samuel exhaled loudly, raising his hand to his head. He ran his finger through his hair and looked at the dark doorway to the barn. "What time is it?"

"Almost eleven," the driver said.

Shaking his head, Samuel turned back to the car. "*Nee*. Best be going home. No one is here."

It had been a long weekend and nothing had seemed to go right for Samuel. He had tried to get back in time for the singing, tried to be there to walk Mary Ruth home. But the train from Philadelphia to Lancaster had broken down, and then he had missed the bus to Intercourse. When he finally decided to take a car service, it was already late. He had missed his chance to be there for Mary Ruth.

The car ride down the lane to his parents' farm felt longer than the two miles that it truly was. They passed a buggy along the way, and Samuel tried to see who was driving it, imagining that it was Elias taking Mary Ruth home. His heart pounded inside of his chest, his blood feeling hot at the thought. But it was too dark to see inside the buggy. Frustrated, Samuel sank against the car seat and closed his eyes.

Yes, the weekend had been a horrible mistake. He knew that now and was glad that he had decided to leave early. Peter Bartlett was simply no *gut*, a young man interested in dark bars and loose women. He had been surprised that Robert had gone along with Peter. Samuel had imagined a weekend of exploring the city, eating at restaurants, and meeting new people. He had imagined going to movies, listening to music, and other benign activities. But once the others decided to go to the bar, Samuel had refused.

That second night, when the others had returned to the motel room, Samuel was shocked to see Paul barely able to walk. His clothes were rumpled and his eyes red. When he tried to speak, nothing made sense. Was that what alcohol did to a man, Samuel wondered. If it was, he wanted nothing to do with it. Robert and Peter had laughed at Paul before turning their attention to Samuel. For the next half an hour, they teased him about his decision to return to the room instead of hanging out at the bar and trying to meet women.

Samuel didn't sleep much that night. He listened to the other men snoring from their bed, Paul sleeping on the floor, which is where he had eventually passed out.

No, Samuel realized, this isn't what I want. He regretted having gone with these men that he had thought were friends. So, early in the morning, he had snuck out of the room and made his way through the streets to the train station and waited to return home early. If getting drunk and chasing bold women was their idea of fun, Samuel realized, he was in the wrong place and clearly he was with the wrong people.

The long wait for the train had given him plenty of time to think. In two weeks, he'd turn twenty-one. For almost five years, he had been running around, doing what he could to experience life before settling down to the church. He had vowed not to rush himself before doing so. However, his recent conversations with Mary Ruth had made him realize that life didn't always wait. If he wanted certain things, he had to seize the opportunity at the moment it presented itself. Otherwise, as Mary Ruth had made him see, he might risk losing it.

Yes, he thought. Even if settling down is a year or more away, there is no reason to let Mary Ruth slip away and become someone else's intended. It was time for him to make his intention known rather than risk seeing her riding home from singings with that Elias Lantz. Any Amish man would be foolish not to jump at the chance to court Mary Ruth Smucker, he told himself. Indeed, he had been acting foolish over the past few months. Well, he decided, no more. Tonight would be that first step.

"Stop here," Samuel said quickly. The driver slowed the car down and pulled over to the side of the dark road. "I'll walk the rest of the way," he said, reaching into his pocket to pull out the money to pay the man.

He walked down the road toward the Smucker farm.

If Elias had brought her home, Samuel would wait for her. He had to let her know that, indeed, he had come back to escort her home from the singing. He needed her to understand that she had been right about the Philadelphia trip. He wanted her to be the first one to learn that he was willing to try to shun the ways of the world and slowly return to the fold with an eye to the future. Yes, he had seen enough to be aware that a non-Amish life was not for him. But it might take time, he realized, before he could commit to the kneeling vow and a wife.

When he heard the familiar clip-clop of the horse's hooves against the macadam and the gentle humming of the buggy wheels, Samuel sank back into the shadows. He didn't want to confront Elias, but he certainly wanted to speak privately to Mary Ruth.

The buggy pulled down the driveway and stopped at the corner of the house. Samuel watched and waited until the door opened and he saw Mary Ruth emerge. He was glad that Elias hadn't brought her home in a courting buggy, for that would surely be a bad sign. And Samuel was going to make certain that no other courting buggy brought her anywhere unless it was his.

She had just reached her parents' front door and Elias had started his buggy back down the driveway when Samuel stepped out from the shadows and walked up behind her.

"Mary Ruth," he said softly.

She jumped and turned around, dropping her hand from the doorknob.

"It's me. Samuel."

"You seem to delight in scaring me," she said, none

too friendly. Clearly, she was still upset with him. "And what on earth are you doing here, anyway?"

He stepped closer to her, emerging from the shadows and standing in the glow of the kerosene lantern that Miriam Smucker had left lit in the window for her daughter. "I tried to get back in time to take you home from the singing," he explained.

"Oh, really?" Her voice gave away her disbelief in what he said. "You're not even dressed for a singing and don't even have your hat!"

Samuel leaned against the porch and stared at her. He wasn't used to her being so confrontational and sarcastic. Where had his Mary Ruth disappeared? "My hat?" His hand went to his head, and sure enough, his hat was missing.

"Any proper man would come calling dressed properly!" She hesitated before quickly adding, "If he was serious, that is. And certainly he would not show up at this hour!"

"Mary Ruth," he started softly, ignoring her hurtful words. "I want to apologize to you."

"Apologize?" she scoffed. "Where would you begin?"

He reached out and grabbed her hand. "Don't be like that, Mary Ruth. I came here tonight to tell you that I'm done with my demons and I'm ready to make that first step toward a real commitment."

She tilted her head, intently listening to his words, for which he was thankful. When she didn't interrupt him, he sensed that she was softening. Clearly, she didn't want to be upset with him, and he knew that he had not lost her heart after all.

"I…" He caressed the back of her hand with his thumb, equally thankful that she had not yanked her hand from his grasp. "I'm willing to take that next move. But only if you are beside me."

In the glow from the kerosene lantern, he saw the expression on her face change. Indeed, she was losing the edge of her anger with him. "Go on," she whispered.

"I can't say that I'm ready to settle down completely," he stammered. Then, realizing how vague that sounded, he quickly added, "But I have seen that no *gut* can come from the Englischer ways. Not for me, anyhow."

"Samuel?" she asked. She hesitated as she tried to understand what his words meant. "What are you saying?"

He cleared his throat. "Well, Mary Ruth," he said then hesitated. What was he saying? The words were falling from his lips faster than he could think. "I reckon I'm saying that, mayhaps I am ready to start courting after all and…well…" He paused. This was the no-turning-back moment. Would she forgive him? "If you can see fit to give me that second chance, I'll do right by you."

There was a pause. It lingered between them, and for a moment, Samuel thought that she was going to say no. So he was quite relieved when she asked cautiously, "Right by me? How so?"

"Well, for starters," he began. "I want you coming home from future singings with me."

"With you?"

"*Ja*," he said and took a deep breath. He had practiced in his head how he was going to say it, but none of the practice words seemed right, not now as he stood before her. "In my courting buggy." There, he thought. It has been said and no taking it back.

A smile lit up her face and she lowered her eyes. He

imagined that if the lighting was better that he would have seen a blush covering her cheeks. "Oh, Samuel," she whispered.

"And I'm going to talk to the bishop about those summer baptismal classes," he continued.

"For the kneeling vow in fall?" she asked, her voice giving away her disbelief.

"*Ja*," he nodded. "The kneeling vow. And I reckon you'll be taking it alongside me, Mary Ruth."

"I... I don't know what to say," she whispered.

His heart pounded inside of his chest. She didn't know what to say? He prayed he wasn't too late and prayed that she still cared. "You could start by saying yes, Mary Ruth," he replied.

She nodded her head and lifted her eyes to meet his. "*Ja*," she said. "That's a yes."

He hesitated to approach her, but after a brief second, decided to take the chance. He walked up the steps so that he stood before her. Reaching for her hands, he stared at her. "I'll not be a fool no more, Mary Ruth. But you might have to be patient with me."

She laughed. "Haven't I always?"

"*Ja*, true." He smiled but remained serious. "But I can't lose you to anyone else. You are Samuel's Mary Ruth, and it's time that I start doing my part."

"I'm awful glad that you realized that," she said softly. "Mayhaps that Philadelphia trip wasn't such a bad idea after all."

Reluctantly, he nodded. He certainly didn't want to tell her about his friends and their behavior that had so upset him. He didn't want her to learn that he had seen the dark side of the non-Amish world. It was a place he hoped to never see again. No, he thought, there was no good that would come out of exposing his Mary Ruth to such worldliness. "Mayhaps."

Mary Ruth laughed again, the noise gentle and joyous to his ears. She let him keep holding her hand as she said, "Samuel's Mary Ruth. I do like the sound of that."

"I'm right glad you do, Mary Ruth." He lifted her hand to his lips and kissed the back of it, his warm breath caressing her skin. "And we have a lot of time ahead of us for you to get used to the sound of it."

There was a moment of silence between them. Samuel could hardly believe what had transpired. Had it really only been two days ago that he had been excited for the adventurous weekend in Philadelphia, still convinced that he would never settle down with any woman? Now, here he was talking about a future with Mary Ruth. It felt right, he realized. Perhaps fighting it had been a bad idea all along. No one was trying to control him, except himself. It was time, he realized, to stop fighting everything and everyone. It was a new dawn for him, one that included Mary Ruth beside him.

Chapter Thirteen

The walk home from the Smuckers' farm seemed to fly by. He didn't care that it was dark and late. He cut through the pastures, knowing the way by heart, despite the darkness. It was faster than the road anyway. Plus, he liked listening to the cows grazing in the night. It just added to his joy. Indeed, Samuel was just plain happy, happier than he could ever remember feeling. He felt as if a weight was off his shoulders. He would not fight the community or his family anymore.

Perhaps everyone had been right, he told himself. *Rumschpringe* was a *gut* time to explore, a *gut* time to answer questions, but it was not a time to think that the pasture was greener on the other side of town. No, Samuel told himself. Going to Philadelphia had shown him that life outside of his community was not any better and, in most ways, was worse than what he had thought. He could never live among those people who drank and chased women. If that was expected of him, he'd never survive.

With his family and community, he knew where he belonged. He knew his place and his support. God had shown him the light, shown him that life in the fast world of the Englische was not for him. Of course, he knew that not all Englische lived like that. But he also knew that none of the Amish did. Any church member who took a misstep in that direction was quickly guided back to the right path or asked to leave the community. Samuel was willing to take that step, the step onto the right path at last.

And now that he had taken that step with Mary Ruth…

He smiled to himself. Yes, she was now his Mary Ruth and they were courting. Unlike some of the other youth, he wouldn't rush into marriage, but when two people were courting, formally courting, that was the end goal. Having known her for all of his life, he knew that she would be his wife. His life partner. His best friend.

All of these glorious thoughts were floating through his mind as he walked home along the hill. He felt warm inside, despite the cool night air. He was so thankful that he had come back from Philadelphia early and had waited for Mary Ruth in the darkness. Elias would be disappointed, that was for sure and certain. But he would accept it like a true Amish man. God's will was never questioned among the Amish.

Of course, Samuel had been disappointed to hear that Mary Ruth would not be helping Lillian for the next week. Her *daed* needed her help with hay cutting in the mornings before the sun got too hot overhead. But just the thought that she'd be his girl, leaving the singings with him and saving her smiles just for him, was enough to help him get through that next week. Soon enough, when he was ready to make that final commitment, he knew that they wouldn't ever be apart again.

So when he cut down the field off of Musser School Lane to get to his parents' farm, he had to do a double-take at the flashing lights from the police cars in the driveway. He stopped in the field, trying to comprehend what he was seeing. Police cars? Flashing lights? At his home? It took him a moment to register what he was seeing. It just didn't make sense.

But they were there. The lights kept flashing and he could see people standing in front of the cars' headlights. He jogged down the hills, his heart suddenly pounding inside of his chest. Could something have happened to his *daed*? His *mamm*? One of the *kinner*? His mind immediately thought of little Jacob and he said a quick prayer to God that no one was harmed, that the police were there by mistake.

The closer he got to the house, the brighter the lights were. He saw that there were two police cars in the driveway. His *daed*, Junior, and Daniel were talking with the police officers. The women were inside the house, and Samuel easily imagined that they were huddled around the window in the kitchen, trying to see what was going on but knowing better than to interfere. He wondered where David was.

"What's wrong?" Samuel asked as he emerged from around the side of the barn, pausing only to catch his breath from having run so fast in the dark.

"Samuel!" his father said and started to approach him, a look of relief on his face.

"Samuel Lapp?" one of the older officers said, putting his arm out to stop Jonas from getting closer to his son. "Are you Samuel Lapp?"

A confused look crossed his face as he looked at

the officer as if trying to understand the question. "*Ja*, I am." He looked at his *daed*. "What's going on here?"

The officer nodded to one of the other men, who proceeded to step forward, grabbing Samuel's arm. "You need to come with us," the first officer said. As the officer repeated strange words, Samuel felt something cold and hard on his wrists. Handcuffs?

"*Daed*?" Samuel stared at his father then looked at Daniel and Junior. "What's happening?" They averted their eyes, their faces pale and drawn. Clearly, they knew that there was nothing they could do, and they felt ashamed by that knowledge.

He could hear the familiar clip-clop of horse hooves approaching but the noise was faster than normal. A horse was cantering down their lane, and as the buggy stopped just behind the police cars, Jake jumped out, having tossed the reins to David who was seated inside beside him. It was apparent that his family had sent David to Sylvia and Jake's to get him for help. But Samuel couldn't figure out why.

"Now hold on there," Jake said, stepping up to the older officer who seemed to be in charge. "What's all this about?"

"Please stand back, sir," the older officer said.

"I will not until someone tells me what is going on," Jake snapped back. "What has this boy supposedly done that you are not only taking him away but are arresting him?"

The older officer ignored Jake and motioned with his head toward the car. Two of the other officers led Samuel to the police car and shoved him, none too gently, into the back seat. "He'll be at the Philadelphia Police Station. I would recommend contacting a lawyer for your son," the older officer said to Jonas and turned to leave.

"Philadelphia?" Jonas gasped and reached out for Junior to support him.

Junior held his father and looked up at Jake. "Jake, please help Samuel!"

Taking a deep breath, Jake stared at his father and brother-in-laws then glanced at the officer who was starting to walk by. Blocking his path, Jake stood up to his full height and made certain that he could not pass. "Not so fast," he said, careful to keep his voice calm and low. "I'm aware of your laws. You have to tell him, if not us, why you are taking him away."

The officer frowned and glanced over his shoulder at the other officers. Seeing that they were focusing on putting Samuel in the back of the police car, he lowered his voice. "Vehicular manslaughter," the officer said. "Leaving the scene of a crime. Drinking and driving."

Jake shook his head in disbelief and frowned. "What are you saying?" But the officer merely turned on his heel and retreated to the police car.

Jonas clung to his oldest son and seemed to collapse against his side. "What did he say?"

Junior steadied his father. "Jake? What does this mean?" He stared at Jake, who had his back to them. Jake was staring at the police car, his mouth hanging open and his hand rubbing his forehead.

Daniel stared at Jake. "Vehicular? As in a car?"

Jonas grabbed at Daniel's arm. "What is this about a car? What did Samuel do?"

The police cars were pulling out of the driveway, their tires making a strange crackling noise against the loose macadam and gravel. Samuel was straining his neck in the back of the car, trying to look out of the window at his family. Jake thought that he saw tears in his eyes, but as the car moved away, Samuel quickly disappeared from sight.

Dropping his eyes, Jake stared at the ground. Vehicular manslaughter? An Amish youth? He couldn't seem to comprehend that what had just happened was real. Had police truly just come to the farm and taken away his brother-in-law? Surely this was not happening, he thought. Just a bad nightmare. But as he saw the lights of the police car pull up the hill and disappear from view, he knew otherwise.

Junior steadied his father. "Let's go inside. We will need to talk. Jake will need to advise us what to do and what this means." He met his brother-in-law's eyes. "You can help him, can't you?"

Without the police cars, there was no light in the driveway. Jake was thankful for that because he certainly didn't want Samuel's family to see his face. "I don't know, Junior," he said. "I just don't know on this one."

Chapter Fourteen

Samuel sat in the cold, empty room, shivering from both the cold and fear. He had no idea what was happening. No one was telling him anything. There was a metal table before him that was bolted to the ground. A mirror was on the far wall and he could stare at his own reflection. He had lost his hat, probably when running through the fields, and his hair was matted with sweat.

The walls were cinderblock and had been painted a pale yellow. He noticed that it was chipped in places and there was writing on it in others. "For a good time call…," read one handwritten scrawl. Samuel shook his head, closing his eyes and trying to figure out what had happened and how he had arrived at this police station.

It must be a mistake, he told himself. Clearly they had brought in the wrong person for questioning about some crime that Samuel had nothing to do with. That much was certain. But he didn't understand why they had left him alone in the room for so long. Time went by until he realized that an hour had passed and no one had entered to check in on him. If he hadn't been so scared, he might have paced the floor, but he was too frightened to get up from where he sat.

God will not desert me, he told himself and shut his eyes in a silent prayer. *Please heavenly Father,* he said. *Let me clear up this matter and return home. I have already promised to turn over a new leaf and return to Your fold. Please do not let me be torn away from this new life that I have chosen to join.*

Hours later, just as a new day dawned, the door finally opened. Samuel's head rested on the table; he had fallen into a very light sleep. When the door creaked, he jumped in his seat and stared at the opening, waiting to see who would walk through it. *Please Lord,* he prayed. *Let it be Jake or Daed and let them be taking me away from this horrible place.*

Instead, two uniformed officers walked in. One sat down at the table while the other lingered behind him. Samuel stared at them, bewildered by their silence. They watched him carefully but said nothing. Seconds passed. Minutes passed. And finally, the one cleared his throat.

"Samuel, do you know why you are here?"

He shook his head. "I don't even know where I am, never mind why I'm here. I just want to go home."

The officer smiled, but it was not a genuine smile. "My name's Officer Reilly. I just want you to answer some questions and then you can be on your way, Samuel."

Samuel nodded enthusiastically. Anything, he thought, to get out of here.

"Where were you at five o'clock on Sunday evening?"

The question startled Samuel. Sunday evening? "You mean last night?" He frowned. "I was on a train to Lancaster."

"Were you with anyone?"

Samuel shook his head. "No. I was alone."

The two officers exchanged a glance before Officer Reilly turned his attention back to Samuel. "You familiar with these boys?" He opened a cream-colored file folder that was on the table, a folder Samuel hadn't noticed before now. Inside were three black-and-white photos. The officer slid two of them across the table so that they were lined up before Samuel.

And he gasped.

"That's Peter Bartlett! And Robert Miller!"

Indeed, it was Peter and Robert, but they did not look like Peter and Robert. Samuel looked away, closing his eyes. He hoped that he could erase from his memory the horrid photos that he had just seen. But he knew that those images would haunt him forever. Clearly, those photos were recent, and clearly both boys were no longer living.

"They're dead, Samuel."

Samuel kept his eyes closed and hung his head so that the officers could not see his face. Tears stung at his eyes and he said a quiet prayer to God for their souls. Whatever had happened had been unexpected and violent.

"Do you know why you are here?"

Samuel glanced up. "To identify them?"

The other unnamed officer laughed, but Officer Reilly glared at him before turning his attention back to Samuel. "You were identified as the driver of the car."

Suddenly, the pieces of the puzzle began to come together and Samuel understood everything, despite understanding nothing. "I don't know how to drive," he said.

"You were identified as the driver of the car," Officer Reilly repeated. "Tell us what happened."

"Nothing happened!" Samuel explained, suddenly feeling a wave of panic wash over him. "I left in the morning. Paul was *gsoffe* the night before." He realized that the two officers didn't understand what he meant. "*Gsoffe*. Drunk. Really drunk like nothing I've seen before and I didn't like that." He paused, trying to remember. "They'd gone to a bar while I was wandering along the riverfront. I liked the ships, especially that old pirate-looking one." When he looked up, he saw that the officers looked bored. Clearly, they didn't care about the details, just the facts. Samuel frowned. "When I got back to the room, the other fellows were still out. I didn't join them. I don't like drinking. When they came back, Paul could hardly walk, that's how *gsoffe* he was."

"What happened next?" the officer prodded.

Samuel shrugged. "I barely slept that night. I wanted to leave at the first light." He stared at the officer. "When the sun rose, I left and walked to the train station. Bought a ticket to come home. Didn't want to be around drunkards and I wanted to see my girl home from the singing!"

The two officers glanced at each other. "You mentioned Paul," Officer Reilly said. He opened the manila folder again and slid the last photo toward Samuel. "You mean this guy?"

Samuel glanced at the photo then quickly looked away. He nodded. "*Ja*, that's Paul." He hesitated, wanting to know the truth, to understand but afraid to ask the next question. "What happened to him?"

"You tell us, Samuel."

Surprised, he looked up. "I already told you that I

wasn't there. When I last saw him, he was drunk. Peter and Robert were carrying him into the room."

Reilly shook his head and smiled. "The motel owner said four men checked into his place on Friday and four left on Sunday. Your name is on the registry and another guest said an Amish man was driving. Any other Amish men on your adventure with Paul, Robert, and Peter?"

Samuel shook his head vehemently. "No," he said. "But it wasn't me driving that car."

"You were the only Amish man in the group, isn't that correct?"

Samuel quickly understood what they were insinuating. "I told you. I wasn't driving! I don't know how to drive. Amish don't drive cars!"

Reilly took a deep breath and pushed his chair back from the table. "You're making this very hard for us, Samuel. I want to know what happened."

The door flew open and a man in a black suit walked through it, bellowing, "Enough!" He was a middle-aged man with thick brown hair and glasses perched on his nose. From his expression, Samuel knew that he was not happy with the proceedings. "Dave Snyder, representing Samuel Lapp here. Unless you've read my client his rights, I suggest that you stop questioning my client and let me take him home. The boy has not done anything and you've no right to detain him."

Officer Reilly rolled his eyes. "He's a flight risk. He fled once already."

"Allegedly fled," Dave snapped back.

"I want to go home," Samuel said. He stared at the lawyer, begging the stranger with his eyes. "I didn't do anything. I don't know what they are talking about."

"Quiet!" Dave shot back, none too kindly. Then,

turning his attention back to the officers, he tilted his chin and motioned to the door. "I'd like a word with both of you in private, if you don't mind."

Samuel watched as the three men disappeared through the door, a freedom he had never thought twice about before. Coming and going from any room was never something he had questioned. But now, he knew that he was simply not permitted to leave of his own free will.

He tried to piece together what had happened. It was obvious that the three boys had gotten into trouble. There must have been an accident from the looks of Peter and Robert. But Paul had been photographed in a hospital bed. He was still alive. If only Samuel knew what had happened so that he could explain that he had been on his way back to see Mary Ruth.

Once again, seconds passed, turning into minutes. Before long, Samuel imagined that at least half an hour had gone by. Surely it was close to four in the morning now…maybe even five. He couldn't keep track of time but he knew that, between the ride back to Philadelphia and the hours of waiting, it was certainly early morning.

The door opened again and Dave walked in. He set his briefcase on the table and sat down opposite Samuel. For a moment, he didn't speak. He seemed to be taking in the situation and studying Samuel.

"Two of your friends were killed, Samuel. A car accident. The third one is in critical condition at the hospital. He might live. He might not." He paused, waiting for Samuel's reaction. When he realized that there wasn't going to be a reaction, he took a deep breath. "Someone claims that there was a fourth man, an Amish man, who drove the car away."

"It wasn't me," Samuel said, his voice flat. He didn't like talking to strangers, and Dave Snyder was certainly not warm and fuzzy. His directness frightened Samuel more than the officers.

"They said there were three men at the accident scene, but no one was behind the driver seat," Dave stated flatly. "An eyewitness saw a man in a hat walk away."

"It wasn't me," Samuel repeated, his voice a soft whisper.

"They have circumstantial evidence at best," Dave agreed. "But you are going to have to prove your story. Do you have an alibi?"

"A what?"

Dave sighed. "An alibi. Someone who can swear that you were not there."

"Amish don't take oaths or swear," Samuel said.

This time, Dave rolled his eyes. "Is there anyone who can vouch for your whereabouts?"

Samuel shrugged. "I was on a train. It broke down. It was late pulling into Lancaster and then I took a cab."

Dave cocked his head. "Do you have a credit card receipt?"

"Don't have a credit card," he stated. "I paid cash."

Again, Dave seemed to become irritated. "Do you have anything to prove that you were on that train? A ticket stub? A receipt for paying cash?"

A wave of fear washed over Samuel. He didn't have any of those things. After all, why would he need a receipt or stub? "No," he replied solemnly.

Once again, Dave sighed. "Your brother-in-law's going to owe me for this one."

Samuel looked up. "Jake?"

"Of course!" Dave snapped. "I wouldn't be here for anyone else, I'll tell you that. Not at this hour in the morning and not for something so..." He hesitated as if searching for the word. "Impossible."

"It's not impossible," Samuel pleaded. "I wasn't there. I went home to see Mary Ruth, to ask her to court me. I was giving up my *rumschpringe*. I didn't like what I saw in Philadelphia."

Dave rubbed his hand over his face. He looked tired and worn. "Here's what's going to happen. I'm going to force them to either charge you or release you. Jake is waiting outside for you and will take you home, given the likelihood that you'll be released. But you better not run."

"Run where?"

"Anywhere! You stay put at your parents' farm."

Samuel exhaled. "That's all I want to do. Stay put."

"I don't think you understand, Samuel." Dave leaned forward and lowered his voice. "If you are charged with vehicular manslaughter, you'll face jail time. We need proof that you weren't there and you are not offering me much, especially given the fact that we have your name on a motel registry and two eyewitnesses that you were at the scene."

"Paul will know," Samuel offered meekly.

"Your friend Paul is clinging to life," Dave retorted and stood up. "You Amish like to pray? Pray for that boy to recover and vouch for your story. Until that time, your future is about as iffy as a lottery ticket." He turned and walked toward the door. "I'll be back and let you know if I can get the officers to release you into Jake's care."

Once the lawyer left the room, Samuel lowered his

head into his hands. He couldn't understand what was happening or why. How could the police have taken him from his home? How could a witness have claimed that he was not only there but driving? Samuel tried to replay what had happened over the weekend, feeling as though he was going crazy. For the first time in a long while he had tried to do the right thing, but it had backfired and he had been accused of driving a car, killing his friends, and leaving the scene of a crime…all the while he had been innocently on a train, trying to get back to declare his intentions to Mary Ruth by picking her up from the Sunday evening singing. How could so much go wrong in such a short period of time?

Chapter Fifteen

The drive back to Leola from Philadelphia was quiet. Jake didn't ask questions and Samuel was grateful for that. He sank into the back seat of the car and shut his eyes, praying his thanks to God for having saved him from the clutches of the Englischer laws, even if only temporarily.

He still didn't understand what had transpired. Everything felt so surreal, as if he was floating above his own body, watching the events unfold. From the conversation he had with Mary Ruth, which had sent him into a tailspin, to the bright lights of the police cars at his parents' house which had brought him back to reality, to the time he had spent at the Philadelphia police station which had sunk him into a living nightmare—nothing seemed to make much sense.

The driver was pulling off the main highway when Samuel finally turned to Jake. "What happens now, Jake?"

Jake shook his head. "I don't know, Samuel. You have ventured into a part of the Englische world that I have never really experienced," he said softly. Despite his own dealings with lawyers, police, and other officials after the death of his wife, it was true that Jake had never been in trouble with the law. He wasn't certain how this would play out, especially given that the prime suspect was an Amish youth.

But Jake also knew that the Englischers' legal system wouldn't care whether Samuel was Amish or not. Laws were laws, and, once broken, everyone had to answer to the American court. He just prayed that the young man in the hospital recovered and could answer some questions that would clear Samuel's name. And he was glad that he had been able to reach his friend, Dave. He had called him from the telephone shanty, catching him early in the morning before he left for work. Dave hadn't hesitated to volunteer to come right away, despite living sixty miles from Philadelphia. Anything for an old friend, he had said to Jake.

During that time, Jake had found a taxi that would take him to the police station. By the time he got there, Dave had already arrived and was inside with the police officers. Jake could hear his friend's voice, loud and demanding, citing laws for holding suspects without reading them their rights. He could hear Dave explaining the concept of holding an Amish man and how the news media would jump all over the officers if they didn't let Samuel return home. In the long run, Dave's belligerent attitude had won Samuel his freedom, at least temporarily.

Now, as they headed home, Jake knew that he was the only bridge that Samuel had between the two worlds. The Amish were able to navigate the laws of the Englische because, for the most part, their ways did not conflict. The Amish also had their own laws within their community that they followed as a collective group. Now that the two words had collided, his wife's family would look to him for answers and explanations; and, given his own experience with the legal system, he knew that the process could be long and drawn-out. There was never an easy ending to these situations.

"Answer me one question, Samuel, and I'll never ask it again," Jake asked, breaking the silence that had befallen them. "Were you there?"

"No!" Samuel proclaimed, his voice sharp and strong. "I was so disgusted by Paul's drunkenness and Robert and Peter's behavior that I left as soon as the sun rose on Sunday morning. All I could think of was coming home," he said, his voice desperate for Jake's support. "You have to believe me. I was not there when that accident happened."

Satisfied that his brother-in-law was telling the truth, Jake took a deep breath and nodded. "*Ja vell*," he said, hoping to alleviate some of Samuel's fears. "Then everything should get cleared up soon enough, I imagine. It sure would be helpful if that Paul would come out of his coma and confirm your story."

Samuel had been so caught up in his own problems that he hadn't really inquired about Paul. "He's in a coma?"

"*Ja*," Jake nodded. "It was a head-on collision. The car crossed the median and ran into a van."

"A van?" Samuel gasped. Vans carried lots of people. Often, when the Amish were traveling great distances to visit family, they rented vans. "Was anyone in it? Was anyone else…?" he paused, unable to actually say the word.

Jake shook his head. "Injured? Yes. Killed? No."

"This is unbelievable," Samuel mumbled, leaning against the back of the seat. "I just don't understand."

"The van driver was knocked out but a passenger claims she saw an Amish-looking fellow driving the car, get out of it, and leave the scene," Jake said. "When the police and ambulances arrived, there were only three people in that car. Well..." He hesitated. "Peter had been tossed out of the vehicle and was found on the side of the road."

"Then he could have been driving!" Samuel exclaimed.

Jake took a deep breath and nodded. "Sounds logical but for the witness. Robert and Paul aren't Amish."

Samuel digested this news for a few minutes, still trying to make sense of what had happened. Nothing made sense to him. Suddenly, his heart began to pound inside of his chest and his blood felt as though it was on fire. If none of this made sense to him, what would his family think? Mary Ruth? The community?

"Samuel?"

He looked at his brother-in-law. His eyes were wide and frightened against his pale skin. The color had drained from his face. "Jake, what will everyone believe?"

"Now that," Jake started slowly, being careful to select his words. "I can't answer, Samuel. I don't know for certain." He paused. "I do know that you've been towing a loose line recently. You've been hanging out with those boys, staying out all night, missing work, sleeping through service. One thing I do know is that people like to think the worst about others."

"The worst meaning that they'll think I actually did

this? I killed those boys and just walked away?" Samuel couldn't believe what he was hearing.

Jake nodded. "I'm not going to sugarcoat it, Samuel. You're going to have a lot of explaining to do, and you must pray that the truth comes out in support of your story."

"Mary Ruth...," he said, letting the sentence hang unfinished between them.

"That's the trouble with running with the wrong crowd, Samuel," Jake replied, his words careful and short. "When they go down, they tend to take you with them."

"She has to know that it isn't true!" His voice sounded panic-stricken.

Jake laid a hand on his youngest brother-in-law's shoulders. "Now, calm down, Samuel. As of right now, no one knows what happened last night. The word will spread, that's for certain. There are three very unhappy families in Leola today. We have to remember that two of your friends died in that accident, and the third one is hanging on by a thread."

"He has to live," Samuel whispered to himself.

"That's up to God, not you and your wishes," Jake pointed out.

"I need to go to their families, make certain they know the truth!" Samuel said, an urgency in his voice.

But Jake brought him back to reality. "You need to get home, talk to your parents, get yourself some much-needed sleep, then sit down with your *daed* and figure out what to say to the bishop."

Samuel frowned. "The...bishop?" Jake's statement confused him. Why would he want to get the bishop involved?

"Oh, yes," Jake replied firmly. "The sooner you get the bishop involved, the better for you, your family, and your future."

"I just don't believe any of this is happening," he said, shaking his head and leaning it against the back of the car seat. How could so much have gone so wrong?

The car was pulling into his parents' driveway. Jake laid a hand on Samuel's shoulders. "Unfortunately, you need to get past that, Samuel, for this is, indeed, really happening." He gave Samuel a reassuring smile as the car came to a stop. "Now, you get on out and spend some time with your parents. Tell them what has happened. Tell them your story. Then sleep. I'll be back later when I've finished my chores and had a good long nap. I'm also going to check in with that lawyer."

"Dave?"

"*Ja*, Dave Snyder. An old friend of mine from my Englischer days. He owed me a few favors, that's for certain. Reckon that score will be settled before this situation clears up." Jake motioned toward the farmhouse. "Now, go into the house and follow my advice. You won't be any good to yourself or that lawyer if you don't get some sleep."

Samuel nodded and exited the car. He stared at the white farmhouse and took a deep breath. He didn't want to go inside, too ashamed at the predicament that he had found himself in. But he knew that he had nowhere else to go and Jake's advice sounded good enough, that was for sure and certain. Talk, eat, and sleep. He just prayed that his family would support him, believe his story, and stand by his side.

Chapter Sixteen

By late Monday afternoon, the bishop and two ministers were standing in Jonas and Katie's kitchen, waiting for Samuel to come downstairs. Word had started to spread throughout the community about the death of Robert Miller and Peter Bartlett. Whispered with that news was the speculation that Samuel Lapp had been involved, perhaps even the driver of the vehicle. And with that, the bishop and ministers descended upon the Lapp farm to offer support for Katie and Jonas. But, more than that, they wanted to meet with Samuel and find out what had happened.

Samuel was groggy when his father woke him in the early evening. He ran his fingers through his hair and followed his *daed* down the stairs, his heart heavy and pounding inside of his chest. He prayed that the bishop would believe him.

The three men were standing in the kitchen, dressed in their Sunday suits. Their black suits, black vests, and black pants seemed even more austere, considering it wasn't even Sunday. Bishop Peachey stared at Samuel as he entered the room, his shoulders slumped forward and his eyes trying to avoid contact with the bishop.

Samuel couldn't help glancing around the kitchen. His father stood by the window, his back toward Samuel. He seemed to be staring outside. And then Samuel saw his mother. Immediately, he felt his pulse quicken. She had seemed to age overnight. Her face was pinched and drawn, with dark circles under her eyes. She sat at the table, her hands folded on her lap and her mouth moving in a silent prayer.

"Samuel," the bishop said, his voice deep and stern. "A most disturbing story has come to my attention."

Samuel lifted his chin and met the bishop's gaze. "I wasn't there, Bishop."

"Two young men are dead, Samuel. Another is in the hands of God."

"I am aware of that," Samuel murmured.

Bishop Peachey took a deep breath. "The story is circulating that you were the one driving the automobile."

"Outrageous." Jonas turned around, his eyes burning and his mouth pressed into a tight grimace. "That's simply outrageous!"

Holding up his hands, Bishop Peachy nodded. "I tend to agree with you, Jonas. The story does sound most unlikely." When he paused, he met Jonas's gaze. "But this would not be the first time that an Amish youth in *rumschpringe* snuck off to obtain a license to drive those worldly vehicles. And..." He looked back at Samuel, his expression stern and solemn. "Your son seems to have a reputation for liking fast cars, raceways, and worldly people."

Samuel looked at his father, pleading with his eyes.

"I have never driven a car, *Daed*," he said. "You have to believe me!"

The door opened and Samuel saw Jake quietly enter the room with Sylvia following close behind him. She slipped over to her mother's side and stood next to her, a shadow of support for Katie. Jake took off his hat and stayed off to the side, listening but not contributing. For Samuel, there was some comfort in having Jake present, and for just the briefest of moments, Samuel felt relieved. At least Jake knows the Englischer laws, he thought, and can help explain them to me.

"You state that you have never driven a car and that you were not the one driving. That is yet to be known," the bishop stated flatly.

"What happens now?" Jonas asked, the one question that was on everyone's minds but not their lips.

"That will depend on the boy in the hospital," the bishop said. "We do not live by the laws of the Englische, but we cannot avoid abiding by them. Should the legal authorities decide to arrest Samuel…" He hesitated and looked at Samuel before he continued. His dark eyes looked sad, and it was clear that he took no joy from this visit. "If they press charges, there is not much that we can do."

Samuel tipped his chin at Jake. "What about that lawyer friend of yours?"

At the mention of a lawyer, the bishop frowned. "What is this?" He turned to look at Jake. Clearly, he wasn't happy with Samuel's question. "A lawyer? What is Samuel talking about?"

The muscles in Jake's jaw tightened as he clenched his teeth. "A friend of mine is a lawyer. He helped me in the past." Jake stared back at the bishop, refusing to act ashamed. "I called him for help and he went to the police station to assist us in getting Samuel released as well as finding out what was happening."

"A lawyer was retained?" the bishop asked, his voice indicating both his disbelief and displeasure. He looked at Jake, his eyes hard and sharp. "We don't hire lawyers, Jake Edwards."

Jake nodded and, curbing his own annoyance, lowered his eyes. "I understand that, Bishop. Yet the suspicion is so severe, I felt it was best to have someone from the Englischer world of law help Samuel with these Englischer charges."

The bishop slammed his hand on the side of the table, the noise resonating throughout the room. Sylvia jumped at the noise and moved closer to her mother. Jonas seemed startled and glanced at Jake before averting his eyes.

"No!" the bishop shouted. He looked around the room at each person standing there as he slowly enunciated each word when he said, "We do not rely on the Englische lawyers but on our Lord to help us through difficult times and challenges! He will lead Samuel through this. It is His will, not yours, Jake Edwards, or anyone else's that determines the outcome of this situation. It is the Lord's will!" He walked slowly in a wide circle, pausing briefly to stare at Jake and again at Samuel. "We will pray for a resolution to this matter and let God handle the outcome."

The room was silent.

The bishop took a deep breath and said, "*For I know the plans I have for you, plans to prosper you and not to harm you, plans to give you hope and a future.*" He snapped his gaze back onto Samuel. "Jeremiah 29:11.

You'd be wise to remember it." He looked back at Jake. "And you, too, Jake Edwards! You left the Englischer ways and shall not return to them! I want no more talk about lawyers!"

No one dared to speak.

Exhaling, the bishop tapped his fingers against the edge of the table. He seemed to be weighing his words. The other ministers stood stoically near the door, never having moved during the bishop's reprimand. Clearly this was a situation that none of them had ever encountered, and the magnitude was so great that they were quite willing to let the bishop handle it.

"We will pray for a favorable resolution," he repeated softly. He turned and started to walk toward the door. His shoulders seemed to slump forward as he walked. "That's all we can do now," he mumbled before disappearing out the door.

There was a deep stillness in the room when the bishop left, the ministers trailing after him. It was heavy and oppressive. Everyone seemed to wait until they heard the familiar rattle of the buggy and horse's hooves on macadam, before they seemed to take a collective sigh. Throughout all of their years living on that farm, they had never experienced such a visit from a church leader. Katie dabbed at her eyes, her will to hold back her tears gone. Instead, she let them fall down her cheeks, quick to take the simple white handkerchief that Sylvia handed to her.

Jake was the first to break the silence. "Well," he said, running his fingers through his hair. "That didn't go over so well now, did it?"

"Jake," Sylvia said softly. "No time for joking."

For a moment, he looked at her. Her reprimand had

been soft and spoken with kindness. Jake knew that she was speaking the truth. So he moved toward the table and sat down. "Sylvia's right. Time for some discussion." He motioned to the other chair. "Samuel, you should sit."

Katie seemed to lose all of the remaining color from her face. "Do you have news, Jake? I don't think I can take much more."

He gestured with a simple nod of his head for Sylvia to help her mother to the table. "Not good news but not bad news, *Mammi* Katie."

"What have you learned, Jake?" Jonas asked.

"I spoke with Dave," he began.

"The lawyer?" Katie gushed. "You could be shunned! We all could! You heard the bishop!"

"*Ja*, I sure did." He laid a hand over Katie's and smiled gently. "Was hard to miss how he felt about the lawyer."

"Jake!" Sylvia whispered.

"Now, now, Sylvia," he said lightly. "We've had enough doom and gloom for the past twenty-four hours, and dare I say, we might have more. Let's try to take a breath here and think reasonably." He turned back toward Katie, hoping to reassure her. "I spoke with the lawyer before the bishop made his opinion known to us. He can't fault me for that."

Jonas spoke up. "What did he say?"

He shifted in his seat. "There was a witness. A witness who says that he saw a man wearing a hat in the driver's seat," Jake said. He leveled his gaze at Samuel. "It was your hat, Samuel."

"My hat?" he repeated, not understanding what Jake

was saying. What did his hat have to do with any of this? "I lost my hat."

"Well, it appears your friends found it and someone was wearing it when the car accident occurred," Jake said.

Samuel rubbed his face with his hands. "I came back. I wasn't in that car." He looked up. "I must have left my hat in the room with the fellows." He stared at the faces that were watching him. He couldn't gauge whether or not they believed him. He wished they would tell him but they remained silent. Jake nodded, as if signaling to him that he believed him. But Samuel wasn't so certain about the rest. They still seemed stunned by the course of events.

"There's more," Jake said slowly, clearing his throat as if to buy time. "The motel attendant says you were with them. Says he saw four men at the room together and your name was in the registry."

Samuel jumped out of his seat, knocking the chair over as he started to pace the floor. "I don't believe this!"

"Try to stay calm," Daniel said, his voice low and composed.

"Calm?" Samuel shot back as he spun around to face his family. His eyes were wild and his face pale. "Calm, you say? How can I be calm?" Everyone was staring at him, their eyes wide and faces pale. "Of course my name was on the registry. I don't deny that I was there with them, that I had checked in with them and chipped in money for the room. But I wasn't there when this accident happened!"

"Where were you, Samuel?" Jonas asked.

"I told you already; I was on my way back here," he

snapped. Immediately, he was sorry for his anger. He wasn't angry at his family but at the situation. He lowered his eyes and stilled his temper. When he spoke again, his voice was unruffled. "I came back to get Mary Ruth from the singing. She wasn't there so I went to her house. Would I do that if I had just killed man?"

Katie pressed her lips together and shook her head. "Oh Samuel," she whispered.

But Samuel pressed his case. "It's true. I went there to tell her what I had learned."

"And what was that, Samuel?" Jake prodded.

"I didn't like what I saw in Philadelphia," he said softly. "I didn't want to risk losing her."

Katie shook her head. "Oh, Samuel," she whispered, her eyes misting over with tears. "You never should have gone, son!"

"You say that, *Mamm*," Samuel started. "But it opened my eyes. I saw what those young men were doing and I didn't like it. I didn't like it at all. And that was what I learned!" He looked around the room at each one of them. "Isn't that what this is about? Discovering the truth before joining the church?" He turned his eyes to his parents. "Isn't that what parents hope for? That their children will venture forth and return? That's what happened this weekend." He paused, then enunciating each word and shaking his open hands at his family, he said firmly, "I was returning!"

A silence fell upon the room. No one knew how to respond. Samuel felt his energy drain from his body. He hadn't slept well the night before and certainly hadn't slept much that day. He was tired, bone-weary tired. Dropping his hands to his sides and slumping his shoulders, he shook his head. "I just can't understand why this would happen to me...at the moment when I made the decision!"

Sylvia placed a hand on his shoulder and rubbed it gently. "God won't desert you now, Samuel. Mayhaps He's testing your newfound faith in Him."

Behind them, they heard footsteps on the porch and a door opened. "I saw the bishop was here," Samuel heard his brother Daniel say. "What happened?"

When Samuel looked over his shoulder, he saw that Junior stood beside Daniel and David was lingering in the doorway. He felt embarrassed at the attention and ashamed of the worry that he had brought to his father's farm. Here was his family, joined together to try to help him figure out what to do. They had joined together to support him, even though he had not always been obedient or responsible. He hung his head in disgrace, too aware that his behavior from the previous months didn't match the truth of what had actually happened.

His brothers listened intently while Jake told them about the events from the previous evening and about the visit from the bishop. With two young men having died, it was clear that the Amish grapevine was in full swing. Despite not having telephones in their homes, it was always surprising how quickly bad news traveled to the different Amish households throughout the community.

Certainly, many of the women were already baking pies and bread to take over to the families of the two young men who had perished. Even if they didn't know the families personally, the Amish would step up to show their support for their neighbors in such a traumatic time. And the families of Paul would have similar support during his hospitalization.

Samuel was certain that many of the community members would attend the funeral. Unlike the Amish who held funerals in their homes, the Mennonites were more likely to hold them in their church. It was still hard for him to believe that his friends were dead, but the sorrow of their tragic passing was overshadowed by the accusations that were hanging over his own head. The conflict of emotions was too much for Samuel, and he covered his face with his hands, weeping silently while Sylvia and the rest of his family consoled him.

Chapter Seventeen

Mary Ruth was working in the garden when she heard the commotion. The sun was barely over the crest of the sky and she had finished her morning chores early in order to work in the garden before it became too hot. The spring was becoming increasingly warm, and while the sunshine was more than welcome, the rapid onset of high temperatures was causing an equal rise in tempers. Although, Mary Ruth thought as she sat back on her heels and wiped the sweat from her brow, that tension could also be caused by the recent events affecting the community.

Over the weekend, Lillian sent word to Mary Ruth that she was not needed to help on Monday. The extra time gave Mary Ruth a chance to spend the morning at home, working with her mother on the morning chores.

No one in the Lapp family had breathed a word to her, and it had been Simon who had informed the family about the recent events at the Lapp farm. He told them over supper on Monday evening. The first reaction from everyone had been complete silence. No one had known how to react. A car accident? Deaths of two young men from the local community? During that silence, there had been quiet prayers said by all and a few tears had fallen from her *mamm*'s eyes. She always cried when young people died too early. Of course, it had been her *daed* who had quickly pointed out that the boys were doing things that they shouldn't have. Mary Ruth had wanted to shake her head and remind him that the facts were not known about what had happened, but she had maintained her own silence, too afraid to upset her father further.

Simon cleared his throat and glanced at his sister. The look had sent a chill down her spine. "There's more," he mumbled, quickly averting his eyes.

Their *daed* took a deep breath and set his fork down, the metal clanking against the side of the plate. The sharp and unexpected noise had startled Mary Ruth, causing her to jump in her seat and snap her gaze to her father. Her *daed* had seemed frustrated, unhappy with such sad news at the supper table. "How could there be more, son? Your *mamm* is already terribly upset."

"It's Samuel," Simon said, his voice flat and emotionless.

Mary Ruth had gasped and dropped her own fork at the surprise of her brother's words. "What about Samuel?" She reached out and grabbed her brother's hand. "Was he hurt? Please, Simon! What happened?"

"He was with them, it seems," Simon said.

Mary Ruth stared at him, shock registering on her face. Her Samuel? In a car accident? Last night? "That's impossible. You must have heard wrong, Simon. He was just here last night!"

Silence. Everyone had looked at her, startled by her confession. Now, as Mary Ruth sat in the garden, the sun beating down upon her neck and her hands dry from having been working in the soil, she felt the color rise to her cheeks. If she could have taken back the words, she would have. But the surprise of hearing Samuel's name associated with those poor young men had made her take leave of her senses. Certainly nothing could have happened to her Samuel, she had thought as she sank back into the chair at the table, too aware of the eyes upon her.

Simon had cleared his throat, refusing to make eye contact with her. "Well, that's surprising, Mary Ruth, since he was taken to the police station last night and kept there until early this morning!"

"Police station?" she asked, confused by his words. Nothing was making sense. The way that he had started to tell the story, she had assumed Samuel had been in the accident, too. So why would he have been taken to an Englische police station? It didn't make sense.

"It happened in Philadelphia, the accident," Simon had explained. "They think Samuel caused it."

At that announcement, her *daed* had slammed his hand on the side of the table, causing the water glasses to jump and water to splash over the sides. "I have told you, daughter, to steer clear of that boy, and now I will do nothing less than demand it! You stay away from Samuel Lapp!"

"*Daed*!" she started to cry out in protest, but her *mamm* had laid a gentle hand on her arm to silence her.

"Amos, please," Miriam had said, pleading with her eyes for him to calm down. Then she turned toward her son in an attempt to redirect the conversation away from the bitter words that were being spoken from father to daughter. In her sensibility, she was able to steer the focus back onto the real matter at hand. "Simon," Miriam had started softly, "please tell us what you heard about our neighbor."

There had been another long moment of silence as Simon caught his breath and seemed to mull over the proper choice of words. He glanced at his sister, wishing that he could spare her any unnecessary pain. Yet he had known that the truth needed to be shared, and it was better to hear it from family than from friends. "There were witnesses saying that he was driving the car and that, when it crashed, he left the scene."

Mary Ruth's hand had quickly covered her mouth, trying to hide the expression on her face. She had to repeat the words in her head, not understanding what her brother was saying. It was impossible. Driving? Car crash? Left the scene? Before she knew it, the tears were rolling down her cheeks. "That's simply not possible," she whispered.

"*Nee*," her brother had said gently. "It might well be the truth, Mary Ruth. That's what everyone is saying."

She digested the words, despite her appetite having vanished in more ways than one. Nothing seemed real. "But he came here to court me," she whispered, not caring that she was revealing too much. Under the circumstances, she wanted to defend Samuel, and, she thought, if they only knew what had happened, they would believe him…just as she did. Or did she? She paused and bit her lip. Could he be guilty? Was it possible?

Immediately, she pushed aside the idea. It was unbelievable…unthinkable.

Her *daed* leaned forward and grabbed her wrist, forcing her to look at him. The move startled her. Her father had never done something like that before. But he didn't release his hold, and when she finally complied, he glared at her and said, "You will stay away from that boy, Mary Ruth. He is trouble, and I will not have this family's good name dragged down with him. There is no hope for that boy."

"*Daed*!"

He had shaken his head. "Don't defend him no more, Mary Ruth. It is your own soul, not his, that needs preservation now." He glanced around the table at the rest of his children. His expression was hard and unforgiving as he said, "I'll have none of you involved with that Lapp boy. He has run wild and will now answer to God as well as the community! Our family must remain out of this."

The rest of the family had bowed their heads in silence, accepting the command from their father and husband. After all, in the Amish household, the man was the head, with no questions asked. But Mary Ruth had plenty of questions. Could her Samuel have done such a thing? And, while Mary Ruth thought not, she couldn't help wondering why everyone was pointing the finger at him. Had something happened that indicated Samuel was, indeed, involved? Why had her *daed* given up faith and hope in Samuel? Why was he encouraging her to do the same? Her heart had been heavy and the night had been long as her mind wrestled with these agonizing thoughts.

Despite that having happened only the evening before, it seemed as if it had occurred weeks ago. She hadn't been able to sleep all night. How could this be, she kept asking herself. Just when Samuel had turned around and committed to a relationship? Just when he was on the verge of accepting Jesus? What had happened in Philadelphia? He had said nothing to her about his weekend, just declared his intention to court her. Certainly he did not *seem* like someone who would leave the scene of a terrible accident. And to come calling after causing such a trauma? No, that didn't seem possible to Mary Ruth.

Nothing had seemed real to her all last night. Thankfully, after the initial conversation, everyone must have sensed her inner conflict and had left her alone to her thoughts.

But now, as she sat in the garden, her heart pounded inside of her chest when she realized that the commotion could only be caused by one thing: Samuel. She suspected that he had come to the farm, wanting to speak to her, and she was fairly certain that her *daed* and brother had intercepted him, forbidding him from seeing her.

She wiped her hands on her skirt and struggled to her feet. The voices that filtered through the air were loud enough as the breeze carried them in her direction. However, they were also too low for her to understand what was actually being said. Yet she knew that one of the voices was her father's and the other was Stephen's. When she heard a third voice, she knew that it was Samuel, and once again, her heart seemed to jump inside her chest.

Her eyes stung from having cried during the night, and she quickly lifted her hand to smooth her hair back under the blue kerchief that covered her head. She hoped that she didn't look as exhausted and upset as she felt. Yet, as her bare feet began to walk in the direction of the noise, she knew that it didn't really matter. Her *daed* would never let her speak to Samuel.

The voices grew louder as she approached the barn. The doors were opened to let light and air into the main section where the cows and horses were kept. It was empty now, except for the three men who were standing in the dim light. Mary Ruth lingered near the door, her hand resting tentatively on the frame as she listened.

"You need to let the situation simmer down, Samuel, before you think about that!"

Mary Ruth frowned at her brother's words. What were they talking about?

"I just want to speak to her," she heard Samuel say.

"You'll see her at church on Sunday," her *daed* replied tersely. "No need interrupting her work." Clearly, Amos had no intention of permitting Samuel to the house for visiting Mary Ruth. The lack of compassion in his voice startled her, and at that moment, she felt ashamed of her father.

"Amos," Samuel said to her *daed*. "I wasn't there with those boys."

"Don't need no explanations to something that ain't my business," her *daed* said, a harshness in his voice that Mary Ruth hadn't heard before. In fact, she had never seen him so protective over her and so insistent on keeping a particular Amish man away from one of his daughters. "And especially to a question that I ain't asked!"

There was a moment of silence and Mary Ruth thought that she heard feet shuffling. Samuel shouted out, "Wait!" and she knew that her father had started to walk away. Quickly, she moved away from the door in case her father emerged. But the doorway to the barn remained empty.

"Leave it be, Samuel," her brother Stephen said softly.

"No!" Samuel shot back. "I need her to know that I meant everything! I need her to know that I wasn't there!" He hesitated then in a calm voice said, "*Die Wahrehti ist untodlich!*" Indeed, no one would be able to stop the truth from coming out, but he needed Mary Ruth to know the truth now.

There was a heavy silence and Mary Ruth shut her eyes, leaning her head on the barn wall. *Truth cannot be killed,* indeed, she thought as she repeated what Samuel had said to her father. She pressed her cheek against the wood and felt tears, once again, coming to her eyes. The sadness in Samuel's voice touched her soul. He was alone, so alone, she thought. If only she could go to him, to comfort him… His words made her want to capture him in an embrace and protect him from these horrible accusations. But she knew that her father would feel much less pity.

And then she heard it. If Samuel had spoken calmly, her *daed* was equally calm. Yet the edge to his voice was more than apparent when he said, "You compare yourself to Balthasar Hubmaier? I dare say that you, Samuel Lapp, will not be seen as a martyr." His father laughed, a single, low laugh that seemed out of place with the discussion. "And quoting the words of such a great man does not make you pious, nor does it mask your recent deeds!"

"Amos…," Samuel pleaded.

"That will be all, Samuel," her *daed* said dismissively. His voice was stern and it was clear that the conversation had ended. As head of his own household, Amos Smucker's decision had been made. "You get yourself back home and help your parents. I reckon you've caused them enough worry. No need to cause the same on my farm or with my family."

Now the shuffling was louder. Mary Ruth knew that her *daed* was leaving the barn and wouldn't be turning back again. Certainly he would look for her and escort her back to the house so that Samuel could not speak with her. Quickly, before he could catch sight of her, she dashed around the corner of the barn, her heart pounding and her hands shaking. She felt as if she was disobeying her father, something that she had never done yet; she also knew that he could fault her if she accidentally encountered Samuel. She just had to find a way to make that happen.

She pressed her back against the back wall of the barn, tilting her head up with her eyes closed. She tried to catch her breath and still her beating heart. He had to come this way, she prayed. Please let him come this way.

And just like that, he stood before her, dressed in his Sunday best. Clearly he had tried to present a more humble image than his reputation permitted at the present moment. That one gesture touched her and she wanted to say as much. But words seemed stuck in her throat.

He started to say her name but stopped, glancing over his shoulder to make certain no one was near. When he looked back at her, she couldn't help but stare at him, taking in his pale face and sunken eyes. He had aged in just two days, she thought. Gone was the youthful look of a rebellious boy, and in its place was the tired and worn face of a very frightened young man.

"Samuel," she whispered, feeling the sting of tears in her eyes once again.

He placed his finger to his lips, indicating that she should not speak. Then, with his other hand, he reached out and took hers. He led her away from the barn and toward the place where he had left his horse and buggy. Around the side of the buggy, he finally released her hand, knowing that no one could see her.

"Samuel," she started again. "What has happened?"

He took off his hat and ran his fingers through his hair. His brown curls drooped over his forehead and he stared over the hill behind them. "I don't know, Mary Ruth. I'm as bewildered as the next person."

She bit her lower lip as she watched him. "They said you were driving the car and just walked away."

His reaction startled her. He stared at her, his blue eyes wide and wild. "And what do you think, Mary Ruth? What do you believe?"

She wasn't certain how to respond so she hesitated. She only knew the story from Simon's words, but she also had seen Samuel that night when he was waiting for her. He hadn't seemed like someone who could have driven a car and walked away from a fatal car accident.

"I sure hope it's not true," she finally whispered.

Clearly, her answer disappointed him. His shoulders seemed to slump as he shook his head and pursed his lips. "Wrong answer," he mumbled.

She felt a sting of guilt. "What do you want me to say?" she pleaded.

He spun around and took a step toward her. "You know I don't know how to drive a car! You know that I traveled all day and evening to try to get back here to take you home from the singing. I told you all of those things, Mary Ruth, the night that I told you my intentions to settle down, join the church, and court you."

She nodded her head, her voice soft and barely audible. "*Ja*, you said those things, for sure and certain."

"How could I have said those things if what they say was true?" He straightened his back and stared into her eyes. "I need to know that you believe me."

"Believe you?"

"Do you or don't you?" he demanded.

"Mary Ruth!" a voice called from the barn. "Is that you out there?"

She hesitated, glancing over her shoulder in the direction of the voice then back at Samuel. "I have to answer him," she said softly.

The muscles in his jaw tightened and he seemed to hesitate. But he didn't say anything. After all, he knew that she was right. If her *daed* caught her talking to him alone, he would be none too pleased that she hadn't responded. Defeated, Samuel lifted his chin in the direction of the barn, indicating that she should answer her *daed.*

"*Ja*, *Daed*! I'm here."

"Your *mamm* needs you in the house," he called back, his feet shuffling on the driveway as he hurried over toward the buggy. Within seconds, he was around the side of the buggy and grabbing for her arm. "Now, Mary Ruth." He cast a dark look at Samuel. "You need to go home now, Samuel. I told you not to be bothering my daughter."

She pulled back, pausing just briefly. "I was headed to the mailbox, *Daed*," she lied, feeling no remorse for the words as they slipped past her tongue.

"I'll get it later," he snapped as he started pulling her toward the house and away from Samuel.

It was clear that she wouldn't have the opportunity to say goodbye to Samuel. It was even clearer that she wouldn't get a chance to talk to him until church Sunday, and even that was unlikely if her *daed* and brothers had their way. Quickly, she looked over her shoulder, her eyes quickly meeting Samuel's. He was watching her being escorted away, too aware that irrevocable damage had been done to his relationship with her father.

The look on his face was of complete despair, and Mary Ruth's heart ached for him. And then, in just one quick moment of defiance, she stopped walking and pulled her arm free, just long enough to turn around and take a few steps toward Samuel. "I believe you," she said. "I do, Samuel. I honestly do."

There was nothing left to say. She felt her father's hand tighten around her arm and pull her, none too gently this time, away from the buggy and toward the house.

But a look of relief washed over his face. Those three words had been just enough to lift a great burden from his shoulders. And she knew that she did, indeed, believe him. She knew that Samuel was innocent and that she would support him as best as she could...as she always had and as she always would.

Chapter Eighteen

The days after Samuel's arrest dragged by, and he retreated to his own thoughts. For the rest of the week, through visiting Sunday, and well into the next week he arose early to get started on his chores, quietly moving about the dairy barn to help with the milking before having breakfast, which he ate without appetite. He found comfort with the cows, despite the years of dreading the morning milking. The lack of judgment from the herd of cattle soothed his soul at a time when there was too much judgment from the people surrounding him. Even at the family table, there was little conversation, everyone drawn into their own private thoughts. For that, Samuel was thankful. He couldn't have handled forced conversation about farming or gardens, not during this time of stress.

During the day, he went about his work at the carpentry shop, quiet and withdrawn. He avoided Simon, although he wished he had the nerve to talk to him about Mary Ruth. He wanted to tell Simon that he had left Philadelphia Sunday morning, had gone looking for Mary Ruth after the singing, and had made a commitment to her that he was a changed man. He wanted to tell Simon that he wanted only to honor her and return the adoration she had shown him throughout the years. But he didn't tell Simon any of these things.

When Mary Ruth had not appeared Tuesday morning to help Lillian, it became clear that Amos Smucker was serious about keeping Mary Ruth away from Samuel and everyone else in his family, at least while the matter was unresolved. The thought that it might *never* be resolved troubled him. Could he really survive two weeks without a chance of seeing Mary Ruth again? Especially now that he needed the comfort of her support and to hear more of those very words that she had spoken. "I believe you," she had said. And his heart had rejoiced. If no one else dared to believe, at least Mary Ruth did. And that saved his soul.

Now, as he sat on the hard bench waiting for worship to begin, Samuel reflected on how tonight's singing still seemed too far away. He knew that the singing held his only chance to speak to Mary Ruth privately about everything that had happened. Would he see her? What would she say?

A song began, and Samuel felt a tightness in his chest as he listened to the words. He suspected that the morning song from the *Ausbund* had been especially selected for him.

At one time, I walked to and fro
In my latter days,
Contemplated how near death was to me,
Then I began to be fearful.
I have no neither day nor hour
And have committed many sins,

All my days have done nothing good,
God's commandments all neglected,
Death has surrounded me.

Samuel kept his eyes on the *Ausbund* in his hands, the German words jumping off the page. He mouthed the words but was not actually singing them with the rest of the congregation. He felt many eyes staring at him, the weight of it heavy on his shoulders. But he kept his back straight and his eyes focused on the words that described the lamentations of the Anabaptist martyr Hans von Bilach. Samuel found it astonishing that those very words from the song, despite having been written four hundred years ago, described exactly how he felt on this early spring morning.

He hadn't wanted to attend church today, but he knew better than to broach the subject with his parents. Besides, he kept telling himself, there is no reason to hide. After all, Samuel knew that he was wrongly suspected. He had prayed all night to God, prayed for his friend Paul, and prayed for Robert and Peter who were no longer alive. He prayed for their families and prayed for his own. It had been a long night of prayers…a long two *weeks* of prayers, he corrected himself; and, for the first time in a long time, he felt closer to God and his faith was stronger than ever before. Now, he thought, if only the rest of the community could see that.

When it was time to kneel for the closing prayer, Samuel was the first one to turn around and press his forehead to his clenched hands, which rested on the bench. He listened to the words from the minister and lifted his heart up to the Lord. He felt the strength of the words in his core, his eyes squeezed shut and his mind open. Then, at that very moment, Samuel felt it. He felt the love of God as the words flowed from the minister's mouth directly into his soul. And he felt spiritually cleansed of the burden that had been placed upon him.

When he stood up, Samuel felt lighter and free. Yes, he thought. God knows what happened, and like Job, I'm being tested. Sylvia was right, indeed. Just like Job, I will pass this test. Whatever happens after that is the will of God. But God will not forsake me and I will not fail Him, Samuel promised to himself.

Looking around the room, Samuel took in a deep breath. He would not judge those who judged him, he decided. He would walk with Jesus and God, following their lead. With the burden removed from his shoulders, he stood tall and kept his head lifted high; and rather than scurry outside to be with his friends, he hurried to help the other men set up the tables for the noon meal.

For the rest of the fellowship time, Samuel remained quiet but with an inner peace. He helped when he could, without having to be asked. He smiled at the older women, ignoring their cold reactions. He steered clear of Mary Ruth, too aware of Amos's stern glare that seemed to follow him around the room. And when the two seatings for the noon fellowship meal ended, Samuel eagerly helped the men disassemble the tables and carry the wooden benches to the wagon for storage until the following week.

As he was leaving the meeting room, he passed by two of his friends. Samuel walked over to them and greeted them casually. "See you fellows tonight, *ja*?" he asked.

Amos Beiler and John Bucher stared at him, their faces blank. Samuel knew that they were surprised to hear that he would be attending the singing. Besides the fact that Samuel hardly ever went to the singings, the fact that he was in trouble with the Englische law compounded their confusion.

Finally, John Bucher spoke up, his voice deep and his words carefully chosen. "It sure would be nice to see you at the singing, Samuel," he said. "I'll be looking for you then."

Amos Beiler said nothing.

Samuel hurried away to hitch up his parents' horse and buggy. He felt better now that his hands were busy with the harness. The fact that his friends were even questioning him was troublesome, but he was sure glad that John Bucher had shown him kindness. Sure learn who your true friends are in times of need, he thought to himself. But, just as quickly as he thought it, he told himself that he needed to forgive Amos Beiler as well as Amos Smucker and everyone else who had cast judgment on him without listening to the facts. Otherwise he was just as guilty.

The ride home from church was quiet. Neither one of his parents talked. Samuel sat in the back, listening to the horse's hooves making their steady rhythmic music against the road. It soothed his nerves and helped him to slow his breathing, which calmed him during the short five-minute ride back to the farm.

Back at home, Samuel quickly changed out of his Sunday's best and hurried out to the barn. He didn't feel like visiting with anyone and felt the need to keep busy. On a Sunday, feigning chores was the best way to do just that. He took his time, mucking the stalls and washing the horse buckets. He even set out the hay for the evening feeding so that his father, David, and Daniel wouldn't have to be bothered.

When it was close to four, he heard them coming into the barn to get started on chores. He was upstairs, resting in the hayloft, and rather than make his presence known, he stayed away from the ladder and kept to the shadows.

"What's this?" Daniel asked, a pitchfork in hand as he walked down the main aisle. "Everything's been cleaned up, *Daed*."

Jonas glanced in the buckets. "Feed's out, too."

Daniel took a heavy breath. "Seems Samuel's been busy, then, *ja*?"

"Busy is *gut* for now, I reckon," his *daed* said. "Must have a lot on his mind, for sure and certain."

Samuel heard his older brother set the pitchfork against the side of the wall. The handle slid and touched a metal bucket hanging from a hook. The sound reverberated throughout the empty barn. "*Daed*, what happens if..."

"Daniel!" his father said sharply, interrupting him. "I won't hear any of that. We must have hope that the system will save our Samuel. He wanted to explore the world of the Englische. *Vell*," his *daed* said, his voice softening. "He'll have his chance now, *ja*?" There was a pause between the two men before Jonas changed the subject. "No work in here for us until milking. So we best go see what help your *mamm* needs setting up the tables for supper, then."

Samuel shut his eyes and leaned against the haystack. Setting up tables for supper meant that the family was going to eat together. It would be a light fare, not much more than what they had at church fellowship. But it meant facing Junior and Lillian, Daniel and Rachel, and all of the children. He wondered if Sylvia and Jake would be coming to visit from their farm, and in a moment of anticipation, he sure hoped so. Jake seemed to keep things light and in perspective. If he had to have supper with everyone, he hoped Jake would be there to keep the conversation flowing and the mood light.

An hour later, Samuel emerged from the hayloft and walked across the driveway toward the house. The tables had already been set up under the shade of a large tree. Linda was watching the younger children, who ran and played near the creek in the cow paddock. He was thankful that young Jacob had been especially quiet this week. He wondered if Lillian had anything to do with that. Samuel suspected that she had told her children to leave him be.

"Samuel," someone called out.

He turned his head in the direction of the voice and was surprised to see Rachel walking around the side of the barn. Inwardly, he groaned. They had never seen eye-to-eye, and this was the first time he had to be in her presence since the police had taken him away. He groaned, wishing the earth would open to swallow him. He didn't fancy having to see her gloat at his misfortune.

"Come help me, *ja*?" she said, waving her hand. "Mayhaps you can take little Katie while I carry this big basket."

Samuel frowned. She had never asked him for help before, especially when it came to her children. Slowly, he turned and began walking up the incline toward the top of the barn. She was already headed back toward the house where she lived with Daniel by the mule shed. With two children, it was certainly getting a bit cramped in there. But she never seemed to complain.

He followed her into the house, a place that he hadn't visited too often. In fact, as he looked around, he realized that he hadn't been inside her house for years. Since they never got along, they tended to spend time in each other's presence only when necessary and that was mostly at gatherings elsewhere.

She pointed to a box on the floor. "Could you lift that up for me, Samuel?"

"Lift it?" he asked, still not understanding what he was doing standing in his sister-in-law's house.

Turning to look at him, she smiled. He was surprised, realizing that it was a genuine smile, not one with any hint of animosity. "It'll be easier to pack it and carry it if you put it on the table for me. I'll get little Katie ready and you could start putting some of those jars in the box, *ja*?"

Still not understanding why Rachel was being so kind to him, he did as he was told. Kindness was not a theme that ran through their relationship, that was for sure and certain. When she had first arrived at the Lapp farm, he had teased her and loved to make her cry. Despite Daniel marrying her, Samuel had never warmed up to his sister-in-law, a distant cousin from Ohio. But, given the situation, he was willing to take kindness from wherever he could get it. Even from Rachel.

She was hustling through the downstairs then disappeared through a doorway and he heard her climbing the stairs. A few minutes later, she came down carrying little Katie, who was still sleeping. Behind them came Lovina, her two-year-old daughter. She also looked as though she had been sleeping as she rubbed her eyes and crawled onto the sofa while her *mamm* finished preparing their bag to take over to Katie's.

"None of that, Lovina," she said gently. "You can't fall back asleep now." Then Rachel walked over to Samuel and handed him the baby. "Would you mind holding her, Samuel? I need to wash Lovina's face and then we can leave."

He responded by taking the baby and realized that it was the first time he had held his youngest niece. He wasn't much of a baby person, preferring the more solid ones who could walk and talk. But as he looked into her face, he felt something tug at his heart.

"Sure is a pretty baby," he replied.

Rachel busied herself with pouring some water onto a washcloth and hurried over to wipe it across Lovina's face. "No prettier than others, I imagine." When she walked back to the sink, she paused to look at the baby in Samuel's arms. Taking a moment to look at her baby, she smiled. "Well, maybe just a tad," she teased.

"Why are you being nice to me?" he blurted out. His candor surprised him as much as it surprised her.

Laying the washcloth across the sink, she turned around to face him. She was definitely a formidable woman and had always stood up against Samuel's antics when she had first arrived at the Lapp farm. Now she studied him with a stern look in her eyes. "Figured it was time that you and I started over, Samuel. Seems you could use a few kind words from someone who knows what it is like to be on the receiving end of unkind ones."

"I had forgotten," he replied, lowering his eyes.

"Don't do that," she snapped angrily.

Surprised, he quickly looked back up, meeting her gaze. "Do what?"

"You said you weren't there. So you don't have to look away from anyone, Samuel Lapp. You hold your head high. Let the others bow their heads in shame. The truth will come out. But even if it doesn't," she said, softening her tone, "you know the truth and God knows the truth. That's all that is important."

"*Danke*," he said softly, humbled by her advice.

Rachel didn't let him get emotional with her. Instead, she waved a hand at him dismissively. "Thanks are not needed, Samuel. We are family, after all." She hoisted the box on her hip and started toward the door, changing the subject and getting back on track. She had always been a no-nonsense, to-the-point kind of woman, he thought. "Now, let's go take this food and these two sleepy children over to your *mamm*'s and have a wonderful Sunday supper."

Following Rachel, Samuel felt an odd sensation in his throat. For the past several years, she had been his adversary. They had not gotten along when she first arrived at the Lapp farm. Now, she was the one that was not questioning his situation but offering him an olive branch? He felt a wave of humility wash over him. How could Rachel, of all people, be so kind and generous of spirit toward him when he had been so awful to her when she first arrived?

As they walked around the corner of the house, he was still thinking about this shift in events. He didn't notice that his family was seated outside on the porch, watching as he helped Rachel with the children. His older brother Daniel was leaving the dairy barn and stopped, leaning against the doorway as his wife walked by, holding the box of food, followed by Samuel holding Lovina's hand and carrying the baby. Had Samuel been aware that Daniel was staring at them, he would have noticed Daniel smile and tug at his growing beard, a look of understanding crossing his face.

"*Onkel! Onkel!*" a small voice called out.

Samuel shifted little Katie in his arms and, releasing Lovina's hand, ruffled Jacob's curly hair. He was a true Lapp, through and through, from the bright blue eyes to the loose curls that covered his head. "Where've you been hiding, Jacob?"

The small boy lowered his eyes. "*Mamm* told me you weren't feeling well. Told me to let you be." He lifted his eyes hopefully. "You feeling better now, ain't so?"

Samuel took a deep breath. Was he feeling better? Until the matter was resolved, he wouldn't be feeling much of anything. Yet, as he hesitated, he noticed Rachel turn back to look at him. She smiled reassuringly. Samuel turned his attention back to his nephew. "*Ja*, I sure am."

Jacob clapped his hands and hopped up and down. "Then you'll play ball with me?"

"Jacob!"

They both turned at the sound of the deep voice that called the boy's name. Junior was standing on the porch. "You let Samuel be now. It's time for relaxing. You go take Lovina inside to Linda. She's going to play with all of you while the grown-ups visit."

Jacob made a face, kicking at some rocks in the driveway. But, obediently, he took Lovina's hand and dragged her toward the house.

"Slowly, Jacob! She's going to fall," Rachel called out.

Samuel smiled as he watched Jacob reluctantly carry

out his task. Having been the youngest of ten, Samuel was often the one being dragged around behind an older brother or sister. He knew how Lovina felt, her little legs trying hard to keep up with Jacob. Samuel had always resented being the one trying to keep up and never the one to lead. At least Lovina would one day lead her baby sister and Katie would surely have plenty of other younger siblings and cousins to drag behind her.

"Rachel, I'll trade you," he said, reaching for the box that she still held in her hands. He took it with one arm and let her take the baby from his other arm.

"See?" Rachel said, a mischievous look on her face. "Holding your niece wasn't so bad after all, was it?"

He wanted to hang his head in shame. He didn't need the reminder that, before this day, he had neglected Daniel and Rachel's new baby. Because he never had gotten along very well with Rachel, he hadn't paid much attention to *either* of her children with his brother, Daniel. *How could I have been so blind,* Samuel wondered.

For once, Samuel decided to take her rebuke in stride. Rather than fight it, he lifted his chin and met her steady gaze. "I reckon not, Rachel. She didn't wet my arm after all."

Rachel laughed, a sound that wasn't very frequently heard. She had always been a bit on the serious side. Daniel approached from behind, smiling at his wife. He leaned over her shoulder and peeked at the sleeping baby in her arms. "Now what is your *mamm* laughing at, I wonder," he said.

"Daniel!" she said, startled by his sudden appearance behind her. "You scared me."

He didn't reply but reached forward to caress the baby's cheek. "She sure is a sleeper, *ja*?"

Samuel carried the box into the house and set it on the counter. Lillian was setting out food, moving slowly as she worked. Katie was beside her, helping her daughter-in-law as they opened glass jars of chow-chow and red beets to put into bowls for the evening meal. It would be an easy meal since no one wanted to work on Sunday. Cold cuts, canned vegetables, bread. The emphasis for the evening was on visiting, not working in the kitchen.

"Here you go, *Mamm*," Samuel said, his hand on the edge of the box.

"*Danke*, Samuel."

He started to turn to leave but hesitated. "You need some help, then? I could carry things outside."

Both Lillian and Katie looked up at the same time. They glanced at each other then turned toward Samuel. Men didn't help in the kitchen and Samuel never volunteered to help anywhere. So his offer to assist them was doubly surprising for both women. Clearly, this was a new Samuel who stood before them, and both women weren't certain how to respond.

It was Lillian who spoke first. "That would be right *gut*, Samuel," she said slowly. She pointed toward the counter by the window. "There's a tray under there, and you could take these bowls out to the table that Junior set up under the oak tree."

He ignored their surprised expressions as he did as he was told. The bowls were on the table, each bowl a different size and color. He carefully arranged them on the tray and carried it outside. As the door opened to the porch, Samuel also ignored the looks of the men. His father was seated in a chair and lifted his eyebrows as Samuel walked by and set the tray on the table. Even Junior and Daniel were speechless.

It was Jake who made the first comment. "Well, well, well," he called out. "What have we here?"

Samuel glanced up at the sound of Jake's voice. He smiled at his brother-in-law, who was helping his wife and children out of the buggy. He hadn't heard the buggy pull into the driveway, but he was glad to see Jake. Everything always seemed lighter when Jake was around. "A little kitchen work never killed a man," Samuel replied.

Jake set his hand on Sylvia's shoulder as they walked across the driveway and toward the gathering. "Well, I wouldn't be so sure about that." He winked at Samuel. "And I'm not about to take any chances."

Sylvia tried to hide her smile as she nudged her husband with her elbow. "Jake!"

Gideon tugged at his *daed*'s pant leg, and when Jake looked down, he waved with his hand urgently. Jake leaned over and let the little boy whisper into his ear. Then, standing back up, he frowned. "Well, seems someone needs a quick visit inside after all," he said, taking his son by the hand and leaving Sylvia with the baby. "I'll be certain to avoid that kitchen, though," he teased over his shoulder.

It was during the meal, while everyone picked at the food on the table, that Junior made a big announcement. The little children were playing with a ball and the dog, throwing the ball as far as they could so that the dog would chase it and bring it back. Jacob, however, was delighting Gideon by throwing the ball toward the dairy barn, the ball rolling into the muck and the dog chasing after it.

"Seems time to think about the future," Junior said, leaning back in his chair.

Jonas looked at his oldest son. "*Ja*? What's going on, son?"

With a quick glance at his wife, Junior met his father's gaze. "Seems like might be a *gut* idea to build a new house back by the carpentry shop. I'll be closer on hand to help Lillian if needed."

"Build a new house?" Katie asked. Clearly she didn't like the thought of the family moving out of the main house. The grandchildren would be farther away, even if only down the back lane. "Oh, Junior! That's so much work."

He nodded. "*Ja*, it is. But I know some fellows who just did this over in Bird-in-Hand. They said they'd be willing to help me with permits and they have the design already." He looked over at his father. "The carpentry shop is doing well. We have a backlog of orders for sheds. I'll have to build the framing in the evenings, but it could be finished by the end of the summer...before the new babies are born."

Samuel spoke up. "I'll help build it, brother."

Junior looked at him. For a long moment, he studied his brother. His offer to help was genuine, so Junior nodded, a gesture of appreciation. "*Danke*, Samuel."

"But the main house?" Samuel asked.

Daniel cleared his throat. "Sure would be nice if Rachel had herself a proper house, now that we have the *kinner*."

Everyone nodded in agreement. And so it was decided. The cycle of life continued on the Lapp farm. Junior and his family would move out; Daniel and his family would move in. The apartment over the mule shed would be empty once again.

It was close to seven when the gathering started to

break up. The women had *kinner* to put to bed, and the men started to put away the table and chairs. Samuel excused himself and hurried into the house to change his clothes in time for the singing. When he pulled out the courting buggy to hitch to his horse, he was too aware that the men stopped working and stared.

But when he went to the singing, Mary Ruth wasn't there. He held his hat in his hand, waiting for her to arrive, but she didn't. Neither was Simon Smucker or Leah Smucker. He waited for an hour, too aware of the eyes that watched him and the whispers that spoke of him. He could ignore those easily enough. But it was the fact that Mary Ruth hadn't shown up and he had to drive home alone in the courting buggy that disappointed him the most.

It was dark when he returned to the farm. Yet there was a glow from a light in the horse barn. He found his brother, David, unharnessing his own horse by the light of a battery-operated lantern.

"*Wie gehts*?" Samuel asked. "You weren't at the singing?"

"Were you?" David asked, the surprise quite apparent in his voice.

"*Ja*," Samuel said. "But Mary Ruth wasn't there."

David nodded. "*Nee*, she wasn't. Her family had relatives over tonight."

Samuel looked up. "But no singing tonight?"

David shrugged. "Can't speak for the Smuckers, but I reckon that she got tied up and her brother was too busy to take her." Noticing the defeated look on his younger brother's face, David walked up to him and placed a hand on his shoulder. "I wouldn't take it personally, Samuel. She may have her own issues going on that you just don't know about."

But they both knew what David was insinuating. If Simon wouldn't have taken Mary Ruth, she couldn't have gone to the singing; and if the family was concerned about Mary Ruth's friendship with Samuel, there was no doubt that Simon might have decided against attending the singing at all. To his disappointment, it was clear that the Smucker family was not happy about the recent happenings at the Lapp farm, and they were trying to keep Mary Ruth away from Samuel, as evidenced by the fact that she had not come recently to help Lillian.

He hung his head, his hand lingering on the side of his horse's neck as he turned to leave the barn. He didn't hear David bid him goodnight as he walked toward the house, a sinking feeling in his chest over the lost opportunity that he figured just passed him by. Decisions, he thought. The wrong ones could destroy lives, and he realized that he might have made some of too strong a magnitude to be remedied.

Chapter Nineteen

Mary Ruth used her scooter, a pale blue one with a basket in the front, to travel down the road to the Lapp farm. Holding the handlebars, she used one foot to push it along the road. It glided easily on the pavement, and the cool breeze felt good against her face. Even though it was early in the morning, the sun was warm already, promising to bless them with a hot summer day.

There had been quite a row in the house when Mary Ruth, alarmed at seeing Lillian so pale and listless at church, insisted that she honor her promise to care for Lillian and her children. For two weeks she had bided her time, knowing that to broach the subject too soon would be sure to raise her father's ire. Still, she had been surprised that she had won the argument that the Lapp family had little to do with Samuel's predicament. After all, Lillian was pregnant with twins and the family still needed her help. Mary Ruth had stood her ground to respectfully argue that a promise was a promise. Hadn't she promised to help Lillian with the *kinner* while she was pregnant?

She had known that the family's main objection was

specifically related to Samuel. Her father didn't want her to spend time on the Lapp farm where it was likely that she would run into Samuel. But even Simon had jumped to Mary Ruth's defense when he stated the obvious.

"Samuel will be at the carpentry shop, *Daed*," Simon had said. When he glanced at his sister, she had to fight the tears in her eyes. His compassion and willingness to stand up to their father was overwhelming to her.

Miriam had also stuck up for Mary Ruth, a rare act of defiance against her husband when she added, "And we all must support the Lapp family, Amos. They need us more than ever, *ja*?" When Amos had hesitated, Miriam had added, "The bishop would want it that way." That solved the issue for once and for all.

So, on the beautiful summer day that was before her, Mary Ruth hurried herself along the road, one push of her foot at a time. Each push brought her closer to the Lapp farm and further into a cloud of confusion. On the one hand, she hoped that she wouldn't see Samuel. She didn't want to openly defy her father's wishes that she not speak to him. Yet, on the other hand, she respected the fact that she had committed to court him, even though she had no idea what had truly happened on that horrible night in Philadelphia.

Lillian was resting on the sofa when Mary Ruth came into the house. She set her basket on the counter and smiled at Lillian. "Feeling poorly, *ja*?"

"So tired," Lillian whispered. "It's just a feeling of complete weariness."

Mary Ruth laughed, the sound light and airy in the house full of heaviness. "It won't last forever. I'll watch the *kinner* so you can rest, *ja*?"

Lillian forced a smile. "Linda, Jacob, and Lena are over at Sylvia's," she said. "And Rachel has Abram and Anna. The baby is napping upstairs." Then, shutting her eyes, Lillian seemed to drift to sleep but managed to whisper, "I'm so glad you're here, Mary Ruth."

For the next hour, Mary Ruth quietly straightened up the kitchen and upstairs. She gathered the soiled clothing to wash while Lillian rested. It was clear that no one had expected Mary Ruth to show up to help. After all, she hadn't been there in two weeks, and with the community in an uproar over the accident and Samuel's involvement, no one blamed Amos and Miriam Smucker if they had decided that Mary Ruth should stay home and not help Lillian during this time of family trouble.

By dinnertime, Mary Ruth had the house in complete order, laundry was hanging outside to dry, and a meal was waiting on the table. She even had time to play with baby James, taking him outside for a walk up the lane so that he could get some fresh air. He had clutched at her fingers, his one-year-old legs stumbling as he tried to walk on his own. She had laughed when he fell down on the grass and refused to get up, lifting up his arms for her to carry him. It had been a busy morning indeed.

She knew that Junior would come home to check on his wife and to share the noon meal with his family. Mary Ruth was happy that the kitchen was clean and the food prepared when Junior walked into the mudroom. Lillian would be pleased that her husband was fed properly prior to returning to work for the afternoon.

"Mary Ruth!" he said when he walked in, the surprise quite apparent from his tone. "I'm so glad you came today!" His appreciation was equally obvious.

He glanced at Lillian, pale and lying on the sofa. "She is not doing well, *ja*?"

Following his gaze, Mary Ruth noticed the pale color of Lillian's skin. There were also beads of sweat on her forehead. "She seems very tired, Junior," was all that Mary Ruth could say.

"Tired," he repeated, as though he was testing the word on his tongue. "She was never tired before with our other *kinner*."

Smiling, Mary Ruth shrugged. "Mayhaps it's the twins. She never was pregnant with twins before, ain't so?"

Junior smiled back but there was little joy in his smile. Instead, his eyes looked tired and his skin pale. "True, Mary Ruth," he said. Yet, the concern on his face was more than apparent. Mary Ruth could tell that Junior had more on his mind than just the noon meal. Instead, he was more concerned that his wife was so tired during this pregnancy. "You be certain to thank your folks for letting you come to help out, Mary Ruth."

If she wanted to ask Junior what was the latest news about Samuel, she did her best to hide the fact. Indeed, she was anxious to know what Samuel was doing, how he was feeling, and whether the law was still chasing after him. But she knew better than to ask. Private matters were kept that way among the Amish. When matters needed to be shared, they were. And, clearly, this one had a long way to go before anyone was going to speak about it.

After the meal, Mary Ruth hurried to clear the table and wash the dishes. It would be another few hours before Linda brought Jacob and Lena back from Sylvia and Jake's farm. Katie and Jonas had gone visiting to

Ephrata, eager to spend some time at Emanuel's, where Steve and his family would be joining them for the afternoon.

Mary Ruth had offered to stay until Katie returned so that Lillian didn't have to worry about the baby or the older children when they would return from visiting. So, while the house was quiet, Mary Ruth hurried outside to bring in the laundry that she had hung to dry earlier in the day. With six *kinner* and one hard-working man, there was plenty of clothing to wash, and it was clear that Lillian hadn't done any the previous week.

It was warm out, as befit a day in July. It hadn't rained in a week and the fields were starting to show the need for water. Mary Ruth stood on her tippy toes as she began to remove the clothing pins from the line. One by one, she folded each article of clothing, stacking everything neatly on a chair as she worked.

She was just getting to the sheets when she heard the door open to the *grossdaadihaus*. Glancing under the clothing line, she saw Samuel as he started walking along the driveway, headed toward the back lane. She knew that he'd be returning to the carpentry shop for the remainder of the day. If she wanted to speak to him, now would be the only time.

"Samuel!" she called out.

Her voice must have startled him for he spun around, surprised to see her standing on the porch. But, when he did, his face changed and he hurried toward her. "Mary Ruth!" He didn't care who was near or watching as he embraced her. "I didn't think your *daed* would let you come here!" He pulled back and gently held her chin in his hand. "You are a sight for sore eyes!"

"Can't be any sorer than my eyes for all the crying I've been doing," she whispered.

He traced her jawbone with his thumb and smiled into her eyes. "No crying, Mary Ruth. I won't be able to breathe if I think you are crying." But as he said it, the tears started to form in her eyes. She blinked and glanced away, hoping that he wouldn't notice. But he did. "No, no," he said gently. "None of that."

"What is going to happen to you?"

He took a deep breath. "The truth, Mary Ruth, will be known," he said. "I know God will not desert me." He spoke what he felt. How could God desert him after he had made the journey away from his people and quickly returned? How could God desert him on the very day when he had made up his mind to abandon worldliness and commit to life with the Amish? "*Nee*, He won't desert me," he said as he wiped the tear from her cheek with his thumb. "But I don't know what will happen after that. There are too many people who may not be so willing to forgive and forget, even if there was never anything to forgive."

She nodded, understanding what he was saying. She wasn't so certain that her own *daed* would ever be willing to accept the truth if it were known. He was growing increasingly stubborn as he advanced in age. "I will be here for you," she said. "Waiting."

"Always waiting, Mary Ruth Smucker," he said softly. "Doesn't seem fair, does it now?"

Despite herself, she laughed at the irony of what he said. "You speak of fairness?" When he raised an eyebrow in an unspoken question, she leaned her head forward against his chest. "Oh, Samuel, how can you speak about fairness to me when all of these horrible things are happening to you? If anyone is having an unfair time, I think you'd be the winner of that award."

He wrapped one arm around her shoulder and held her tight, not caring if anyone walked by or saw them. He needed this closeness with the one person that he knew believed in him, the one person that he wanted to know believed in him. Her body against his, so soft and supple, comforted him. For a long while, he shut his eyes and let this special moment engrave itself into his memory. Then, reluctantly, he pulled away. "Best to not have anyone spying on us," he said lightly, although his heart was heavy as he knew that he had to return to work. "I'm surprised you're here, Mary Ruth," he said, changing the subject as best as he could.

"*Mamm* said a promise is a promise," she replied. "And Simon also promised to keep an eye on me."

Samuel raised an eyebrow. "Bit hard to do when he's down there at the shop and I'm here with you, ain't so?"

She smiled and shrugged innocently. "Mayhaps you have a point, but I wasn't about to argue. Just so long as I could be here, helping Lillian and…" She hesitated. "Being nearby in case I could see you."

He was about to reply when they heard a loud cry from within the house. Mary Ruth looked up at Samuel, questioning him with her eyes. Simultaneously, it dawned on both of them that something was wrong inside. Samuel flung the door open, entering the house first with Mary Ruth close behind him. They found Lillian on the ground, curled up in a fetal position with her dress soaked through.

"Lillian!" Samuel shouted and ran to her side. He lifted her head and cradled it gently on his lap. "What happened?"

"My water broke. Get Junior," she whispered, her voice cracking and barely audible.

He looked up at Mary Ruth. "Can you run for Junior, Mary Ruth? Get him down here right away?" She didn't even answer as she spun around and ran out the door, racing across the yard and through the garden to shortcut over to the lane down to the carpentry shop.

The minutes seemed to pass like hours while Samuel held Lillian on his lap. He said a quick prayer to God, asking for Junior to hurry and for God to protect Lillian and her unborn babies. Whatever was wrong with her looked serious to him, and he knew that it would require Englische medicine. He wondered if he shouldn't have instructed Mary Ruth to call for medical help before going for Junior. Too many thoughts ran through his head at the same time and he felt confused as to what was the right thing to do. He just prayed that whatever decision he had made was sufficient for the beloved wife of his oldest brother.

When Junior finally burst into the kitchen, his face was pale and his eyes large with fright. He quickly took in the situation and hurried to Lillian's side. Kneeling before her, he clasped her hand in his. "Lillian," he whispered. "Are you all right?"

She nodded and tried to speak, but her lips moved without any sound coming out. Junior looked up at Samuel, questioning him with his eyes.

"We heard her cry out and found her like this when we came into the kitchen," he said.

Junior nodded, doing his best to remain calm. "Best be calling for some medical attention. Would you mind going to the phone shanty and making the call?"

Mary Ruth volunteered. "I'll do it," she said then

quickly turned and hurried outside, running toward the little shack where the family telephone was housed by the mule shed.

"You'll stay with the *kinner, ja*?" Junior asked.

"Of course," Samuel replied, nodding his head. "They'll be fine. You just take care of your wife."

"Junior," she whispered, her voice barely audible.

"Don't speak," he said softly. He rubbed her hand in his, trying to comfort her as best as he could. "I don't want to move you until medical people come, Lillian."

"It's too soon," she managed to say.

"*Nee*," Junior said, forcing a tender and comforting smile on his face that he didn't feel in his heart. "That's up to God to decide, isn't it?"

It was fifteen minutes later when the paramedics arrived and quickly took over the scene. Samuel stood back, his arm protectively around Mary Ruth's waist as they watched the two men in white uniforms work swiftly over Lillian, getting her onto a stretcher and wheeling her out of the house. Junior followed, uncertain of what to do. It was Rachel who, having settled the children down inside her own home, had come over to see what was happening and quickly urged Junior to go with Lillian in the vehicle.

"She'll need you and we have your *kinner* taken care of," she said.

Junior didn't need more urging as he jumped into the back of the vehicle with Lillian. When the doors shut and it drove away, Samuel felt an emptiness inside of him. He had never seen anyone taken away like that. It was a surreal feeling to watch the ambulance pull away, the image of Junior's hat in the small window of the back door. Samuel wondered if this was how his own family had felt when the police had taken him away.

No one spoke for a few minutes, the silence needed after so much excitement. Samuel didn't have to imagine how Lillian felt, being taken away from her home and family. He had lived that very same feeling just a week ago, and the threat of it happening again seemed to linger over his head. He rubbed his forehead with his hand and looked at the two women before him.

"What do we do now, Rachel?" he asked.

With a heavy sigh, Rachel took charge. "Mary Ruth, Linda will be home soon with the other three. She can help you get supper started. Samuel, you should get started on evening chores since you'll be needed to help with the little ones. Jacob will surely have a lot of questions and needs your attention." Rachel looked up at the sky. The sun was beating down on them. "Mary Ruth, you should keep Linda busy with Jacob, Lena, and Abram. Have them water the garden and their *mamm*'s flowers. That will keep their mind off of the house being empty and free you up for the little ones."

"What will we tell them?" Mary Ruth asked.

Rachel shook her head. "Haven't figured that one out yet. We'll know when we see them, *ja*?"

Mary Ruth nodded and hurried into the house to start preparing for the children's return. It would be hard to explain to them about their *mamm* being away. Mary Ruth was certain that Lillian had rarely left her children unattended. Sure, there might be short errands during the day but never over the evening hours. Their *mamm*'s disappearance would not be easy for the smaller ones to accept. Mary Ruth knew that she'd have to shield them from knowing that Lillian had been taken to an

Englische hospital, for that would cause them all unnecessary worry.

As it was nearly three o'clock, Mary Ruth stared out the window, eager for the children to walk across the field from the direction of Sylvia and Jake's farm. The kitchen smelled of fresh-baked sugar cookies, a hopeful attempt at distraction on Mary Ruth's part. She knew that Rachel had left the door to her house open and was listening for the phone to ring with any word from Junior. Since her house was right next to the mule shed, it would be easiest for her to answer whenever it rang.

But it remained silent.

"*Mamm*! *Mamm*!" a voice called from the doorway.

Mary Ruth turned around in time to see Jacob flying into the door, tossing his hat on the bench and his books on the counter. Linda followed, holding Abram's hand while Lena stayed outside, stopping to pet one of the barn cats that was lounging in a sunbeam. Not seeing his mother, Jacob ran toward Mary Ruth and hugged her legs.

Laughing, Mary Ruth knelt down before him. "That's a lovely greeting, Jacob! Did you have a nice time visiting your *aendi* and *onkel*?"

He nodded, but before he could answer, he looked around the room. "I smell cookies."

"You sure do," she said, standing up and walking over to the counter. "I made you some. Thought you'd be hungry after such a long walk."

"He already had some at Sylvia's," Linda offered.

"Tattle-tail!" he shot back.

"Now, now," a deep male voice said from the doorway. Jacob whirled around, smiling when he saw Samuel. Hesitating, Samuel walked into the room and took the plate of cookies from Mary Ruth. "I'd say one cookie each is in order and in keeping with *Mammi* Katie's rule, *ja*?" He turned back to the children and let them select a cookie from the plate.

"Where's *Mamm*?" Lena asked, looking around the kitchen. At seven years old, she trailed behind the large personality of Jacob and authoritative role of Linda. It was rare that she spoke up unless someone directly asked her a question. So both Mary Ruth and Samuel were surprised that she had not only noticed her *mamm*'s disappearance but had ventured to ask about it.

Samuel glanced at Mary Ruth. She raised an eyebrow but didn't speak. It wasn't her place to discuss what had happened to Lillian. She took the plate of cookies from him and hurried over to the sink to finish washing the dishes. Taking a deep breath, Samuel turned back to the anxious faces staring at him.

"That's a good question," he started. "I'm not exactly certain how to answer it."

Jacob's eyes grew wide. "Did the police come and take her like they took you?"

For a moment, Samuel flinched and felt his pulse quicken. How had Jacob heard about that? Certainly not from the family, he realized. It must have been a story spread after church service yesterday since school had been out for the summer season weeks ago. "Your *mamm* is with your *daed* at the doctor's," he said, quickly deciding to ignore Jacob's question. "We are waiting to hear what is happening with her and the babies."

"Babies?" Linda asked. "What's wrong with the babies?"

"I don't know if anything is wrong with them," Samuel quickly said, hoping to alleviate any fears. "She just wanted to make certain that everything is fine."

Abram licked his fingers. "She be home by dinner?" he asked.

"I don't think so," Samuel said, slowly shaking his head.

The five-year old looked up, his eyes starting tears as he realized his mother wouldn't be home. "When she coming home?"

"Mayhaps tomorrow," Samuel said. He wished that Junior had called. He wished that he had some real answers for these children. He wished that everything would be all right.

For the rest of the evening, David and Samuel took Jacob and Abram under their care. Samuel had asked the young boys to help with the evening milking, a ploy to help distract them. Jacob was eager to show Abram "how it was done," dragging his five-year-old brother through the dairy. Samuel smiled as he listened to Jacob instructing Abram as to the proper way to wash the udders before Daniel, David, and Samuel milked each cow.

They were just about ready to finish for the evening when they heard the buggy pull down the lane. Daniel wiped his hands on his pants and started walking to the door, hoping that the buggy brought some good news. He looked over at his two brothers who were washing the buckets. "Amos has come," he said flatly.

"Mary Ruth!" a deep male voice called out.

Samuel took a deep breath. Indeed, it was Amos Smucker. He'd recognize that voice anywhere. Certainly Amos hadn't been too pleased when Simon had returned home without Mary Ruth. With Katie and Jonas visiting Emanuel's and Steve's families while Junior had rushed Lillian to the hospital, Mary Ruth was virtually unsupervised with Samuel Lapp in an isolated home for the evening. Despite her gracious offer to stay and help with the children, even Samuel knew how precarious a position that had put Mary Ruth in. Only he hadn't realized just how serious such a position truly was.

"She's watching the *kinner*," Daniel said, pointing toward the house. "Lillian went to hospital."

Amos nodded once. "So I heard."

Daniel paused, waiting for Amos to say something, perhaps to ask how Lillian was doing. But Amos sat in the buggy, holding the reins in his weathered hands, staring sternly at Daniel. His hostility toward the family was apparent and surprising to Daniel. Where had it come from? For years, the two families had raised their families together, sharing fellowship, and enjoying friendship. All because of Samuel?

"She was a great help today, Amos," Daniel finally said, trying to defuse the situation. He caught sight of Samuel in the doorway of the dairy barn, listening to the conversation.

"She'll be coming home with me now," Amos said. "Won't be back. Needed by her *mamm*" was the only explanation he gave. But Daniel and Samuel knew the truth. Her *daed* simply didn't want his daughter alone on a farm with Samuel Lapp, even if his other brothers were there.

Daniel nodded. "I'll get her, Amos," he said and started to walk toward the house to fetch her. Samuel hung back in the shadows, not wanting to provoke Amos. He knew that the father was the authority over his children in all matters, save anything that involved the church leaders; and that meant that Samuel had to honor that relationship or risk alienating himself even further.

It was at that moment that Rachel ran through the barn, having entered from the open doorway near her own house. Her bare feet raced toward Samuel, not caring that she was running through muck in the aisle way. She called out for Daniel as she ran. Samuel emerged from the shadows and collided with her.

"What is it, Rachel?"

"Where's Daniel?" she asked, breathless from running. She looked over his shoulder, trying to see if Daniel was behind Samuel. She hadn't seen him walk toward the house when Amos had arrived. Not seeing Daniel, Rachel looked at Samuel, her eyes wide and bright. "Your *daed* called. He's at the hospital with Junior."

"Daniel's there," Samuel said, giving a quick gesture toward the house that sent Rachel running in that direction. She passed Amos without any acknowledgment in her hurry to find her husband. Samuel followed, not caring about Amos's reaction to seeing him. It was clear how he felt and nothing Samuel did or didn't do at that moment would change it.

"She's going to be fine," Rachel said between gulps of air as she stood before Daniel on the porch. "Junior sent a driver over to Ephrata for your *mamm* and *daed*. Your *daed* called from the hospital to share the good news!"

"Thanks be to God," Daniel said, the relief apparent in his voice as he lifted his eyes toward the sky.

Samuel stood behind them, his eyes looking at Mary Ruth as she walked out of the kitchen door. She stopped on the porch, seeing her father peering from the buggy as he watched.

"What happened?" she asked.

Rachel smiled and laughed. "She's going to be fine, Mary Ruth. The babies are all right, too!"

"Oh!" Mary Ruth gasped, her hand fluttering to her chest. "I was so worried!"

"What did they say?" Samuel asked.

Rachel looked at him, confused for a second about his question. "Say?"

"What did the doctors say about Lillian?" he repeated slowly.

Laughing, she lifted her fingers to her head, touching her forehead gently as if trying to think. Samuel noticed that she was shaking. "Of course, of course," Rachel flustered. "Her water broke and she's going to have the babies. But they have her on some special medicine to try to delay birthing for a day or two. The babies are early but they should be fine. Might have to stay in the hospital for a few weeks, but they should live."

A day or two? Samuel glanced at Daniel first then Mary Ruth second. Junior would never leave her side, and their *mamm* was too old to care for six *kinner* by herself, even with Linda being old enough to help. Both Rachel and Sylvia had their own small children to watch. Who would watch the children? "I can sleep here with the children," Samuel offered. "But during the day…"

Raising his hand to stop Samuel from saying more, Daniel nodded. "Understood, brother." He glanced over his shoulder at the buggy. Amos was leaning out the open door, a scowl on his face. "Mary Ruth, I'll walk you over to your *daed* since he's waiting for you," he said slowly. "Like to have a word with him."

Rather than wait on the porch, Samuel went inside the house, not wanting to leave Linda with the responsibility of watching the other five children by herself. Despite being capable, Linda was certainly worried about her *mamm* as much as the younger ones. Having an adult nearby would be reassuring to her. Yet he stood in the window, watching as Daniel talked to Amos. He didn't have to be nearby to know what was being said. Daniel was trying to convince Amos to let Mary Ruth come back to help with the children. But Amos stared straight ahead, not saying one word in response. When Mary Ruth finally climbed into the buggy, her *daed* merely clicked his tongue and slapped the reins on the horse's back. It lurched forward and rolled down the driveway. With that, Mary Ruth was gone and not likely to return.

Samuel turned away from the window, his heart heavy. Just when the family needed help the most, Amos Smucker would turn his back on their need? He wondered if anyone else in the community would offer to help. He doubted it. Anyone with young women at home wouldn't want their daughters exposed to Samuel, not while he was being investigated for driving that car and causing that accident. It was because of Samuel that no one would come to help them. The weight of that fact was more than he could bear.

Later that evening, Rachel brought Lovina and baby Katie over to the main house. She set Linda to work helping her with the finishing touches on the evening meal while Lena watched the smaller children and babies. It was comforting to have a woman's presence in the house, and Samuel took the time to escape for a few minutes. He needed a break from children and the emotions that seemed to be hanging over his head like a dark thundercloud.

Chapter Twenty

The next few days fell into a chaotic routine for Samuel, as he didn't have so much as one minute to himself. He slept in the main house, reassuring his parents that he'd be fine with the children. After all, Linda was there to help him, if he needed it. The truth was that Samuel didn't want his parents sleeping in a different bed, one that was unfamiliar to them. After all of the stress that the family had been going through, he wanted his parents to have the comfort of their own bed at night.

In the mornings, he woke up before five in order to help with the early milking. By the time he returned to the house, Linda had already arisen and tended to the baby. Samuel would help get the other children ready before taking over the care of the baby until Katie came over to relieve him.

After breakfast, Samuel would walk with Jacob to the carpentry shop. Earlier, the family agreed that Jacob could help out at the shop if Samuel was willing to keep an eye on him. Jacob was delighted with this arrangement, especially since he worshipped his *Onkel* Samuel. So, besides working on his regular tasks at the shop,

Samuel had to invent chores for Jacob to do. It didn't take long for Samuel to get creative, asking Jacob to practice hitting nails into blocks of wood or having him pick up wood scraps for burning later.

For dinner, they would walk down the gravel lane to the house. Jacob would talk about all of his plans for building his own shed for the mother cat and its kittens while Samuel listened. It was clear that Jacob had an endless amount of energy. The more time they spent together, the more Samuel realized how amazing Jacob truly was. His love for the animals and nature was apparent as was his ability to see everything with large eyes and a passion for life. Samuel was also amazed at how inquisitive Jacob was, asking questions that caused him to really think before answering.

Every day, after the noon meal, Samuel headed back to the carpentry shop alone. By the third day, he realized that he missed Jacob's presence in the afternoons. The silence gave him too much time to think. It had been almost two weeks now and there had been no word from the police about Paul's recovery. Since Jake had been forbidden to contact the lawyer, Samuel had no idea whether that lawyer man, Dave, was still in contact with the authorities.

What he did know was that, every second of every day, he lived in fear. There was too real of a threat looming overhead, like a dark cloud that threatened to pour rain. Whenever a car drove over the hill, Samuel would find his heart suddenly beating faster until he was certain it wasn't someone pulling into their driveway. The thought of being dragged away from the farm frightened him. He had never realized how much he loved his home and his family. Having been forcibly separated from them had certainly changed his perception on how important they were to him. He certainly didn't want that to ever happen again.

The news from the hospital had been good. Junior called every morning and again in the afternoon. By Thursday, the doctors had performed a Cesarean section on Lillian, welcoming her two new daughters to the world. Little Jacob had cheered at the news, happy to know that he wasn't going to have too much competition for his *daed*'s attention until Linda pointed out that meant he'd have fewer brothers to help with chores. His jubilation quickly dissipated and he sulked off to play with the kittens that were rough-housing near the shed.

Indeed, the celebration had been brief as the premature babies had to be whisked away to the neonatal unit at the hospital. Lillian was recovering while Junior stayed by her side. There wasn't much Junior could do at home. His mind would be on Lillian and the two new babies. Everyone understood that he had no choice but to stay with his wife. Without one complaint, the rest of the family stepped up to help with the children. Even Sylvia came over one day, bringing her own children, so that she could lend a hand with cooking, cleaning, and entertaining the *kinner*.

The week seemed to drag by slowly. Each day was filled with unexpected surprises. Little Anna fell and bruised her nose. Abram tore the seat of his pants climbing a fence. Linda grew increasingly quiet, the worry for her *mamm* too obvious, yet there simply wasn't time to spare for a private discussion with her. Samuel tried his best to relieve his *mamm* and Rachel, both of whom seemed increasingly worn out by the end of the day.

On Saturday, Katie and Jonas hired a driver to take

them to the hospital, leaving Samuel and David alone with the *kinner* for the day. The two brothers had recruited Jacob and Abram to help with chores around the barnyard while Linda stayed inside with the smaller children. With Lena to help, Linda would have no problem managing the morning house chores. Samuel had promised them an afternoon picnic by the pond over the hill if they finished their chores on time. That was all the motivation that the smaller children needed.

It was a hot and muggy day. The air felt oppressive and powerful. As the sun rose overhead, it became stifling, and Samuel was increasingly sorry that he had mentioned the picnic. Yet he knew that the house would be just as sticky warm, so keeping the children outdoors was not such a bad plan, after all. Plus, the more time they spent outside, the less time they had to make a mess inside.

It was two in the afternoon when Samuel walked with David, leading the five children across the pasture. Rachel had volunteered to watch the baby so that Samuel and David only had to worry about the older children. Samuel had little Anna on his shoulders, his hands holding her bare ankles while she pulled at his hair. Jacob tagged along behind him while Lena and Abram stuck by David. Linda walked alone between her two uncles.

"I'm gonna catch me a big ole fish!" Jacob announced, running ahead toward the water's edge.

Abram quickly followed, releasing David's hands to race after his brother toward the water. "Me, too," he yelled, his little legs moving quickly as he tried to catch up to Jacob.

"Careful now!" David called out.

Linda watched her two little brothers. "I bet *Mamm* would sure like to be here," she sighed.

Samuel wished that he had something to say in response to Linda's statement, something that would make her feel better. Unfortunately, he knew that Linda was probably correct. Lillian would be missing her children something fierce by now, especially twelve-year-old Linda. Since the birth of her first child, Lillian hadn't spent even one night away from her children. But now she had a decision to make. Leave the newborn twins in the hospital, or trust that her other six children were being well tended.

Samuel smiled at his niece. "She'll be home soon. In time for plenty of picnics, I'm sure."

Linda shrugged, her face drawn tight and expression a level of sorrow that Samuel hadn't noticed before this moment. "Not with the babies. She'll be too preoccupied and needing my help. Won't be time for picnics this summer." She paused, lowering her head. "Won't be time for much at all with these two new babies."

She was probably right, and that made Samuel realize how powerful strong the ties to family truly were. While he was facing the threat of being arrested for a crime that he did not commit, he had not realized that life continued around him. His niece, this gloriously wonderful girl, was more worried about spending quality time alone with her mother than anything else. All she wanted was to sip meadow tea on the porch, having her mother's undivided attention for even just thirty minutes. Yet she knew that moment would never come. The celebration of two new babies, daughters at that, meant that Linda would have much more work at home for the next few years. And by the time the moment of quiet sharing arose once again, Linda herself might have become a mother and be fighting the same battles with her own daughters.

"Aw, Linda," Samuel said. His heart was breaking for this lovely girl. She had always been so kind, so pleasant, so beautiful on the inside as well as outside. To see her heart so heavy with sadness made him realize how much he had missed by thinking only of himself for so long. "You need something, you come to me. I'm not your *mamm*," he said gently, "but I can be your friend."

She looked up at him, blinking her large blue eyes twice. There were tears on her lashes. "Thanks, *Onkel* Samuel." She paused, glancing away for a minute. Then, with a strength that he didn't imagine she possessed, she stared him straight in the eye. "And I don't believe anything that people are saying. I know you weren't driving that car. I know you didn't kill those boys and just walk away. You would never do that, *Onkel* Samuel."

For a moment, Samuel couldn't walk any further. His feet simply stopped moving. Was that what people were saying? Was that what people thought about him? The weight of the accusations clung to him and he realized that his own behavior had brought this situation upon himself. Had he been kind and true during the years, more people would have felt like Linda. Had he been hard-working and honorable, no one would have questioned him. Yet, during the years, he had not been kind, nor had he been true, hard-working, or honorable. So the consensus was that he was guilty. It was easier to believe he was guilty than to suspect that, maybe, he was innocent.

"Samuel! Come quick!"

Samuel looked up, his train of thought broken by the

piercing cry of Jacob. David was wading into the pond water, his hands breaking the surface. "What on earth?" Samuel said. Taking baby Anna from his shoulders, he set her on the ground in front of Linda then started running toward the pond.

"It's Abram! He's missing!" Jacob screamed.

Samuel jumped into the pond. "Where?"

Jacob pointed toward where David was trying to find the little boy. "He was over there a minute ago!"

Without waiting for more details, Samuel dove under the surface of the water. It was dark and murky. He couldn't see anything so he began feeling the water before him. He swam until his lungs felt as though they would burst. Only then, would he surface to refuel himself with fresh oxygen before diving back down under the water. When he rose up gasping for air, he heard Lena crying and Linda weeping by the side of the pond. With fierce determination, he dove back down again, reaching before his face in the murky water, hoping beyond hope to touch the arm or foot of the little boy.

Samuel broke through the water one more time, gasping for air, filling his lungs as best as he could. He thought he heard Jacob crying out for him to keep looking for his brother but Samuel didn't bother with his nephew's pleas. Instead, he dove back under the water.

His hands groped in the darkness, feeling through some weeds until he finally bumped against something. At first, he thought it was a tree limb, but he quickly felt the soft fabric of pants and realized it was Abram. His hand grabbed frantically at the ankle of the little boy and he pushed himself to the surface, pulling Abram's limp body through the water.

"I got him!" he cried out as he frantically clawed

at the water, trying to pull the little boy's head above water. Samuel tossed Abram over his shoulder and swam as best as he could to the edge of the pond.

Linda was holding Lena, both girls sobbing uncontrollably. Little Anna had been plopped down in the grass, a safe enough distance from the edge of the pond so no one had to worry about her. She was crying, however, from the tension in the air and the fact that no one was paying attention to her. And Jacob…sweet Jacob… was kneeling by the edge of the pond, his hands clasped in silent prayer and his eyes squeezed shut.

Samuel pulled himself from the water and quickly dropped Abram onto the ground, the impact of the fall causing some water to pour out of the sides of his mouth. Lena screamed and buried her head into Linda's stomach. Samuel ignored them and began pumping on the little boy's chest. One, two, three. Then, leaning forward, he pinched the boy's nose and blew into his mouth.

"What's he doing to Abram?" Lena screamed.

Linda tried to console her, but Lena continued to scream. David had emerged from the water, hurrying to the girls to hold them in his arms and protect them from watching what Samuel was doing. He tucked Linda and Lena into his body, shielding them enough but still being able to look over his own shoulder to watch.

One, two, three. Breathe. One, two, three. Breathe. Samuel felt his heart stop when he realized that Abram was not responding. One, two, three. Breathe. Please God, he prayed silently, adding a plea for no more tragedy for his family.

One, two, three… Samuel refused to give up. He continued to pump at the little boy's chest between breathing into Abram's mouth. How long had the child been underwater? One, two, three. Breathe. It couldn't have been that long. His mind quickly thought back, trying to figure it out. After all, David was watching them while he and Linda were talking. One, two, three. Breathe. He thought of Lillian's struggle with her new babies. There was no way he could give up, to have Lillian return home from giving birth to have to deal with burying a child. One, two, three…

Abram's chest jumped and a puddle of water poured out of the sides of his mouth. He began to cough and Samuel quickly turned him onto his side. Holding the boy on his lap, Samuel began to cry, the tears pouring down his cheeks. How close had God come to taking poor Abram, he wondered. He clutched the little boy to his chest and wept. How would he have been able to tell Lillian that he had failed? That he had let her sweet baby boy drown? The thought of even having to tell her about this near miss forced more tears down his face.

"What were you doing, Abram?" Samuel sobbed, rocking the little boy back and forth while Abram sobbed. "Why did you go into the water?" The little boy didn't answer. His voice was choked with sobs and he clung to Samuel's chest. Samuel held him tightly, kissing the boy's head and crying with him. "Don't ever do that again, you hear me?" he asked between his own grief. To his relief, the little boy nodded, his wet hair tickling the underside of Samuel's chin.

David walked over to Samuel and placed a hand on his shoulder. "Well done, Samuel," he said solemnly, his own voice cracking. Samuel didn't have to look up to know that there were tears in his brother's eyes. "Without you, he'd be gone for certain."

"Don't say such a thing," Samuel whispered, glancing at the two older girls. He was relieved to see Linda leave Lena to console Anna, who was still crying in the tall grass. "What's done is done, *ja*?"

"But you saved him, Samuel," David said, his voice dropping so that the girls couldn't hear. "One minute he was there, the next he was just gone! I couldn't find him. He just slipped under the water, and by the time I got out there, I couldn't find him." He lifted a hand to his eyes, Samuel suspected to wipe away tears. "How you did it, I have no idea."

"Luck. Love. I don't know," Samuel said quickly, still holding Abram. He rocked the little boy in his arms, holding him as tight as he could to his chest. They were both soaking wet and covered in dirt from the pond and the ground. Abram trembled, sobbing as he clung to Samuel. "It just wasn't his time, thanks be to God."

No one felt in the mood for the picnic and it was quickly decided that everyone wanted to head back home to the safety of the farm, where things were familiar and the dangers of the pond well behind them. Samuel carried Abram in his arms, too aware that the little boy refused to release his hold around Samuel's neck. Samuel didn't care. The fact that the little boy was alive and breathing was a miracle, as far as he was concerned. A true miracle gifted to them by God.

Katie sat in her chair, listening to the story as David and Samuel stood before her. Her hand went to her mouth as she gasped when she realized how close she had come to losing her grandson Abram. The color drained from her face and Samuel realized how old she was looking. There was simply too much stress in the family for his aging mother to cope. Jonas stood by the window, his hands behind his back as he looked outside. He didn't speak during the confession from his two sons, nor did he turn around when they finished.

David paused, glancing at his *daed*. "Samuel saved Abram's life," he said. "I would never have known what to do."

Katie shut her eyes for a moment, her mouth moving in silent prayer. Samuel knew that she was thinking of the many nieces and nephews that her own siblings had buried. Every year, they had attended at least one or two funerals for children that had been killed from falling out of buggies or getting kicked by horses. Other children died from illness. But such tragedy had, so far, escaped their own immediate family.

His parents had just returned home. Both David and Samuel had dreaded the moment that they would have to explain what happened. While they knew it was an accident, they both felt responsible, as if it reflected poorly on their ability to watch the children. It had been decided that David would be the one to speak, Samuel feeling that his own recent contributions to family stress and heartache was enough for one lifetime.

When Katie finally spoke, she had leveled her gaze directly at Samuel. "God has a message for you," she said softly. Her eyes were brimming with tears, but she fought having them stream down her cheeks. There was a gentle smile on her face.

"For me?" Samuel asked, not understanding what his *mamm* was saying. He had expected her to yell at them, be upset with them for not having watched the young boy more closely. Even Jonas turned from the window to look at his wife, a question in his expression.

She nodded. "You didn't give up on Abram," she continued. "He doesn't want you to give up on Him, either, just as He is not about to give up on you."

For a moment, no one spoke. Katie's words seemed to echo in Samuel's mind. Perhaps she was right, he thought. When he had been straying from the church and community, bad things had happened to him. When he had made the decision to turn his life around, tragedy had struck. What Samuel had perceived as God turning His back was actually God showing him just how alone he would be without his family, community, and church. Now that he was living his life in a more Christian manner, Samuel had just witnessed a miracle about not giving up, no matter how difficult or insurmountable the task may appear.

"God is telling you how powerful He is. He can give and He can take. You need to learn a lesson from this, Samuel. God wants you to learn from His decisions," she said, pausing to make certain that he was paying attention to her. "You follow Him and He will take care of you. But," she said, lifting up one finger and pointing it at him. "If you stray, you will find yourself walking down a very lonely path."

"Katie," Jonas said sharply. "We should never presume to know what God is thinking."

For the first time in Samuel's memory, he watched as his mother voiced disagreement with her husband. She shook her head. "No, Jonas," she said. "He wants Samuel to learn this lesson."

"If the bishop hears…," Jonas said.

"The bishop won't hear," she snapped. The tension was apparent. Samuel had never heard his parents bicker before this moment. Those discussions were saved for behind closed doors and away from any of the children.

Yet he could see from the dark circles under his *mamm*'s eyes that she was, indeed, feeling the weight of so much hardship. "I can speak freely in my own home without fear of the bishop!"

"*Mamm*," Samuel said, placing his hand over hers. He didn't want to hear his parents fight, not because of him. "Words spoken can't be retrieved," he whispered, repeating the saying that she had often said to him.

His words seemed to jolt her back to her normal calm self and she looked at him, studying his face. Her eyes flickered back and forth as they seemed to memorize everything she saw. She looked tired. These past weeks had been hard on her, perhaps harder than on anyone else, except Samuel. Finally, a faint smile lightened her face and she squeezed his hand. "I see it has worked, Samuel. You have indeed learned a lot from this experience. God has moved you."

There was nothing left to say. Samuel smiled back, although the happiness was not showing in his eyes. While his heart rejoiced that Abram had not drowned, his spirit was still weak. With Jake not being able to call the lawyer, there was no way for them to know what was going on with Paul's recovery or the police investigation. It left a terrible dark cloud over his soul, a cloud that followed him wherever he went.

"If you don't mind," Samuel said, his voice soft enough to let everyone know that he, too, was emotional about the events of the day. "I'm going to retire early tonight." And he disappeared up the stairwell and into the darkness, hoping that a good night's sleep would help erase the pain of the day.

Chapter Twenty-One

After a long day helping her *daed* in the fields with haying, Mary Ruth was tired. Her muscles ached and the back of her neck was sunburned. It was hot and humid, the weight of the air draining her of any energy. She was thankful when her *mamm* told her to sit outside on the porch where an early evening breeze could refresh her. Sitting on a folding chair, she leaned her head back and shut her eyes, holding the cool glass of meadow tea that her *mamm* had brought out for her.

She hadn't been permitted back to the Lapp farm since being banished a week ago. Her father had been adamant about that fact, reminding both her and her mother that, promise or no promise, he was the head of the household and he didn't want Mary Ruth returning to the Lapps'.

"Not until matters are cleared up," he stated firmly, leveling a stern look at his daughter. Mary Ruth wasn't too certain that even if matters cleared up he would permit her back to the Lapp farm.

Even when Mary Ruth tried to argue, that had only made things worse.

"I found you with that boy and no chaperone!" he retorted to her pleas.

"I was watching the children!" she said, finding the strength to talk back to her *daed*. "Lillian was taken to the hospital. Would you have me leave the *kinner* alone? Unattended?"

"I will not have your reputation tarnished because of his!"

"*Daed*!" Mary Ruth had started to argue back, feeling more bold than usual. After all, she had pledged herself to Samuel and she believed in his innocence. "The Lapps need our help. No one would question my presence there. You cannot have young men watching six *kinner*, and one just barely walking!"

"Amos," Miriam had said, speaking up. "You know that Lillian is with her *boppoli* in the hospital. Someone needs to watch those *kinner*. They need our help."

Shaking his head and holding up his hand, Amos had stopped the conversation. "They have family. They are not alone. Rachel, Sylvia, even that Shana can help them!" He frowned at the disapproving look on his wife's face. "I'll hear no more about this, Miriam. Not from you either," he said with a pointed finger at Mary Ruth. "You are becoming quite outspoken in recent days, and that just proves my point that your contact with that Lapp boy is no *gut*!"

With that, Amos had stalked out of the house, slamming his hat on his head before he disappeared out the kitchen door. Miriam had tried to say something to her daughter but, after trying to find the words, she realized that there was nothing to say that would excuse Amos' behavior.

Now, as Mary Ruth realized that she hadn't seen

Samuel in over a week, she found herself wondering how he was holding up against the pressure and suspicion of the community. Yesterday, several of her *mamm*'s friends had come visiting and Mary Ruth had overheard their conversations, talking about Samuel's involvement in the accident that had killed two young men. Oh, how she had wanted to speak up, to defend Samuel and declare his innocence. But she knew better. To do so would only cause the talk to shift away from Samuel and onto her. Mary Ruth knew that would only cause more problems with her *daed* in the long run.

She thought back to all that had happened over the previous few months. What should she have done differently, she thought, to show her feelings toward Samuel. She smiled as she remembered the day that he had kissed her in the buggy, not once but twice. She remembered how angry she had been, hurt and upset that he had stolen what rightfully belonged to her future husband. Now, she realized, the dream that Samuel might one day be that husband was balanced with a stronger decision: Would she be forced to choose between Samuel and her family? The smile faded from her face as she felt the weight of that decision upon her shoulders.

"*Mamm*," she called, knowing that her mother would be able to hear her through the open window. "Going for a walk to cool down," she said. There was some shuffling from inside the house and a quick acknowledgment from her mother. That sufficed for Mary Ruth as an approval. She certainly didn't want her *daed* accusing her of sneaking off, especially the way he was watching her every move.

Setting her glass on the floor beside her chair, she stood up and stretched. Her back ached and her shoulders were sore from helping in the fields all day. Yet the work had been peaceful and gave her time to think.

However, the more she thought, the more confused she became about her *daed*'s staunch position against Samuel. It was not the Amish way to be so unforgiving, to judge another person. In many ways, she had lost faith in her father as the head of the house. How could she respect a man that insisted on following the Ordnung and Amish ways, but broke it so quickly when it came to Samuel Lapp? Why did he not like Samuel?

She knew that Samuel had a reputation amongst the people. He had always been outspoken and rash, even as a child. But, to Mary Ruth, that was what made him so interesting. After all, he didn't follow without questioning. He had a mind of his own and the strength to speak up when pushed into a corner. He had a passion for life that she had not seen in many other Amish men. She had always appreciated his liveliness, despite the rest of the community frowning upon it.

Still, she knew that he was a good man. She had seen him caring for his horse, so gentle and patient. He was never abrupt with the animals like others sometimes were; and the children… She smiled to herself. Despite claiming that he didn't want children of his own and that children were for women, she had watched him with Jacob in the mornings before he had gone to the carpentry shop. She had seen the small wooden toys that Jacob played with, made by his *Onkel* Samuel. Mary Ruth knew that, as much as Samuel had tried to create a strong and independent image, the truth was that he was just as *gut* a man as the next. Perhaps more so, she thought.

All of these things had crossed her mind as she had

worked all day under the scorching sun, sweating in the humid air. Still, she didn't mind working in the fields, although she preferred time in the garden and helping her *mamm* in the kitchen. She missed the Lapp children, having enjoyed herself during her time helping Lillian. Yes, she realized, she truly missed the *kinner*, especially young Jacob with his funny sense of curiosity and little Abram with his devotion to do anything and everything his older brother did.

She walked through the freshly plowed hay fields toward the large hill behind her house. It dipped down into a small valley, and if she stood at the top, she'd be able to see the Lapp farm in the distance. With a quick glance over her shoulder to insure that no one was watching, she started down the hill and found herself wandering in that direction. She knew better than to actually go to the farm. That would be far too forward and was certain to get back to her *daed*, especially if Simon saw her. But it was comforting to be able to see the buildings and the cows and the freshly laundered clothing hanging on the line to dry.

For a long while, she sat on the top of the hill. The grass was not too high and it waved in the breeze. She was glad to feel that it was cooling down for the evening. Otherwise, it would be another sleepless night in her second-story bedroom. Even with the windows opened, her room would still be uncomfortable on such hot, sticky nights. But a cool breeze was always more than welcome.

It was just about time for the evening feeding, and the black and white cows were beginning to wander toward the dairy barn. She loved watching the cows, mesmerized by how they walked single file through the chute between the paddocks, a long line of sixty or more cows, heading toward their barn as if an invisible hand led them. Of course, there were a few younger cows that refused to join the line. Mary Ruth laughed, watching them. They were like naughty children, disobedient and rebellious. Someone would have to chase them into the barn if they decided to hold out and not join the rest.

"Mary Ruth," a voice said from behind her.

Startled, she jumped at her name and a hand fluttered to her chest. She looked up in time to see Samuel approach her from the other side of the hill. "Samuel! What are you doing here?" Instinctively, she looked around to make certain no one else could see that he was now standing next to her.

He shrugged. "Was over there," he said, pointing toward the far paddock of his *daed*'s farm. "Saw you here." He smiled but there was little life in his eyes. The sparkle was gone, and Mary Ruth wondered how long it would take to return. He squatted beside her, his knees cracking as he did so. "You watching the cows, then?"

She nodded, feeling shy for the first time in his presence. "*Ja*. I love watching their evening march into the dairy." She watched as he nodded and turned his gaze to watch the cows, too. "It's like poetry, isn't it? They just know to go home."

"I imagine," he said. "Not too familiar with poetry."

For a moment, neither spoke. The silence was awkward, an indicator of so many unspoken questions between them. Mary Ruth wanted to know how he was doing, whether he had heard anything, how were the *kinner*, when was Lillian coming home. But she asked nothing. Instead, she just sat near him, glad to be in his presence. There was an aura of humility about Samuel now, and she found that, despite the circumstances, she liked it. He was becoming a man at last, shedding his wild side and his crazy ideas of exploring the world. Indeed, she realized, there was finally hope that he could actually settle down and be the man that she had always known was inside of him.

"You doing okay?" he asked, breaking the silence. He squinted in the harsh light from the sun as it set behind them.

"You ask me that when I want to ask you the very same," she replied.

He took a deep breath. "No, I'm not," he replied, staring into the distance. "You see, I finally decided to take the next step with this girl. I told her my intentions to see her, to court her, to explore the possibilities of a future." He plucked at the grass by his feet and tossed it into the breeze, watching as it fluttered to the ground. "But I can't see her right now, can't take her for ice cream in my courting buggy or see her at singings."

"Samuel," she whispered.

He nodded. "I know. It's terrible, isn't it? I finally took that step, that step toward the future." He sighed. "I wanted to show her what life could be like, to make her laugh and smile, to make her live a little, and, most importantly, to mayhaps have her fall in love with me." With a quick glance at her, he paused. She felt her cheeks turn pink at both his words and his look. "*Ja*, to fall in love with me so that I could marry her in the spring when I take my baptism."

"Oh," she gasped, pressing her hands against her cheeks to hide the color.

"But I can't now, can I?" He reached out and took one of her hands in his, removing it from her cheek.

She saw him smile, but this smile was genuine. "She blushes," he murmured.

"You embarrass me," she said. But the pounding of her heart against her chest told her that she would treasure his words forever.

He clasped her hand in his, holding it gently. "I need to see you, Mary Ruth. I can't go on like this." He waited until she met his gaze. "I feel like I'm walking in a cloud, waiting for something else terrible to happen, and that would be that you decided not to wait for me."

How could he think that, she wondered, alarmed at his words. "Oh no, Samuel," she cried out. "I will wait! Don't doubt that!"

"Everything keeps going from bad to worse, Mary Ruth," he said. He told her the story about Abram and how the little boy had almost drowned. He told her about his mother's words regarding God's message and how Samuel believed that she was correct. He told her about how much he just needed to take her into his arms and hold her. Her embrace was all that he thought about, longing to have it so that his pain could be washed away. And she listened to him, his words so honest and from the heart that she felt tears invading her eyes. How much pain could this man endure, she wondered, and how glorious that his faith in God increased, rather than the alternative!

"This will end soon, Samuel," she reassured him.

"Will it?"

She nodded. "It has to end soon."

"And if it doesn't?" He raised an eyebrow at her. "What then? I cannot ask you to ruin your life."

How many times had she asked herself the same question? Yet, at this moment, as she sat beside him with his hand holding hers, she knew that the answer would be yes. She would, indeed, give up everything if that meant being with Samuel. "Let's pray for a happy outcome," she replied.

He was silent for a moment, but he never took his eyes off hers. She wondered what he was thinking, wondered if she had said the wrong thing. She knew that she couldn't tell him that she'd give up her family and community if he asked. She hoped that she hadn't upset him. However, when he finally responded, she knew that what she offered as a solution was the right thing to have said.

"Yes, Mary Ruth," he said solemnly. "We should pray, indeed." And he shut his eyes and bowed his head, his hand still holding hers.

His action impressed her, and she felt her heart. This new Samuel behaved in a much more—and surprisingly!—humble manner. Gone was the bravado and puffery that had been so much a part of his outer persona. She had always known that her Samuel wasn't truly like that. Now it appeared that he knew it, too. Life had changed him, but the change was powerful and deep. She found herself lowering her own head and joining him in a long, silent prayer.

When they finished, Samuel stood up and reached down to help Mary Ruth stand before him. She felt small in his shadow. He towered over her by at least half a foot, and his shoulders were so broad and strong. He still held her hand, caressing it gently as they stood there, staring at each other. She kept her eyes on his and waited for him to say something. But there was nothing to say. His steady gaze expressed what he was thinking and feeling.

"You may kiss me," she heard herself say.

The words surprised her as much as they surprised him. For a moment, she thought he was going to bend down and press his lips against hers. He seemed to contemplate it. But then, he shook his head. "*Nee*," he said. "I want to wait for our wedding day, Mary Ruth." He smiled, raising her hand to his lips and kissing the back of it.

She blushed and lowered her eyes, embarrassed by her offer and fearful that he would think she was too forward and dishonorable. How could she have said something like that? To offer a kiss? For a moment, she thought she might actually cry with shame.

Sensing her discomfort, Samuel chuckled under his breath and tilted her chin so that she had to look at him again. "But don't think I don't want to kiss you. I just want to do it properly, Mary Ruth. For you and for me." He leaned down and planted a soft kiss on her cheek. "That shall do for now, *ja*?"

Not trusting her voice, she nodded.

"Now," he said. "Let me walk you back. I won't walk with you all the way, mind you. No need to give your father reason to dislike me anymore than he already does." He kept her hand in his as he turned toward her father's farm. She appreciated his acceptance of her *daed*'s position during this uncertain time. It would make life much easier if he didn't fight Amos, as her *daed* could be a force to reckon with, his temper and opinions well known throughout the community.

When the farm was closer, Samuel stopped and nodded in its direction. "You go on now, Mary Ruth, but know that I walk beside you in my heart, *ja*?"

The color flooded to her cheeks again. "Samuel, and I with you," she responded softly.

"I shall see you at church this Sunday and, mayhaps, the singing that night?"

The singing, she thought. If only her *daed* would let her go. He had refused to permit her to leave the house the previous church Sunday. He had claimed that she couldn't leave because his brother and family were visiting, although she knew the real reason was to keep her away from Samuel. She wondered what his excuse would be for this upcoming Sunday? How long could her *daed* stand in her way? Unfortunately, she knew that he could and most certainly would. Once an idea was planted in his mind, Amos Smucker didn't often change his position. Short of openly defying him, Mary Ruth had few choices before her.

"I'll try," she said, her words sounding more convincing than she felt.

"*Gut*!" he replied with a smile, a touch of the sparkle back in his eyes. "Until then," he said, backing away from her as he waited for her to turn and continue walking toward the farm. He walked slowly, watching her.

She turned around and waved once. She didn't want to have any problems with her parents, but she hated leaving Samuel. However, knowing that he was thinking about her and would be waiting for her at the singing gave her something to look forward to over the next few days. With his sweet words still lingering in her ears and planted firmly in her heart, she hurried back down the hill toward her parents' farm.

Chapter Twenty-Two

When the two buggies rolled into the driveway Tuesday afternoon, Samuel caught his breath. He had been standing in the doorway, letting a cool summer breeze cool his sweaty body. He had just come into the house from the fields, after working with his *daed* and brothers at cutting the hay. Junior had released Samuel from work that day so that he could help his brothers. They would begin baling it when it had dried in a few days. While he stood in the doorway, he had heard the buggies before he actually saw them. When the buggies rounded the driveway by the back of the dairy barn, Samuel watched them as he leaned against the doorframe, a refreshing glass of meadow tea in his hand.

The buggies came to stop in front of the hitching post by the barn. One was Jake's and the other was the bishop's. He felt his heart begin to quicken. The expressions on their faces were solemn and severe, giving a clear indication that their visit was most serious. Certainly that could not be good news, he told himself.

Turning just slightly, he watched as his mother leaned over the counter to look out the window. She lifted the white curtain that covered the lower part of the window just enough to see the two men emerge from the buggies. Her eyes flickered over to Samuel's, and seeing that he was watching her, she quickly looked away. Yet the look of fear in her expression did not go unnoticed. She, too, suspected bad news.

"Looks important," she said, her voice cracking slightly. She refused to meet his gaze. "Best go find your *daed*."

Samuel didn't move from the doorway but nodded in the direction of the barn. "No need, *Mamm*," he said, as his father emerged from the dairy barn. He watched as his father greeted Jake and the bishop with a stiff handshake. They exchanged some words before Samuel saw his *daed* gesture toward the house and turn to lead the two men toward the porch. His father's shoulders were slumped over and his feet seemed to shuffle as he walked. His father had definitely aged over the past three weeks, and for a fleeting moment, Samuel felt guilt for what his father was going through. Yet, he also knew that he had nothing to feel shamed about, despite the feelings of responsibility.

As the men approached the porch, Samuel stood up straight in the doorway and greeted them. "*Guder Owed*, Bishop," he said solemnly. Indeed, he hoped it would be a good evening, but when the bishop barely responded, Samuel took that as another bad sign. Whatever the bishop had come to say, it wasn't something that he wanted to hear. Of that, Samuel was certain. His heart started to pound inside of his chest and he turned toward Jake, hoping to see some glimmer of hope. But Jake's expression was just as somber as the bishop's.

"Bishop's come to speak with you, Samuel," his *daed*

finally said. His stare was blank and expressionless, making it obvious that the bishop had not shared any news with his father when they spoke at the barn.

Samuel felt his heart lurch into his throat, his fears confirmed. Surely this was not a social visit, but could the news be so awful? If something terrible had happened, wouldn't the police have come, too? Samuel stepped aside to let them enter the house. He tried to get Jake to look at him, hoping to get an indicator about how bad the news truly was. But Jake kept his eyes straight and followed the bishop into the kitchen.

The men stood near the door, waiting for Samuel to join them. He took his time, his heart pounding inside of his chest. Time seemed to stand still, and the ticking of the clock on the wall echoed in his ears. He didn't want to stand before them. It seemed too serious, too severe. Was he to be judged before them? Jonas stood next to Jake, looking small and frail next to him. The men were facing Samuel and he felt alone, as though facing a jury of his peers. In a way, he thought, that's what this is, indeed.

Everyone was silent, waiting for the bishop to speak first. But he remained deep in thought, perhaps praying for guidance about how to say what was on his mind. His face was drawn, the wrinkles under his eyes speaking of his own sleepless nights since the car accident had brought such tragedy to his church district. Once again, Samuel realized how far-reaching the implications of his actions were, those actions that he had done and even those that he had not done. The realization caught him off-guard, and once again, Samuel found himself regretting his poor decisions of the past.

Finally, after what seemed like an eternity to Samuel, the bishop cleared his throat and looked up. "Paul has died, Samuel."

Katie's hand flew to her mouth and she leaned against the counter, a sob escaping her throat. Samuel glanced at her, knowing that his *mamm* was crying for many different reasons. While Paul had been Mennonite, and a rebellious one at that, he was still the son of two grieving parents. Katie's heart broke for the family of the young man, of the wasted years that he'd never live, the family he'd never raise, and the love he'd never share.

But, for Samuel, there was a different reason to mourn. With Paul dead, how would Samuel's name be cleared? But no one asked that question. Instead, they focused on his death.

"He's with God, I'm sure," Samuel said slowly, the moisture gone from his mouth. His lips felt dry and his throat parched.

Jake took a deep breath and shuffled his straw hat from hand to hand. "There is more news, Samuel." When Samuel met his gaze, Jake nodded once, the first glimmer of hope that was given to him. "*Gut* news for you."

A frown crossed his face. Paul had died and, with him, any chance of clearing his name. "*Gut* news? I don't understand, Jake."

Jake cleared his throat and glanced at the bishop. "Apparently, the police were able to interview him before he died. He had moments of lucidity during the past week before he slipped away," Jake said slowly, each word carefully chosen. He glanced at the bishop then back to Samuel. "He was able to tell them that you weren't with them, that you had left earlier to return home."

Katie gasped and Jonas looked up, startled at the news that Jake had just shared. It was clear that Samuel was not the only one who had expected the worst with Paul's death. Jonas was the first one to ask the question on everyone's mind. "How?"

The bishop glanced at Jake, his expression stern and fierce. It was clear that another struggle was happening in the room, one between Jake and the bishop. Immediately Samuel knew without asking that Jake had spoken to the lawyer, despite the bishop's warning to the contrary. The disregard for the bishop's demand of no interaction with the Englische laws would cause Jake trouble, of that Samuel was certain. But, for now, the bishop remained silent about that.

"Go on," the bishop urged Jake. "Tell them what you have learned."

"Well," Jake began. "Paul woke from the coma earlier in the week and faded in and out of consciousness. His brain wasn't impacted, but the damage to his organs was too much. Apparently, he died two days ago."

Samuel frowned. "Two days ago?" He wondered why it had taken so long to learn about this. The Amish grapevine usually worked much faster than that.

"The police notified the lawyer, and he contacted me." Jake nodded to the bishop. "As soon as I received his message, I went to Bishop Peachey and asked for permission to speak to the lawyer for an update. That's how we learned today of the situation."

Samuel tried to digest what Jake was saying. It had been over three weeks since the accident. Yet Jake had said that Paul had moments of awareness and had been able to communicate. Something didn't compute and Samuel needed to know. "When did they know about my innocence?" he asked, his voice barely above a whisper.

Before Jake could answer, Bishop Peachey held up his hand. "I don't think that's important, Samuel."

His frown deepened. For three weeks, he had been living on the edge, worrying and waiting. His community had virtually shunned him, Mary Ruth's father wouldn't let her off of the farm, and people believed the worst about him. How could the bishop not realize how important it was for Samuel to know the answer to this question? "It is important," he said respectfully. "To me."

"That's the Englischer way, Samuel, and not our way to question it," the bishop rebuked strongly.

"Last week," Jake added, ignoring the angry look on the bishop's face. "The police cleared your name last week."

Catching his breath, Samuel looked around the room. He couldn't believe what he was hearing and was quickly trying to make sense of everything. For over an entire week, he had been officially innocent, yet no one had known? The police had been quick to drag him down to their station but not quite as quick to inform him about his innocence. Of course, the lawyer would have known, but the bishop had forbidden Jake from contacting him. Certainly the lawyer had a difficult time tracking down Jake, too. He shared a phone with a neighbor and probably didn't get a message right away.

Jonas stared at Jake, his eyes wide with questions. "But Samuel's hat? And the witness?"

Jake shrugged, turning toward his father-in-law. "Samuel must have left his hat behind, just like he said. It appears that Peter was wearing it when he was driving the car. The police think that Peter was not actually thrown from the car but was actually able to walk away before collapsing on the side of the road from his internal injuries."

Jonas nodded. "*Ja*, that would explain the witness's version."

Feeling weak in his knees, Samuel reached for the table and pulled out a chair. He sat down, the wheels of the chair rolling slightly away from the table. He had to lean forward, his elbow on the edge of the table and his hand on his forehead. His heart still beat rapidly as he tried to reconcile all that was being said. But he couldn't. Not without feeling angry about the bishop's previous ruling that Jake couldn't speak with the lawyer. That had prevented him from moving on with his life. That had prevented Mary Ruth from being permitted at the farm. That had almost resulted in the death of Abram. Too many conflicting thoughts flooded through his mind that he quickly decided to think about nothing at all. It was easier.

"Samuel," Jake said slowly. "Do you understand what that means?" When he didn't answer, Jake moved toward him and knelt before his brother-in-law. He reached out and took Samuel's hand in his. "Samuel?"

Moving his hand away from his face, Samuel lifted his eyes and looked at Jake. "What, Jake?"

"Did you hear me? Did you hear what I said?"

Samuel nodded. "*Ja*, I heard you."

"Do you understand what it means?" Jake repeated. When Samuel didn't respond, Jake smiled. "You are no longer a suspect. The police won't be bothering you anymore."

It took a moment for the words to sink in. But when they did, Samuel felt the tidal wave of emotion pour over him. He covered his face with his hands and sobbed, letting the tears flow as the pain and suffering of the past three weeks resurfaced. He couldn't hold it back any longer. Jake stood up and laid a hand on Samuel's shoulder, letting him cry. It was clear that Samuel had lost more than just three friends. He had also lost his hope that others would believe him. Now the truth was out and the stress was lifted.

The bishop waited a minute before clearing his throat again. Samuel rubbed at his eyes with the back of his hands and looked up. "The road to redemption will not be easy, Samuel," he said.

"What?" He looked at his parents, shocked to see tears streaming down both of their faces. He realized that they had been walking beside him during the past weeks, feeling the burden of stress and suffering with him. Bewildered, Samuel looked back at the bishop. "What do you mean?"

"There will be those who won't be so quick to forgive," the bishop said.

"Forgive?" Samuel stood up, the chair rolling backwards from his sudden movement. "What is there to forgive? I did nothing wrong."

Jake touched Samuel's arm. "It might take time, Samuel."

"Time?" He didn't understand what they were saying. "Time for what?"

The bishop tugged at his beard and shook his head. "I've seen this type of thing happen before, Samuel.

The community casts judgment and when it is discovered to be in error, it's not always easy for some to ask for forgiveness. In this case, they will say that you were still in Philadelphia, playing with the worldly lifestyle of the Englische. They'll justify their judgment because of that."

Jake nodded. "I've seen it before in the Englische world. People can do such irrational things, Samuel."

"So what does that mean?" he demanded.

"I think the bishop is trying to tell you that it'll take time for things to go back to normal," Jake said.

"Have patience, Samuel," the bishop said before nodding his good-bye to Katie and turning to leave.

"I'll see you out," Jonas said and reached for his hat to accompany the bishop to his buggy.

There was a heavy silence in the room when the bishop and Jonas left. The air seemed to drain, depleting the energy. Samuel stared at the empty doorway that the bishop had just walked through. He couldn't believe what he had heard. Despite being innocent, he'd have to deal with more judgment? That seemed neither fair nor right; and he couldn't believe that the bishop would just accept it at face value.

Jake was the first one to break the silence. He glanced at Katie. "Reckon we have some praying to do for the family of that boy." He looked back at Samuel. "You'll be all right, Samuel. Just don't expect everyone to immediately forget the negative feelings they had toward you." He placed his hat on his head. "Reckon we need to send some prayers to those folks in our own community, too, *ja*?" Then, with a slight smile and nod at Katie, he slipped out the door to journey back to his own farm for the early evening chores.

Chapter Twenty-Three

Samuel waited patiently for Bishop Peachey to finish his conversation with Eli Hostetler. He held his hat in his hand, nervously fiddling with it as he waited. The Sunday sermon had seemed longer than usual this week since he had so much on his mind. All week, he had been practicing what he wanted to say in his mind, re-playing the words over and over again.

Since the news that Paul had confirmed Samuel had not been with the other boys began to spread throughout the community, Samuel had been certain to keep his eyes straight ahead and his chin lifted, humbling him-self rather than looking for apologies from his neighbors and friends for the silent treatment that he had received. Instead, Samuel had made certain to be at work on time every day, helped around the farm as much as he could, and even ran errands for his *mamm*.

Lillian had come home the day after the bishop's visit, having to leave the twins in the hospital until they gained more weight. Samuel made certain to take Jacob and Abram under his wing during the evening chores in order to give her a break while she recovered, both physically and emotionally, from the trauma of giving birth to two children that were not yet home with her, as well as the worry of leaving behind her other children for ten days.

On Friday evening, Samuel had taken the two smaller boys for a ride into Intercourse to get ice cream. He had used the courting buggy, wishing that Mary Ruth was with them, but he was giving Amos Smucker time to cool down from his poor behavior during Samuel's troubles. Samuel knew that the bishop had spoken true when stating that some people would need more time to come around and accept the fact that they had been wrong in judging Samuel so quickly.

Now, as Samuel waited in the wings for the bishop, he felt his heart racing. He had learned a lot during the past month. From realizing that his place was with his people to understanding how important Mary Ruth was to him, Samuel had finally grown up. Now, he wanted to take the next step to become a true man…and an Amish man at that.

"Samuel," the bishop said when Eli and Whitey turned to join some of the other men. He laid his hand on Samuel's arm. "I trust things are easing up, *ja*?"

Samuel nodded. "For certain, Bishop," he said.

There was a long hesitation and the bishop waited patiently. Despite the fact that the bishop was one of their own, chosen by lot to lead the people, he was well aware that many of the younger members of the church district held him in great reverence. "Did you need something, Samuel?" he finally said.

"*Ja*," he said, stumbling over his words. "I wanted to talk to you about baptism classes."

The bishop raised an eyebrow. "Baptism classes? They began last month."

Samuel nodded. "I know, Bishop. But I was thinking toward the spring baptism. I wanted you to know that I'm ready to start my studies, and if my reflection holds true, I'm of the mindset to make that commitment to God and our church."

For a moment, the bishop studied Samuel, his steady gaze making Samuel feel uncomfortable. "Sometimes tragedy and hardship make people turn to God before they are ready, son," he finally said, his words low and slow. "You should not react so quickly to such an important and lifelong commitment."

Shaking his head, Samuel lowered his eyes. "*Nee,*" he replied. He had already considered that the bishop might question his timing. Certainly the congregation would question it too. It had been four weeks ago when he had decided to take this step. He had shared his desire with Mary Ruth that night, and Samuel had originally hoped to talk the bishop into a fall baptism. But his plan had been shattered with the car accident and accusations. He had already accepted that he'd have to focus on the spring baptism. He was prepared to address that issue.

"That's not so, Bishop. I was ready to turn to God before this happened. That very weekend, I had decided to speak with you." He looked up. "I didn't feel it was right to express my intent while there was still doubt about my involvement in the accident. Now that my name has been cleared, I thought it was best to let you know. The accident and accusations were tragic, *ja*. But the situation has certainly confirmed my desire for a life of following His will."

He waited for the bishop's reaction. After all, this was an important moment. If the bishop accepted his request for baptism, Samuel would be expected to begin acting as if he had already joined the church. There would be a probationary period, where his behavior was monitored and watched for conformity. In January, he'd begin attending the instructional sessions at the beginning of each worship service until the baptism ceremony took place at the end of April.

But all of that hinged on how the bishop perceived Samuel's request. Would he believe Samuel? Would he accept his request as sincere? Or would he doubt Samuel, thinking that he was just reacting to the stress of the past month?

To Samuel's delight, a smile broke onto the bishop's face. "*Vell*, then, I'm glad to hear it," he said. "I'm sure I speak for the others when I say that we shall be pleased to have you join the church, Samuel Lapp." He had spoken the last part loud enough so that several of the other men standing nearby would overhear him. There would be no end to the Amish grapevine over that announcement, Samuel thought. He just hoped that it would travel quickly to the Smucker farm.

"*Danke*," Samuel said, feeling his throat tighten as he fought back the tears of relief that threatened to cloud his eyes.

Holding Samuel's arm in his hand, the bishop leaned forward. "That should start the healing process, too," he whispered. "And the community sure could use some healing these days, *ja*?"

During the second seating for the noon meal, Samuel sat next to David and his friend, John Bucher. He was quiet during the meal but quickly noticed that many of the youth were staring at him. When he looked up, they would cast an uneasy smile at him before quickly lowering their eyes. Samuel wasn't certain how to interpret that, but he didn't ask. He stayed focused on his meal and listened to John Bucher's conversation with David.

A soft hand touched his shoulder. When he looked up, he saw Mary Ruth behind him. She held a pitcher of meadow tea and smiled at him. "Samuel, would you like some more tea?" she asked, loud enough so that several people turned to look at her. It was clear by her actions that she was sending a message to everyone. Not only was she publicly acknowledging his innocence, but she was also making a statement about their relationship.

"*Ja*," he said quietly. "That would sure be nice, Mary Ruth." He reached for his cup and turned as he handed it to her. "*Danke*," he whispered when he took it back from her.

She took a deep breath, smiled, and said, "*Gem gschehne!*" Then she reached for David's cup to pour him some tea as she continued around the table. The rest of the table seemed to silently watch, too aware of the message Mary Ruth had just sent. While her devotion to Samuel didn't surprise anyone, her public display certainly did. And, with that, the ice seemed to be broken.

"Bet you're sure glad to have that whole Philadelphia incident behind you," one young man said.

Silence fell across the table. For what seemed like a long time, no one moved or spoke. Everyone was staring at Samuel, waiting for his response. He felt uncomfortable under their attention. It was too direct and too apparent that they were actually waiting for him to respond. Clearly, this was a question on everyone's minds, but only one person had the nerve to actually ask it.

Taking a deep breath, Samuel frowned and looked at the man, Irv Beiler. If they wanted an answer, Samuel thought, they would get one. But he weighed the words in his mind before responding. How could he possibly tell them what he was really thinking and feeling? How could he let them see the change within him? What words could be so powerful strong as to start the healing process?

Everyone else seemed to be holding their breath, waiting for Samuel's response. "I feel right awful for their families, *ja*," he said. "It's always sad when someone gets called home to God at such a young age."

However, that wasn't what Irv Beiler meant, and they all knew it. No one spoke. They continued watching Samuel, waiting for more. He even noticed that several of the older women who were sitting by the wall near the open windows were paying attention, too. He knew that his words would be repeated. This was his opportunity to clear the air, to set the record straight.

So, knowing that everyone who was nearby was listening, Samuel felt compelled to share more. "I knew that what those fellows did was a mistake. I knew that I shouldn't be in Philadelphia with them from the moment we arrived. Sometimes we learn from our mistakes faster than other times. I sure learned right quick that I didn't like their behavior, and I left as soon as I realized it. I just wanted to come home, to return to my family and community. It was because of that trip that I knew where I belonged, and it wasn't with those men." He sighed. "*Ja*, I left as fast as I could. Lucky for me or I may have been one of them."

He looked around the table at the faces staring at him. How often had he pondered how close he could have come to being the one that was mourned? If he hadn't left, he would have been in that car and undoubtedly injured or even killed. His decision to return to his community had most likely saved his life on more than one level. God had saved him. He cleared his throat and added, "Still, I'm sure sorry that their families will be missing them."

"We're glad you weren't there," John said.

Samuel nodded. "*Ja*, sure do appreciate that, John." He glanced at the faces staring at him. "I can tell you one thing I learned and that is how I won't be straying from the church again, that's for sure and certain."

John Bucher clapped him on the back as he stood to leave, carrying his dirty plate in his other hand. "*Willkumm home*, *bruder*," he said lightly and the other men laughed, some of them looking uncomfortable, but all of them nodding their heads.

It was almost time for the evening singing. Samuel had spent the afternoon polishing the courting buggy. He had spent almost an hour, shining the wood panels until they sparkled, making certain that they were completely smudge free. By the time he was finished, even David had whistled under his breath at how beautiful it looked.

"If that buggy could talk," he said to Samuel.

"*Ja*, how many of us have used it," he replied, not caring that his brother knew why Samuel was using it this evening.

David didn't reply but placed his hand on Samuel's shoulder. "You don't get your hopes up, Samuel. Her *daed* might not let her go, you know."

With a casual shrug of his shoulders, Samuel tried

to act as though it was of no importance. But they both knew otherwise. Mary Ruth had made her own intentions quite clear at the fellowship meal after church services earlier in the day. There was no way that Amos would not have learned how Mary Ruth had made a point to approach Samuel first and refill his cup of iced tea. Now, the question was whether or not Amos would permit her to attend the singing.

Despite the fact that the Smucker's farm was along the hill by the edge of the Lapp farm, Samuel felt as though the buggy ride took too long. He worried that something would happen. What if a car ran him off the road? What if his horse spooked? He knew those thoughts were irrational, but he couldn't stop them from flooding into his mind.

His hands were sweaty and he wished that he could unbutton his shirt at the neckline. But if he wanted to come calling on Mary Ruth, he wanted to be dressed in his Sunday best. So that meant the white shirt buttoned to the neck and his black vest covering it. He was glad he didn't have to wear his black felt winter hat. His Sunday straw hat was more than sufficient, given that summer was in full swing and the heat was oppressive.

When he pulled the buggy into the Smucker's driveway, he couldn't help but flashback to the last time he had been there. Her *daed* had thrown him off the farm, telling him to stay away from Mary Ruth. Samuel's heart pounded inside of his chest. What would Amos's reaction be now? Mary Ruth was free to court whomever she liked, that was true. But most young women preferred to have their parents' approval, even if it wasn't discussed. Amos had made it quite clear that he did not approve of Mary Ruth and Samuel as a courting couple, even without any such discussion.

Samuel stopped the horse near the hitching post, and after securing the horse, he turned toward the house. It was early to leave for the singing. However, Samuel had wanted to arrive early so that Simon or Stephen didn't take Mary Ruth instead. Now, however, he wished that he had stuck to the traditional plan of taking Mary Ruth home after the singing. That would have avoided any sort of confrontation with Amos. Most courting couples didn't drive to the singings until their relationship was well established and an announcement eminent. Samuel was making his intention known right up front, especially since he had already expressed his interest in that eventuality to Mary Ruth.

Standing at the door, he knocked once, twice. Then he took a step back, smoothing down the front of his vest and flicking a piece of hay from his sleeve. Seconds seemed like minutes as he heard the heavy footsteps of a man walking toward the door.

Earlier that afternoon, David had tried to talk Samuel out of taking the courting buggy over to the Smucker's farm to come calling on Mary Ruth. "It's too soon," he had said with as much compassion as he could muster. "You have to give Amos some time. You know he was right sore about everything."

But Samuel had been adamant. He wanted everyone to see that his actions matched his words. Hiding from the people would only continue the gossip. He knew that he had to face them in order to remind everyone that he had not done anything wrong.

"But it's a reminder that they did something wrong,"

David pointed out. "They judged you. All of them. I think you are being too hasty, brother."

"*Nee*," Samuel said. "I'm being true to myself and to God," he had replied, continuing to clear the courting buggy and ignoring any further comments or looks from his brother. Part of being a man, he told himself, was making decisions like a man.

Now, as he waited for the door to open, Samuel wondered if his brother hadn't been correct. Mayhaps Amos Smucker would need more time, he thought. Mayhaps he'd be too ashamed of himself to ever forgive Samuel. Yet Samuel knew that too much time had gone by already and he had made a promise to Mary Ruth, a promise he intended to keep.

"Samuel," Simon said as he opened the door. He glanced over his shoulder, a worried expression on his face. Blocking the door, he lowered his voice. "What are you doing here?"

Straightening his shoulders, Samuel took a deep breath, and with as much confidence as he could muster, he said, "I've come calling for Mary Ruth. I would like to take her to the singing this evening."

"Who's there?" A gruff voice called out.

Simon cringed and shook his head slightly at Samuel, as if indicating that he should leave. But a hand fell onto his shoulder, and Simon backed away from the door as his father pushed him aside.

Amos stood at the door, blocking Samuel's vision into the room. If Mary Ruth was in there behind him, Samuel couldn't see. He was a tall man with large, broad shoulders. The look on Amos's face was stern and harsh. He studied Samuel's face for the briefest of seconds before he snapped, "What are you doing on my doorstep, Samuel Lapp?" There was no forgiveness in his voice.

Once again, Samuel tried to act calmer than he felt. "I've come calling for Mary Ruth. I'd like to take her to the singing, Amos," Samuel said. His pulse raced and he felt the color drain from his face as he waited for Amos's reaction.

"You would now, eh?"

"Yes, sir," Samuel said. He hesitated, wondering how far to push the issue.

"After everything you have put this community through, you show up on my doorstep, asking to see my daughter?"

"Yes sir," Samuel said meekly.

"That's very bold of you, Samuel." Clearly Amos was not happy with his presence on his porch. His expression was too full of disapproval to be mistaken for anything else. "I told you not to come to our house."

"You did, Amos. But that was before. I have the right to come asking for her." Samuel pushed his shoulders back and stood tall, leveling his eyes at Amos. "And I intend to come every Sunday singing until springtime."

"Springtime?" Amos glared at him. "That's a long way off. Best be focusing on tonight before you starting planning for springtime!"

For a moment, Samuel didn't respond. He wasn't about to take back what he had said. By stating his intentions, Samuel had made it clear for Amos to understand where Samuel wanted this relationship to go. Amos's response had made his own position clear, too. There was no response needed, nothing that would move the situation forward, so silence worked just as well.

"I heard what you did to that little boy," Amos said

sharply, breaking the silence. His eyes were piercing, staring at Samuel. The look on his face and the harshness of his words sounded accusatory and caught Samuel off-guard. Was Amos talking about Abram? Or was he referencing Paul and how he had died?

"Little boy?"

"Your brother's boy. The one that almost drowned," Amos said impatiently, waving his hand in the air. Then, with a stern look and a finger pointed directly at Samuel's chest, he said, "God worked a miracle through you that day."

Samuel didn't speak. He wasn't certain what he should say. To admit such a statement was to be immodest and vain. To downplay it would be dishonest. It *had* been a miracle. Yet, as he stood before Amos, he noticed something soften in the old man's face.

"I heard you were quite helpful to your family during that crisis, too. You took some responsibility and saw it through." Amos cleared his throat but refused to look away from Samuel. "I also heard that you were telling the truth about those boys. You weren't with them," Amos continued.

"I wasn't with them," Samuel said softly.

Amos reached out and placed a hand on Samuel's shoulder. The gesture startled him, and he jumped at the man's touch. "Reckon you've had quite a scare, son. Reckon you've learned quite a lesson." He hesitated. "More importantly, I imagine we have all learned a lesson."

Samuel nodded, too afraid of his voice to speak.

With a simple nod of his head, Amos seemed to indicate his own lessons learned. "Even still, I'll be watching you, Samuel. Don't make any missteps, not when it comes to my daughter. But I'm willing to admit when I was wrong and offer you a second chance." And with that, he leaned back and called out, "Mary Ruth! Someone's at the door for you!" He narrowed his eyes again at Samuel but backed away as Mary Ruth approached from another room.

She seemed surprised to see Samuel standing there and glanced at her *daed*, uncertain how to react. When her *daed* stood there, unmoving, she looked back at Samuel. Clearly, she was confused, wondering what to say and why her *daed* had called her to the door. "*Guder Owed*, Samuel."

Samuel glanced over her shoulder at Amos before he cleared his throat. "Thought you might like to ride over to the singing with me this evening." He hesitated, not wanting to presume that she could go along for such a long period of time. "If you aren't needed at home, that is," he added.

Mary Ruth bit her lower lip and turned to her father. His face remained hard and serious, but he hadn't spoken against Samuel. In fact, there was something new in his eyes. He tried to appear fierce and strong, but there was a sparkle in his eye as he watched his daughter with Samuel. The sparkle gave her strength, and despite feeling nervous, she managed to ask, "*Daed*, might I be excused from the rest of my chores?"

Amos hesitated, his eyes shifting from Mary Ruth to Samuel then back to Mary Ruth. Finally, after what seemed like an eternity but was only a few seconds, he nodded once then turned and walked away. As he left, they stared at the place where he had stood, their eyes full of questions but their mouths remaining silent. If

Amos Smucker had suddenly changed his mind, neither Samuel nor Mary Ruth were about to question it.

"I'll be out in a minute, then," she said softly, her eyes suddenly glowing with life.

Samuel helped her into the buggy before climbing up beside her. With a single slap of the reins on the horse's back, he backed up the buggy before driving out of the driveway. They were silent for the first few minutes, both wrapped up in their own thoughts. Samuel was trying to understand what Amos had said. If he had expected a reaction from Amos, that had not been it. Acceptance? A hint of forgiveness? Indeed, Samuel had been prepared for quite a different outcome. What's more, he was certain that Mary Ruth was equally as surprised by her *daed* giving in so easily.

"So this is how it begins," she whispered, looking over at him.

She was nervous. That made him smile. "Sure does seem that way." He reached out and took her hand in his, holding it comfortably in his. For the rest of the ride, neither spoke. There were no words to say that would express the joy that filled them.

Epilogue

As they stood outside the mule shed, the stars in the night sky casting a blue glow around them, Samuel held Mary Ruth's hands. He stared down at her and smiled. "Mrs. Samuel Lapp," he whispered and laughed softly as she lowered her eyes. "Samuel's Mary Ruth. No one can ever change that now," he said.

"They couldn't change it before, could they?" she asked softly.

It had been a long day and both of them were exhausted. Yet they knew that their wedding day and night could only happen once in their lifetime. They wanted to cherish every second of it before retiring for the evening.

"Won't seem like home for a while, *ja*?" he said, nodding his head toward the small house that was connected to the main house and built over the mule shed. All fall and winter, Samuel and Daniel had helped Junior with building his new house by the carpentry shop. By springtime, Lillian was able to move into the house with their eight children, which freed up the main house for Rachel and Daniel to occupy. The timing coincided with Samuel's announcement of his marriage to Mary Ruth.

Their courtship had passed quickly, ten months of singings, long walks, and buggy rides. Samuel had lived up to his promises and worked hard at proving himself honorable. Even Amos Smucker had noticed and nodded as if indicating his favor of the new Samuel. So when the early spring baptism had come and gone, no one was surprised that the bishop had announced Samuel and Mary Ruth's upcoming marriage.

That had only been three weeks ago. From the time their wedding was announced until this very moment when they were standing on the porch of their new home, clinging to the final moments of this wonderful day, time had seemed to fly by on wings of happiness.

"Will it take a while to seem like home?" she repeated his question, breaking the silence. "*Nee.* Not if you are here with me. Then it will seem like home right away." She hesitated, rocking on her heels so that she bumped gently against him. "I've been waiting for this day for a long time, Samuel Lapp."

"When did you know you wanted to marry me, Mary Ruth?" he heard himself ask.

"Oh, Samuel, that's not so important now, is it?" she asked, her voice soft. She was embarrassed and that intrigued him even more.

"Tell me, dear wife," he teased.

She hesitated, trying to find the right way to tell him. He let her ponder the question as it gave him time to just enjoy being in her presence. Their time alone had always been very short-lived, strictly limited to buggy rides or walks. When they enjoyed fellowship together, it had been after church service or with other family members. Just standing alone, holding hands under the glow of the stars and moon, was a completely new experience for him.

"*Die Wahrehti ist untodlich,*" she whispered.

For a moment, Samuel thought that he had misheard her. *The truth cannot be killed?* It was an old Amish saying, spoken from the lips of an Anabaptist martyr in the seventeenth century. "What does Balthasar Hubmaier have to do with marrying me?"

"You said it to my father when you came to talk to me about your troubles," she said.

He frowned. "You knew you wanted to marry me then?"

She shook her head. "No, silly. That's when I knew you were telling the truth about not being involved with the accident. You were sending me a sign when you said '*Die Wahrehti ist untodlich,*' *ja?*"

Now he was truly perplexed. He wasn't following what she was saying. A sign? "I don't understand, Mary Ruth."

She squeezed his hands. "Think back. Don't you remember?"

Slowly, a faded memory started to emerge. They had been in school. She had been no more than nine and Samuel was almost twelve. Someone had accused him of tripping one of the girls in the schoolyard. She had fallen and her nose bled for nearly an hour. It had been Mary Ruth who had stood by him, insisting that Samuel was innocent, claiming that she had seen the entire scene and it had truly been an accident. But everyone else believed the worse, that Samuel had intentionally hurt the girl.

Probably unconsciously, this had always been engraved in his memory as a defining moment in their relationship. From that point onward, he had always made certain that she would not find herself at the receiving end of this or that particular mischief one of their peers wanted to play on her. Often times, without truly realizing why, he had found himself acting as her champion and her protector. Could that be because she had believed in him and whispered the four simple words to comfort him?

"*Die Wahrehti ist untodlich*," he whispered, remembering the words that she had said to him as they had sat under the shade of a large oak tree, sharing their noon meal while being shunned by their peers.

She smiled. "*Die Wahrehti ist untodlich*," she repeated. "When you said those words at my *daed*'s farm, I knew you were telling me to believe in you. Just as I had, back then, in the schoolyard, Samuel." She lifted her eyes and stared into his face. "That was the moment when I knew we would be together forever, Samuel."

He pulled her close and wrapped his arms around her. "Mary Ruth, you truly touch my heart." He caressed her cheek with his fingertips and sighed. "How could I be so deserving of such a gift from God?"

"Speaking of gifts," she said softly. "There is one more thing."

"What is it, Mary Ruth?" he said, his voice low as he held her in his arms. "Anything that I can give you, I will."

"We are married now and you promised me something." She tilted her chin so that she was looking up and into his face. "A kiss. Now that we are married, I would like to have my kiss."

In the darkness, Samuel nodded. He held her tight in his arms and placed one hand gently on the back of her neck, leaning down to brush his lips against hers. The kiss was soft and gentle, a fulfillment of a promise that had been unspoken so many years ago in that schoolyard but had grown throughout the years. The future was theirs, and that night was just the beginning.

* * * * *

SPECIAL EXCERPT FROM
Love Inspired®

Deborah Miller is living a double life.
Can she keep the truth from her Amish family—and Amos Burkholder?

Read on for a sneak preview of
Courting Her Secret Heart *by Mary Davis,*
the next book in Prodigal Daughters miniseries,
available in September 2018 from Love Inspired

Tugging her coat closed, Deborah slipped out past the garden. She hurried out to the cluster of bare sycamore trees near the pond at the edge of their property. After retrieving her backpack from the tangled base of the largest tree, she headed for the meeting spot. No one would miss her. They never did. *Vater's* trip to the hospital had been proof of that.

Deborah tramped through the still-fallow field. This year would be the year this field was planted again. She came out the other side and dashed down the road. At the intersection, an idling car waited. She opened the passenger door and climbed in.

When the driver dropped her off, Deborah ducked into the gas station restroom to change from her Amish clothing into a pair of jeans and a sweatshirt, and let down her hair. When she wore these clothes with her hair freed, she felt like a different person. What would Amos think of her appearance? Disapprove, for sure.

She hurried to the photography studio and entered silently.

Hudson stood behind his camera giving instructions to the model sitting on a fake rock wall in front of a backdrop featuring an old building. In his late twenties, Hudson had ambitions to move to New York City and become a famous photographer. His dashing good looks said he could likely succeed on the other side of the camera as well. When she'd first started modeling for him a year ago, she'd developed a crush from all his praise and attention. Two things she rarely received at home.

He pulled back from his camera and swung Deborah's direction. "Debo! There you are."

When she hadn't wanted to use her real name, Hudson had dubbed her Debo. She didn't much care for it, but it was better than using Deborah and risk being discovered. No Amish would guess that was her even if they ever found out. The likelihood that any of them would see her in one of these *Englisher* catalogues was slim to none.

He walked over to her. "You're my best model. Go see about wardrobe, hair, and make-up." He stared at her.

"What is it? Is something wrong?"

"It just amazes me how different you look from your Amish self. I would never guess you were the same person."

Deborah counted on that. If her Amish brothers and sisters knew about this, she would be shunned. If the media found out she was an Amish girl modeling, they would exploit that. But Hudson kept her secret, and as long as he did, she could continue to model. She wasn't hurting anyone and wasn't doing anything illegal. The money she earned would help her and her future husband buy a house and farm. She would quit as soon as someone special took interest and asked to court her. Someday.

Don't miss
Courting Her Secret Heart *by Mary Davis,*
available September 2018 wherever
Love Inspired books and ebooks are sold.
www.LoveInspired.com

Amos Burkholder steps in to help the Miller family when their vater is injured. But middle daughter Deborah disappears for hours at a time. Where does she go? What does she do?

Read on for a sneak preview of Courting Her Secret Heart, *by* Mary Davis, *available September 2018 from Love Inspired!*

Amos Burkholder looked out over the Millers' fields to be plowed in the spring. He couldn't help but think of them as partly his. Of course, they weren't his fields, and he might not even be here to do the plowing and the planting. But if he was, he would take pride in that work.

Bartholomew Miller appreciated everything he did around the farm, so Amos worked harder than he ever had at home.

Bartholomew had never had a son to help him with all the work around the farm. How had he run this place without sons?

But on the flip side, Amos's *mutter* had been alone doing the house chores, cooking, cleaning and laundry for six men. How did she do it without help?

On the far side of one of the fields, a woman emerged from a bare stand of sycamore trees nestled next to a pond. She walked across the field.

The woman came closer and closer.

Deborah.

LIEXP00600

Where did she go all the time? She had disappeared every day this week and would be gone for hours. He was about to find out.

With her head down, she didn't see him approaching. He stepped directly into her path a few yards in front of her. When it looked as though she might literally run into him, he cleared his throat.

She halted a foot away. She was so startled to see him there, she appeared to lose her balance. Her arms swung out to keep herself upright.

He reached out and took hold of her upper arms to stop her from tumbling to the ground. "Whoa, there."

She gasped. "I'm sorry. I didn't see you."

"Where have you been all day?"

"What? Nowhere." She tried to pull free of his grip, but he held fast.

He shook his head. "You've been somewhere. You've left every day this week and been gone for most of the day."

"I—I went for a walk."

"Where? Ohio?"

"We have a pond just over there. I like to sit and watch the ducks. It's a nice place to think and be alone. You should go some time."

"I did. Today. You weren't there."

Her self-satisfied expression fell. "I was for a while, then I walked farther."

He sensed there was more to her absence than a walk. "Where?"

"Why do you care?"

"With your *vater* laid up, I'm responsible for everyone on this farm."

"I'm fine. I can take care of myself. May I go now?"

He didn't want to let her go but did. "I don't want you to leave the farm without telling me where you're going."

"Are you serious?"

LIEXP00600

He gave her his serious look.

She huffed and strode away.

Where did she go every day? He had wanted to follow her, but he realized it was none of his business. But curiosity pushed hard on him. He still might follow her if she didn't obey. Just to see. Just to watch her from a distance. Just to know her secret.

Something inside him feared for her. Feared she would walk out across this field and never return. Feared her secret would consume them both. She was a mystery.

A mystery he was drawn to solve.

*

Deborah heaved a sigh of relief. She marched the rest of the way through the field. After two weeks, Amos Burkholder already paid more attention to her comings and goings than her own family had her whole life—they thought her an airhead. Fanciful. Her head full of dreams and nonsense.

Well, she did have dreams. And to prove to everyone that she was someone to be noticed, she'd become a church member younger than any of her older sisters, at age sixteen. She'd basically skipped her Rumspringa.

No one had congratulated her or told her how wonderful it was that she'd joined so young. Anything to be noticed, just once.

Wasn't she as important as any of her sisters? Wasn't she just as much in need of being noticed?

So, she started taking advantage of her invisibility. Experimenting with being gone from the family for longer and longer periods of time, until she could be gone all day without hardly a word. She would claim to go for a walk and be gone for hours. When she returned home, she would be told to get her head out of the clouds and keep track of time.

But they never came looking for her.

So, Deborah wandered farther and farther from home. Until she'd ended up at the edge of a photo shoot over a year ago.

The photographer, Hudson, had seen her and said she'd be perfect for the shot. She hadn't wanted to do it. She knew she shouldn't. Hudson told her that there would be no harm in it. That no one would ever know.

She'd been thrilled at the idea of being special, being different. At being noticed. At no longer being invisible.

Hudson praised her and told her that she was a natural. He'd asked her to come to another shoot the following week. Soon, she participated in weekly shoots with him. And she had enjoyed it. She wasn't hurting anyone and was earning money for her future.

She felt free and no longer invisible. She felt important. She felt like somebody.

But now her absence had been noticed. She certainly couldn't tell Amos where she went. But how many times could she claim to go for a walk and have him still believe her? Or worse yet, ask to go with her?

If she had been going for a simple walk, she would welcome his company and attention. She smiled at the thought.

She sighed. That could never happen. She needed to figure something out before her next photo shoot.

LIEXP00600